4

A THIEF OF HEARTS

"Dear lady," said the cultured voice lazily, while the deep blue eyes swept over her. "Do you know that your pulse is very fast and that something remarkably erratic has happened to your breathing?"

"If it has, it's because I am understandably nervous," said Eleanor. She could feel herself getting flushed. Why should the fellow think it necessary to be rude? He seemed to wear his arrogance as casually as his shirt. "Whether you are drunk or not, sir, you are behaving disgracefully."

"Nowhere near as disgracefully as I am about to behave," said the stranger with a sudden grin.

Before Eleanor had time to react, he had grasped her outstretched hand and pulled her onto the couch beside him. She landed against his chest in a flurry of sprigged muslin, one hand still imprisoned by his, the other clutching desperately at her shawl. In the next instant he had bent her head back against his arm. Firm fingers ran gently over her hair before smoothing down the curve of her cheek.

"You have the most beautiful skin I have ever touched," said the owner of the violet eyes, as he bent his head over hers and began to kiss her without mercy on the lips . . .

* * *

"Leander is a hero to die for. This is a book no Regency lover—no historical lover—no romance lover—should miss."

—*Rendezvous* on ***Rogue's Reward***

Rogue's Reward

Jean R. Ewing

ZEBRA BOOKS
KENSINGTON PUBLISHING CORP.

ZEBRA BOOKS are published by

Kensington Publishing Corp.
850 Third Avenue
New York, NY 10022

First Printing: November, 1995

Printed in the United States of America

Having flown over many knavish professions,
he settled only in rogue.

—*The Winter's Tale*

One

"What a grim place!" said Helena, laughing. "How can you bear it, Eleanor?"

"Languishing in jail like the Pearl of Brittany?" Lady Eleanor Acton warmly embraced her sister-in-law. "I admit I do feel a little like a medieval princess, wickedly imprisoned! Which would you prefer: the chair or the sofa? Both are equally ill-favored."

Helena surveyed the uncomfortable furniture considered suitable for the parlor of Miss Able's Select Academy for Young Ladies. Her stylish dark blue traveling dress elegantly disguised an interesting condition, in distinct contrast to Eleanor who was clad in the demure white muslin considered suitable by Miss Able for her pupils, even if they were the daughters of the peerage. "I shall take the horsehair sofa," she said. "It will remind me of my own schooldays in Exeter. Richard and I just met the formidable Miss Able. Your brother is now trapped in her office making polite inquiries about his little sisters, but I had to make my escape and see you right away. Now I find you don't even have a seat worthy of the name!"

Eleanor dropped to the offending wooden chair and lifted amused brown eyes. "At this moment poor Joanna is agonizing over an elegy she must learn by heart, and little Milly is memorizing *'The Malays are ferocious and unprincipled to a high degree,' 'Patagonia is a desolate country, where men have been seen of a gigantic size,'* and *'The inhabitants of the United States are both proud and ignorant.'* But my captivity is soon to be over! I've a letter from Mama. I'm to come out in London this Season."

"Oh, Eleanor! And be presented at court?"

"Mama says it's high time her brown hen was married, and that I have surely learned enough French and embroidery to be considered perfectly accomplished. I'll have to curtsy to the Queen with a feather on my head! Can you think of anything more absurd? But more remarkable still, first I go with Mama to Norfolk for Easter."

Helena swallowed her smile. Eleanor might have chestnut hair and nut-brown eyes, but she was hardly a brown hen. "To Norfolk? But why?"

"We visit Hawksley Park, home of my friend Lady Diana Hart and her mother, the ominous Dowager Countess Augusta, who undoubtedly counts as being regal enough for practice. Since I understand that Mama and Lady Augusta are always at daggers drawn, it wouldn't appear to be the most amiable undertaking. No doubt I shall be grateful that it's essential to polite society for countesses to be civil to each other! Diana did invite me for Christmas . . ."

"But you came to us at Acton Mead instead!"

"Because I wanted more to meet Richard's new wife, of course. And it was positively splendid, in spite of the most frightful ague and the presence of all my motley brothers and sisters! Pray do not think for a moment it was any sacrifice. But it'll be good to see Diana again. She was the loveliest thing in this school and she's been out for a year."

Helena met this with genuine surprise. "She's not wed?"

"She received innumerable offers, but Lady Augusta turned down every one, angling for a spectacular match, no doubt. Since Diana is sole heir to Hawksley Park, she may well get one."

"As eldest daughter to the Earl of Acton," said Helena, smiling, "so might you. But you won't meet anyone in Norfolk."

"Exactly. Which makes me wonder why on earth Mama wants to take me there. For you know as well as I that my mother, the beautiful Countess of Acton, never did a thing without an ulterior motive in her life."

Helena remembered her own encounters with Lady Acton and laughed, but her attention was diverted by the sound of firm footsteps striding down the corridor. Her heart sang within her as she recognized her husband's step. Eleanor's brother Richard, Lord Lenwood, heir of the Earl of Acton, was at the door. Both ladies jumped up and Helena said softly, "Marry for love, Eleanor."

Eleanor grinned at her sister-in-law. "Don't be silly! Just because you and my splendid brother are as entwined as Philemon and Baucis doesn't mean there's usually a connection between love and marriage among the peerage. Anyone the least interesting would be bound to give Papa apoplexy on the spot and I'll never experience the wild adventures you did." She slipped an arm around Helena's waist, and whispered her next comment into her ear as the door began to open. "My parents' idea of a suitable match will be some fatuous lord in need of my portion, but I must be dutiful and clear the way for my sisters, I suppose. In the meantime, anything is better than school. I intend to thoroughly enjoy a dull stay in Norfolk and practice my curtsies."

The tennis ball bounced sharply, cracked into the waiting racket, and came flying back at the heedless blond head of Walter Feveril Downe. Mr. Downe's wandering attention returned too late. He lunged clumsily and sent the ball careening into the solid wall of the court. The London dandies watching from the gallery clapped and cheered.

"Game, set, and match to me, sir," said Leander Campbell. He laughed and tossed his racket into the air before deftly catching it again in his other hand. "And sixty guineas, I believe?"

"Devil take it, Lee!" Mr. Downe frowned at his friend and thrust one hand through his disordered hair. "How the hell is a fellow supposed to win against you?"

"If that fellow had been paying the slightest attention to the game, instead of dreaming like a lotus-eater, he would have stood a better chance. What's on your mind? A member of the frail sex, no doubt."

Walter grimaced. "If you knew what it was like to have normal human feelings, you wouldn't be so damned cynical about love. I would willingly lay down my life for an angel like Lady Diana Hart."

Lee's dark blue eyes widened very slightly at this fervent sally. "But of course as a hardened rake and gambler, angels are above my touch." He walked casually to the net and held out his hand. Walter shook it, trying to avoid the sardonic expression on the victor's face. But he was to get no mercy from Leander Campbell, in spite of the smile that still lurked at the corner of his mouth. "Have you proposed to this paragon of female grace and been rejected, or are you merely pining from a distance, the lady oblivious to your devotion? Either way, to effect an instant demise seems a very odd way of demonstrating your affection."

"Damn it, Campbell. This is serious! I'm in a devilish quandary. I worship the very hem of her skirt, yet how can I propose to her? I am only plain Mr. Downe, destined to become a vicar!"

"The Honorable Mr. Walter Feveril Downe," corrected Lee, who was the untitled plain Mr. Campbell.

"Yes, but what on earth are my prospects?"

"Considerably better than mine," said Lee with a wry grin. "You are a viscount's younger son. You will become a model churchman, and Lady Diana will make you a faultless wife. I am to assume that the lady returns your regard and would wed you willingly if only her dragon of a mama would allow it?"

"Well, I don't know," said Walter, coloring a little. "I think she likes me, but it's impossible, don't you see? How can I, in honor, address her? She's heiress to a fortune. Lady Augusta will make her marry a duke."

The men had walked into the dressing room of the tennis club, and Leander Campbell peeled off his shirt and trousers, and stepped under the shower. At the pull of a chain, cold water dumped over his dark head and ran down over the firm muscling of his body. "And you will stand aside and allow this outrage against all your finer sensibilities to take place?" he questioned as he soaped himself. "How on earth can you allow the lady to be consumed by a duke when there is your infinitely superior self available? She would hate being a duchess. In fact, I think you should elope with her."

"Lee, for God's sake!"

"Why not? Court her, secure her affection, and run off with her. What else could Lady Augusta do then but agree to welcome you as her son-in-law? Alas, I see that your scrupulous honor forbids you stealing an heiress unless her family gave their consent. If I were in your shoes, I shouldn't let the fortune stand in my way." He pulled another chain and rinsed the soap off his body. Grabbing a towel, he began to dry himself. "Think of the family connections! There's no sense in living in poverty if you have a chance at some comfort. There must be several rich livings within the gift of Hawksley. In fact, you would undoubtedly end up a bishop. Lady Diana would much rather be a parson's wife than a duchess, you know."

Walter Downe had been steadily turning puce as his friend casually made this outrageous speech. "If I didn't know that you would mow me down like a blade of grass," he sputtered at last, "I would call you out, sir. Damn me, if I wouldn't!"

Lee stepped out of the shower and began to rub at his hair. His eyes shone with violet lights as he laughed. "Your righteous indignation would carry the day, Downe. I could never prevail against it and I concede the duel in advance."

"How dare you presume to know what Lady Diana Hart of Hawksley Park would like?"

"Because she's my sister, of course. Here, hand me that dry towel, would you?"

Downe sat suddenly on the bench, as if he had been punched. "What do you mean? She's an only child, isn't she?"

"Lady Augusta's only child. My half-sister, I should have said. Lady Diana and I had the misfortune to share the same father, the late Lord Hawksley. Sadly in my case, he neglected to marry my mother. As far as I know he never learned of my existence. He must have been a remarkably careless fellow."

"I had no idea," said Walter Downe faintly.

"No, many people haven't. They only know that I'm not respectable." Lee shrugged into a spotlessly clean white shirt, then sat to pull on a pair of beige breeches.

"Then you're son to an earl!"

"But the title died with him. I am that most sorry of creatures, I'm afraid: a bastard. I use my mother's last name. She was Scottish and died in the Highlands when I was little. I never knew her."

Walter was still gaping a little. "And Lady Diana knows about this?"

"Of course. We grew up together. My stepmother took me in and raised me, but I have no claim on Hawksley."

"For heaven's sake, Lee! What an extraordinary act of generosity! How did the dowager countess know you were not an impostor?"

"I was accompanied by a birth certificate naming her late husband as my father. But I do see your point. Lady Augusta is not generally thought of as the soul of charity, is she? No, I have the additional misfortune of looking exactly like the late Lord Hawksley. Apparently one glance at my infant face was sufficient to prevent any possibility of denying the connection. Besides, there was St. John Crabtree to advertise my existence to the world."

"Crabtree?"

"Major Sir Robert St. John Crabtree, the impeccable military gentleman you have met at every rout and soirée for the last several years. He found me in Ireland where I'd been sent as a baby and brought me back, then bought the very place next to Hawksley. After he had been so gallant as to rescue a by-blow of the English peerage from the bogs of the Emerald Isle, it would have been excessively awkward for Lady Augusta to attempt to deny the affair and dump me in the foundling hospital."

"Wasn't it rather humiliating to be raised by your father's wife, after he had abandoned your mother?"

"My dear fellow," said Lee with a grin. "I was actually raised by a succession of rather brutal schoolmasters at Eton, as were you. Lady Augusta gave me every advantage that she could and did more than her duty, don't you think? I have received the normal education of an English gentleman and am thus able to make my own way in the world. I am grateful to her."

"But you would never be able to marry into any of the best families," said the Honorable Mr. Downe sympathetically. "And I suppose you have no property and no chance at all at any number of professions. I am sorry, old chap, for wailing on about my own problems."

His reply was an open and genuine burst of laughter. "Save your compassion for your future flock! Unlike you, dear fellow, I am not in love with a scion of the peerage and don't intend to be so. Having grown up in the knowledge of my unfortunate birth all my life, I don't view it as any kind of calamity, but rather as the source of a blessed freedom. I have never had the least problem living by my wits. Now, for God's sake, get washed and changed."

Walter Feveril Downe began to strip off his tennis clothes when the door to the dressing room burst open to reveal the white face of one of London's most famous dandies.

"Thank God I found you, Campbell," he said. "Come quick! Manton Barnes just shot himself!"

Lee thrust on his boots and took up his coat. He seemed neither particularly surprised nor visibly distressed, but the violet eyes had turned almost black. "Where?"

"In his lodgings on Ryder Street. He left a note addressed to you!"

"The damned silly fool!" Lee's face was set like a mask. "Later, Downe!" he said over his shoulder to his half-dressed friend as he ran lightly from the club.

Manton Barnes's door stood open and a couple of young men were gaping at the body which lay on the floor. Lee knelt over it for a moment, but it was obviously useless to feel for a pulse.

"We came to fetch him for a drive and found him like this," said one of the men shakily. "What will his family think?"

"That he met with an accident cleaning his gun," replied Lee. He stood and went to the mantelpiece and took down the note which lay there. "I trust that no word of this will pass any of your honorable lips?"

"Of course not," said one of the men indignantly. It didn't seem to be out of the ordinary to any of them that a landless rake was the first man they should turn to in trouble, and that they should all so willingly let him take charge.

"Good," said Leander Campbell. His voice betrayed nothing of anger or pain, though both burned within him. "Then please leave. There's nothing more you can do here. I shall see that he's not buried at the crossroads."

"But why on earth did he do it?" asked the dandy who had first carried the news.

"Is it any of your business?"

The dandy colored and looked away from the blue gaze. "Of course," he mumbled and Lee was left alone.

He tore open the note and rapidly scanned the contents before tearing it in pieces and casting it onto the fire. Then without hesitation he began to search the room, and several other documents joined the note in the flames. Satisfied that nothing else incriminating remained, Lee took out the gun-cleaning kit that he found in the closet and began to arrange the body as if there had been only an unfortunate accident. He had barely finished when there was a noise at the door and Walter Downe burst into the room. The blond head was still damp from the shower and his cravat was twisted.

"For God's sake, Lee! Why did he do it?"

"Barnes died rather than have that come out, dear friend. I think we might respect the peace of the dead, don't you?"

Downe blushed. "Which is why you are moving his body?"

"He thought it was worth his fortune and finally his life for his family not to know about his little scandal. There's no need at all for them to suspect as much."

"Good God! The affair with Blanche Haricot? He was being blackmailed! Did he leave a note? Who forced him to such desperation?"

Lee looked at the other man. "I don't know. Had he told me, the blackmailer would not live to see another dawn. But he did give me a clue."

"Which was?"

"Dear Walter, you are too full of questions. Why don't you go and tell the Bow Street men that we have found our poor friend dead of an accident, there's a good chap."

Walter Downe bowed and left the room. Lee sat in a chair beside the body and waited. He had told his friend the truth. He had no idea who the blackmailer had been, but he would go down to Norfolk and try to find out. In the meantime the final sentence of poor Barnes's note meant no sense at all.

"The cad is impossible to stop, Campbell," the note had read. *"I am bled dry. Once he has his claws into you, it's worse than the punishment of Prometheus. Ask Lady Acton."*

* * *

Lady Eleanor Acton allowed her maid to unhook the fasteners at the back of her dress, then dismissed the girl for the night. She was alone in the shadowed bedroom of the Three Feathers, one of the better post-houses on the Norwich road. Her mother had a room just down the hall and their maids were to share a chamber at the back of the house. Eleanor slipped out of her beige-and-blue sprigged muslin. As she began to take down her hair, her fingers brushed the bare skin at the back of her neck.

"Damnation," she said aloud, in the most unladylike manner. "I've lost my locket."

She sat on the chair beside the bed and thought for a moment. It had been there at dinner, because Lady Acton had commented that it looked very well and asked about it. Thus it must have slipped off somewhere between the private parlor where they had dined and her bedchamber. Richard and Helena had given it to her after that amazing Christmas at Acton Mead, and she realized with a sudden pang that it was really the most precious thing that she had. It was impossible to reach all the hooks on her dress by herself, but maybe a shawl would cover the gaps. Without further hesitation, Eleanor pulled on her muslin, fastened it as best as she could, wrapped herself in her paisley shawl, and stepped out into the inn corridor.

There was no sign of the locket in the hallway or on the stairs. Perhaps it had fallen in their dining room? She knocked tentatively at the solid oak door to the private parlor, then pushed it open and stepped inside. The room was almost dark, except for the dancing light of the fireplace, so Eleanor went to the grate and took up a taper to light some candles.

"I wish you would not," said a soft voice.

Eleanor whirled around. A man was lying full length on the couch at the side of the room. His booted feet were crossed on one arm of the sofa and his dark head was propped carelessly at the other end. A very white shirt lay open at the neck and for some reason she noticed the way the firelight caressed the little hollows at the base of his throat. Then she raised her eyes to his and stopped in her tracks. Between thick lashes a deep violet gaze seemed to be devouring her.

"Forgive me, sir," she said, with the oddest catch in her voice. "I had no idea that anyone was in here. You didn't answer my knock."

"As it turned out, it didn't matter, did it? For you came in anyway. But please don't light any multitude of candles. It would be more than I could stand."

"Why?" said Eleanor simply.

"Because I am extremely drunk. Which means, of course, that it is more than foolish of you to remain in here with me."

"I only came to search for something I might have dropped. It won't take me a moment to look about the room, and I'll leave the instant I find it."

"You obviously didn't listen to what I said. No lady of quality would remain for one second in a private parlor with a stranger at an inn. Especially when that stranger is as regrettably foxed as I am at this instant."

"Then perhaps I should introduce myself, sir . . ."

The violet eyes closed for a moment, as if in pain. "Please leave, young lady. For you must be either a schoolgirl or a hussy. Either way we shall both regret it if you stay a moment longer."

"Stuff!" said Eleanor. "This is a perfectly respectable inn. You seem to be a gentleman. Surely you can remain on your sofa until I discover my locket?"

"Ah," said the gentlemen softly. "Then this is what you were looking for?"

He sat up in a remarkably smooth and fluid movement and held out something on the palm of his hand. Eleanor recognized it instantly.

"Thank heavens. Yes, that's mine and I'm very glad to have it back. My brother gave it to me."

There was the slightest change in the blue eyes, but the subtle voice betrayed nothing. "Then the handsome devil whose miniature lies inside is your brother? And the beautiful blonde . . ."

". . . Is his wife, Helena. Now if you would be so kind as to restore my property to me forthwith?" Eleanor marched boldly up to the man and held out her hand.

"Dear lady," said the cultured voice lazily, while the deep blue eyes swept over her. "Do you know that your pulse is very fast and that something remarkably erratic has happened to your breathing?"

"If it has, it's because I am understandably nervous," said Eleanor. She could feel herself getting flushed. Why should the fellow think it necessary to be rude? He seemed to wear his arrogance as casually as his shirt. "Whether you are drunk or not, sir, you are behaving disgracefully."

"Nowhere near as disgracefully as I am about to behave," said the stranger with a sudden grin.

Before Eleanor had time to react, he had grasped her outstretched hand and pulled her onto the couch beside him. She landed against his chest in a flurry of sprigged muslin, one hand still imprisoned by his, the other clutching desperately at her shawl. In the next instant he had bent her head back against his arm. Firm fingers ran gently over her hair before smoothing down the curve of her cheek.

"You have the most beautiful skin I have ever touched," said the owner of the violet eyes, as he bent his head over hers and began to kiss her without mercy on the lips.

Two

Eleanor didn't struggle, though she knew in the last coherent thought left to her that she should. Instead it was as if a paralysis had seized her and the whole world had slowed to allow her to savor every delicious sensation. His lips caressed hers until she could taste sugar, then his teeth began the most subtle nibbling until her mouth opened and his tongue was running delicately over hers. She had drunk hot honeyed wine at Christmas; it was the nearest thing she could think of to the sensation. Then his fingers pushed aside her shawl and he was kissing the side of her neck as his hands ran down her back. Which left her mouth free to shout for help. And to bring down the inn staff and her mother to witness her disgrace.

"Well," she said instead, with what remained of her wits. "Which is it?"

The warm breath left her neck and he was looking down at her, the lids very slightly slack over the dark blue depths of his eyes. "Which is what?" he said with a smile.

Eleanor's heart turned over. There was an oddly languorous sensation in the pit of her stomach. She did her best to summon every ounce of defiance. "Schoolgirl or hussy? I warn you that I shall take either description as an insult."

It was a devastating smile. "Hardly a hussy, in spite of your rather odd state of undress."

So he had noticed her gaping hooks! Eleanor felt the blood

race to her cheeks. His fingers were still gently caressing at the side of her neck.

"Then what on earth is your excuse for showing so little respect for my reputation?" she said desperately. "For if I'm not a hussy, I must be a schoolgirl, in which case you are committing a form of robbery."

"No, your composure betrays you, madam. You can hardly have come straight from the schoolroom. Not a schoolgirl either, I think."

"Which shows you to be excessively wanting in judgment—for that is exactly what I am."

And then she had the satisfaction of seeing the rather lazy, comfortable look in his eyes replaced with one of pure astonishment, to be followed by what seemed like a strange delight. "I did warn you," he said at last.

"No, you didn't. For how could a schoolgirl possibly be expected to understand what you intended?"

The sardonic mask had slipped back over his face, but he had also released her, so that Eleanor could sit up and clasp her shawl around her shoulders as if it were a coat of chain mail. Firelight ran brightly over the folds of his white shirt, hinting at the lithe strength beneath. "You might have been a hussy after all, in spite of being sister to the fellow in the locket. Since your dress is unhooked and you displayed no appropriate maidenly vapors, the odds seemed to be in my favor."

"Your profession is to take risks?"

"Only calculated ones, of course. I make my living at the gaming tables."

Eleanor stood up. Her knees were shaking a little. "Then perhaps you should have done a little more calculating before accosting me. I am Lady Eleanor Acton, my father is the earl, and I would very much appreciate my locket."

And then she was bewildered, for instead of looking impressed the gentleman with the violet eyes threw back his head and began to laugh. The sound was muted since he put both hands over his face. Extremely well-made and well-cared-for hands, noted Eleanor distractedly. She began to back away from him toward the door.

"No, no," he said, suddenly regaining control. "After all your intrepid bravery, don't leave without it."

He was on his feet and giving her an elaborate court bow. If he was really drunk, it didn't show in his athletic movements. Then he caught her hand and deposited the locket into her palm.

"I don't imagine that you will forgive me, my lady," he said. "But I might as well be hung for a sheep as a lamb. I'm afraid that I can't let you leave quite yet."

Her brown eyes flashed with anger. "Why not? Am I to be ravished next? I assure you that would make me kick and scream with no decorum or composure at all, before becoming hysterically vaporish, of course. But since I'm known in my family as the 'brown hen,' I can hardly be tempting enough to someone of your undoubtedly wide experience."

"Do you always talk this way to gentlemen, my lady?"

"Never. But it doesn't seem that I'm in the presence of a gentleman. You have told me that you're a gambler and I suppose you're also a rake? I insist on leaving this instant."

"Not yet." The beautiful fingers closed on her wrist. "First you must tell me what you know about blackmail, brown hen."

It was Eleanor's turn to look astonished. "Blackmail?" she said. "Is that your game? You really are a bastard, aren't you?"

"Yes," said the smiling lips. "I am."

"What's your plan? To inform my family that you kissed me at the Three Feathers and then demand money to tell no one else? For God's sake, sir. My brother would kill you."

"The gentleman in the locket?" said Leander Campbell. "Richard, Lord Lenwood, eldest son to the Earl of Acton: he's not actually a terribly good shot. I pray you won't make him challenge me, because I would kill him, and then you really would never forgive me."

"You recognized him? Then you knew who I was all along?"

"Perhaps you meant your other brother, Harry? He's reputed to be a crack shot, though I've never seen him with a gun. I have to admit it's enough to give me pause, though I flatter myself I could match him."

"I also have a little brother, John, who's excellent with a slingshot, and two sisters who would stop at nothing in my defense. And my mother stays with me in this inn, sir, and would very likely have you hanged for your conceit. Now, are you going to let me go or am I going to have to bring the house down?"

"Your mother the countess, Lady Acton? Oh, Lord," he said, and laughed. "Your family name is the same as the name of the earldom, isn't it? I told you I was foxed." He raised her hand to his lips and kissed her fingers, then pulled her to him and kissed her once more, fleetingly, on the lips. His breath was warm on her cheek as he whispered against her ear. "Get the hell out of here, brown hen, and I beg you'll forget you ever met me."

The coach rattled up the drive of Hawksley Park the following afternoon, and the Countess of Acton gently tapped at her cheeks and checked the angle of her dashing little hat in the small mirror that she carried in her reticule. Eleanor watched her mother with an indulgent smile. It wasn't so unusual to have sisters who outshone one in beauty, she thought a little wistfully, but for one's own mother to be so very lovely! Well, the man at the inn hadn't seemed to care if she was plain. Then she blushed scarlet. To have been so used by a self-confessed rake for a moment's amusement did very little for one's already slightly shaky pride. And his absurd threats of blackmail! The only thing worse was to have to admit to oneself that it had been the most interesting experience so far in a remarkably ordinary life. For Eleanor tried very hard to be honest with herself.

The coachman's voice called to the horses and the carriage stopped. Moments later a footman was dropping the steps and helping the ladies from the chaise. Hawksley Park stood before them in all its Palladian glory and Lady Diana was at the door.

"Lady Acton, Eleanor! I'm so glad you could come! I just couldn't wait in the drawing room with Mama as I ought!" She shook the countess by the hand and dropped her a respectful curtsy, before grasping Eleanor by the shoulders and kissing her on the cheek. "As soon as you have had tea, you must come with me and I'll show you around. You're to have the very next bedroom to mine, so we can have the most comfortable coze imaginable!"

Linking arms, the two girls followed the countess into the hallway, where several maids and footmen stood ready to aid the travelers.

"I'm in the most dreadful tangle, Eleanor," whispered Lady Diana as soon as her friend was divested of her coat and bonnet, and they were following behind the countess and the guiding butler. "There's no hope for me at all."

"Which sounds excessively melodramatic, Di! Is it something I can help you with?"

"You kind creature! You're always the soul of good sense; I'm just a ninny in comparison. But I'm lost this time, truly. Have you ever met someone and known right away you were meant for each other, but it could never be?"

Eleanor shook her head. She dismissed the irrelevant image of a pair of violet eyes that annoyingly came to mind. "No, I haven't. Don't tell me you're in love? And it's someone your Mama thinks totally ineligible?"

Diana stopped and looked at her friend with wide blue eyes. "However did you know?"

"Because nothing else would make you look quite so like Hapless Clara who pined away for love."

"Don't make fun, please! His name's Walter Feveril Downe. It's a splendid name, isn't it? We met last year when I first came out and I knew right away. He was at so many dances and dinners, but nothing was ever declared between us, of course. Yet he's written to me."

"Diana! I'm shocked!" Eleanor didn't look in the least shocked. "I'm to assume that Lady Augusta knows nothing of this and would have the vapors if she were to find out? Is he the son of a coal merchant?"

"Eleanor, do be sensible. Of course not! His father is Viscount Clare, but he's a younger son and you know how Mama is."

"Well, no, actually I don't, except by reputation, since I'm about to meet her for the first time. But pray, don't sink into a final decline between here and the drawing room. If there's anything I can do for such very deserving star-crossed lovers, you have my word to help. I'm a splendid conspirator; being one of six children teaches you all kinds of useful skills."

"No, there's nothing anyone can do! It's hopeless, really!"

Eleanor gave Diana's hand a little squeeze. "Surely not! I know you would never really give your heart to someone ineligible. Only a creature as lost to all decency as me would do that."

"Whatever do you mean?"

Eleanor looked at her friend's woebegone face and laughed. She had no idea why she had said that. "Nothing at all. I'm just trying to cheer you up. Now smile, or else I shall lose all courage to face the dragon."

Lady Augusta, Dowager Countess of Hawksley, did look something like a dragon, Eleanor thought as that lady sailed toward them. She had prematurely graying hair caught up beneath a cap of stiff lace shingles and her eyes were small and sharp. Diana had certainly not inherited her lovely blue eyes from her mother. Yet Lady Hawksley wasn't actually breathing fire. Instead, having absolutely no affection for her guests, she was preparing an effusion of greeting.

"Ma chére Felicity!" she said, holding out both hands to Lady Acton, who had entered the room ahead of the girls. "Hawksley is honored." Then she looked past the countess's shoulder at her daughter. "So this is Eleanor? Diana has told me so much about her. What a pity that she is not more *'ravissante'*—so unfortunate for a girl about to come out." Then she continued archly in French which Eleanor had no problem translating: "Such a shame when all the beauty belongs to the mother and none to the daughter."

Lady Acton leaned forward and kissed the dowager countess on both cheeks, her perfect features in marked contrast to the lines of perpetual discontent on the other face. "Then how very gratifying for you," she said, also in perfect French, "that in your case it's the other way around."

Lady Augusta didn't hesitate for a moment, though she returned to her native tongue. "Diana was the belle of last season, indeed. She was drowned in offers, but I believe Lord Ranking will be brought up to snuff this spring and he is to be Duke of May. It would be a most appropriate match for the heiress of Hawksley Park."

"He has such a drooping air about him." Lady Acton smiled. "So very elegant. I'm sure he and Diana will be very happy."

Eleanor squeezed Diana's arm and gave her a supportive smile, but the countesses had changed the subject.

"Major Sir Robert St. John Crabtree sends his compliments," Lady Augusta was saying. "And will no doubt call tomorrow. He's the very model of courtesy, of course. A most amiable neighbor."

"Then we'll look forward to an enchanting morning. Unless it should rain. We can hardly expect casual visits in bad weather." Lady Acton sank gracefully into a chair by the fire. "On the other hand," she continued lazily, "I believe him to be very indifferent to weather. Don't you remember,

Augusta, how the major escorted Miss Haricot from Vauxhall in that appalling storm last summer? She was almost hysterical about something, had forgotten her umbrella, and Sir Robert gave her his cloak. So very gallant! He was soaked to the skin!"

"A most inelegant scene!" sniffed Lady Augusta as the maid came in with the tea tray. "Blanche Haricot should have shown more restraint."

A dish of tea was offered and taken, and nothing more was said about the amiable major. Eleanor was left to wonder if she had imagined the fleeting look of genuine pleasure and anticipation on her mother's matchless face.

At last the girls were released from the drawing room and Eleanor could go up to her room to wash and change for dinner.

"Who's this Major Crabtree?" she asked Diana as they went up the great marble staircase.

"Oh, just a neighbor. He sports the most enormous military mustaches and has some huge fortune. Deerfield is his. See, that's it over there, near the river."

Eleanor stopped by the window and looked where her friend was pointing. The slightly rolling landscape stretched away into a blue haze of fields and lanes, outlined by new plantings of trees. Near the river, she could just make out the tall chimneys of an imposing edifice of red brick. It was not a great seat like Hawksley, but it was certainly more than one might expect for the residence of a retired major.

"Is his family well connected?" she asked.

"I really have no idea. Who cares about Crabtree? He's as old as my father would have been. He probably made a mint in India or something. Eleanor, I know there's no time now, but I have to talk to you about Walter and we won't be able to escape our maids for hours. I can't marry Lord Ranking, truly, even if Mama were to get him to offer. His nose drips."

"Then marry your Mr. Downe. You'll be twenty-one in the summer. Can't you wait until then?"

"You don't understand. I can't marry without the permission of the head of the family until I'm five-and-twenty—and that's Mama. If only I'd been born a boy! Then I'd be the earl and could do as I liked! I wouldn't care for myself if I were as poor as a church mouse, but it would ruin Walter if we ran away, don't you see? He would never get a decent living. Oh, Eleanor, what am I to do?"

"Yes, it's a problem, I see. But don't despair, dear Di. I'll help you if I can, I promise. In the meantime, I confess I'm dying to get out of these clothes and take a bath."

"Can you meet me in the long gallery as soon as you're changed? It is urgent. You see, Walter's coming to Norfolk!"

"Very well, the long gallery as soon as I'm presentable."

An hour later, Eleanor emerged from her chamber and took a critical look at herself in the huge mirror in the hall. She had bathed and was dressed in a fine white silk dinner gown, which was caught up under her breasts with a sash of pale apricot. The ends trailed down the front of her skirts to finish with two gold tassels. Small pleated sleeves gathered into apricot trimming showed off her long smooth arms. At least she had nice arms and hands, she thought ruefully. As for the rest, Lady Augusta was right: it certainly wasn't ravishing—perfectly ordinary, in fact. Brown hair, brown eyes, a nose and a mouth occupying all the right places. What more could a girl want? She laughed at herself and walked rapidly in the direction that Diana had described.

The long gallery was hung with portraits from one end to the other on one paneled wall, the other was lined with bookcases punctuated with tall windows. Each window had its own window seat, and Eleanor perched herself on one of these and composed herself to think about Diana's problem. It was already getting dark outside, though she paid it no attention, and the room began to fill with shadows.

"I hope you have hooked up your dress this time," said a cultured voice. "Have you lost another locket?"

Eleanor spun around and leapt to her feet. As she did so, she heard a small tearing sound and looked down to see that she must have been sitting on one of her gold tassels and in her haste she had ripped it off. She caught at it in her hand and held on to it as if it were a lifeline.

"Of course not," she said calmly, though her heart was pounding loudly enough to summon at least three footmen. "But instead, it seems I have lost my composure and ruined my sash. May I ask what you're doing here?"

"I might ask the same, mightn't I?" said the owner of the violet eyes, leaning back casually against a bookshelf and crossing his arms over his chest. Except for a newly changed shirt and cravat, he was dressed in the same traveling clothes he had worn at the inn, his coat as dark as his head. There was just the faintest sheen of moisture on his hair, as if he had just washed it. Eleanor had to crush the most unholy impulse to reach out and see.

"It's raining outside," he said dryly. "Hadn't you noticed? I would have thought an earl's daughter more observant. And must I answer my own question? Though it's probably easy enough: Lady Eleanor Acton and Lady Diana Hart were at school together?"

"And is Lady Diana another of your attempted schoolgirl conquests?"

He looked extremely amused. "Why, do you think I'm her type?"

"Not in the least," she snapped immediately. "Lady Diana has flawless taste and is guided always by the strictest propriety. She would never fall for a conceited libertine, without honor or scruple, who likes to practice idle flirtations on girls half his age."

"Half his age? My dear Lady Eleanor, I am only five-and-twenty. Surely you're at least seventeen?"

"Eighteen. Does Diana love you?"

"I hope so, for I love her very dearly back."

"You're an accomplished liar, too, I see. How did you get in?"

"Why, the butler opened the front door, in the usual way."

"You mean you're a guest of Lady Augusta?" It came out as a distinctly undignified squeak.

"I'm on my way to visit Major St. John Crabtree, as it happens."

"But how dare you stop at Hawksley and skulk about the private rooms?"

"I'm really not sure that I have to answer all these questions. Don't you have any of the social graces, Lady Eleanor? It's more usual, isn't it, to make small talk about the weather or some book of poetry?"

"When first introduced to another guest, I suppose it is. But not when one's first meeting was intimate enough to bring up a subject like blackmail."

"As I remember," he said perfectly seriously, "our intimacy began even before that."

Eleanor knew that her cheeks were flaming. "If you were a gentleman, sir, you would never refer to your despicable behavior at the Three Feathers. I assure you that I have forgotten it."

The depths of the blue eyes were lit with laughter. "Surely not, brown hen? I pride myself that my kisses are extremely memorable. Should I do it again, do you think, in order to refresh your memory?" He reached out one hand and gently stroked her cheek.

"You have no shame at all, have you? How can you speak so to me when you have been writing to Diana? If Lady Diana's fortune is your goal here, then I give you notice right now that I shall do everything in my power to put a spoke in your wheel."

"Ah," he said, smiling. "Hawksley. Quite a dowry for such a rattlebrain as Diana."

"You will never get it. I shall tell her of your behavior to me."

"Now that I would rather you didn't do. She is dreadfully fond of me, you know, and would be shocked to think I could behave with so little probity."

"I imagine you care nothing for her feelings, or anyone else's. Hawksley is your only aim!"

"It would be dishonest if I claimed not to love Hawksley Park, but I don't begrudge it. And I have no intention whatsoever of stealing it from Diana. How could I?"

"By marrying her, of course. No wonder she won't tell Lady Augusta about your infamous attentions. You wouldn't dare ask permission to address her only daughter, would you? What do you intend to do? Elope to Gretna Green with the heiress?"

The smile was now full of delight. At my expense, thought Eleanor, almost blind with fury. "Who exactly do you think I am, my lady?"

"I must suppose you are a certain Mr. Downe," said Eleanor. "Diana told me about you. You have been acting toward her with a complete lack of honor."

"Have I?" he said. "How very odd. As a matter of fact, I am not poor Walter, who is actually the Honorable Mr. Downe, I am . . ."

"Lee!" squealed Lady Diana Hart, hurtling into the room and straight into the man's chest. Her golden hair was bright against his dark coat as she crushed him in her arms. Eleanor had to annihilate the humiliatingly ungenerous feelings that rose in her breast.

"I've just been hearing that you're a paragon of feminine rectitude, Di," said Lee, hugging her, then holding her at arm's length to plant a kiss on her forehead. "Firstly from your humble faithful knight, the Honorable Feveril Downe, and now from your furious school-friend. And the minute you see me you act like a fishwife. What would Lady Augusta think?"

"That you're a bad influence, but then she's thought that for years. Why is Eleanor furious?"

"She thought that I was the suitor, come to steal away the heiress."

"Oh, Eleanor, you didn't?" Diana laughed. "How could you be such an idiot? This is my half-brother, Leander Campbell, and next to Walter I love him more than anyone in the world."

Three

"Your half-brother?"

"Pray, don't gape, my lady," said Lee with the smallest of winks. "Alas, it's true. Such accidents happen in even the best of families."

He walked across to the shadowed portrait that hung in pride of place above the fireplace. Eleanor had paid it no attention until this moment. But Leander Campbell lit a brace of candles and held them up before the painting. It was that of a young man in the dress of some twenty years before. The flickering light played over high cheekbones and carved nostrils and brought out deep blue highlights in the eyes. The man in the portrait wore an elegant high-collared green brocade coat with matching breeches. One hand caressed the head of a hound and the other sat on the hilt of his sword. The beautiful long fingers were identical to those that supported the candlestick, and it was the same face, with an echo of the same charm and the same infuriating arrogance. Beneath the painting lay a small gilt plaque: "Gerald Arthur Richard Hart, fifth Earl of Hawksley."

"My father," said Lee cheerfully. "And Di's, of course. An embarrassing likeness. And we share more than our looks. He was, like me, an infamous reprobate."

"Oh, fiddlesticks," said Diana. "Everybody was in those days. You would never behave as recklessly as he did."

"Wouldn't I? You have a rosy view of my character, dear sister. But Lady Eleanor doesn't know what we're talking about. She's beginning to look worried, and it's becoming impolite to leave her in the dark any longer."

Diana turned to Eleanor. "My father met Lee's mother in Scotland on his Highland tour. He returned to England just in time for the Season and never went back. But she, poor thing, was left in an interesting condition without benefit of a marriage ceremony. It was ages before he married Mama."

"Four and a half years to be exact. Which hardly excuses him, does it?" said Lee. "Her name was Moira Campbell. My grandfather, Ian Campbell, tried to hide the family scandal by shipping me off to Ireland as a baby. I was left in a convent which smelled of herbs as I remember—and sanctity, of course. The scrubby orphan was rescued and brought back to England by a passing soldier—Sir Robert St. John Crabtree, as it happens. He turned up at Hawksley Park with the foundling, only to find that the heedless younger son who had seduced my mother had become Earl of Hawksley when his brother died, married an heiress, and had then been careless enough to break his own neck, leaving Lady Augusta alone in her turn to produce Diana. I wonder when he found time to have his portrait painted?"

"You remember all this?" said Eleanor a little unsteadily.

The violet eyes were filled suddenly with amusement. "Only the nuns," he said. "They wore white sails on their heads sufficient to blow them unaided out to sea. Now don't you think we should go downstairs? We stop only long enough to pay our respects, then my friend and I hurry on to Deerfield."

"A friend?" said Lady Diana, turning pale, then pink. "Not Walter!"

"Of course Walter," replied her brother. "I came up here to warn you so that you wouldn't swoon when you found him in the house. Though it took an ungodly amount of persuasion for me to overcome his finer scruples, which is why we sojourn with Sir Robert. Not even my mesmerizing talents could make Mr. Downe stay at Hawksley, and it seemed perhaps a trifle impolitic to ask Lady Augusta to be his hostess. What do you think?"

"You brought him here? He said he would come! I think I love you to distraction," cried Diana. "But don't tell me you have left him with Mama in the drawing room!"

"Don't worry. Lady Acton is there to protect him and your mother believes him just a casual friend of mine. She's being condescending and gracious and asking him about his family."

"You mean she's being absolutely horrid and trying to make him feel inferior that his father's only a viscount."

"Which is proving a source of great concern, isn't it? Never mind, I told him to elope with you."

"Lee! How could you?"

"Of course he has far too much moral fiber and my attempts at corrupting him seem to be falling on deaf ears. So I suppose it's to be the drooping offshoot of the Duke of May? Just don't ask me to dance at the wedding."

"If you don't stop this instant, I shall never forgive you!"

"You could always go hand in hand to Lady Augusta and ask her permission for a love match, dear child," he said gently. "I believe that beneath all that starch and venom, she does care for you."

"She would never—oh, Lee, it's hopeless, truly."

"Then the only possibility is for me to undermine your lover's finer principles, isn't it?" he said, as Diana's blue eyes filled suddenly with tears.

They went together to the doorway, which Lee held open for each of the girls in turn. As Eleanor passed him he leant down and whispered in her ear.

"You see, I told you I was a bastard."

Which left Eleanor with nothing to say. She was unreservedly relieved that at least he wasn't the Walter Feveril Downe who had stolen Lady Diana's heart. Yet it would appear that the men were friends. Eleanor bit her lip. At no cost would she discuss with Diana anything about the infuriating Mr. Campbell. For how did you tell a friend that her beloved illegitimate half-brother had kissed you like a chambermaid in an inn and then offered to blackmail you over it?

As promised, Leander Campbell did little more than shake hands with the company in the drawing room before he hustled Walter back out to their carriage. Diana, however, had first made a point of clinging to Lee's arm and introducing him to Lady Acton as her brother. Eleanor's beautiful mother had no problem at all in instantly leaping to the correct conclusion.

"My dear Augusta!" she cried with considerable glee, as soon as the young men had left. "So the infamous Mr. Campbell is connected with your family! Gerald was more than a little indiscreet before he became earl, wasn't he? But I had no idea! Campbell! Was she Scottish? It was all the rage when we were young to tour the Highlands and admire the clans—I don't suppose Gerald was the only man to leave such a mark of his admiration behind. What a cross for you to bear!"

"I never realized that you would move in such circles in society that you would have made Leander's acquaintance," shot back the dowager.

"Oh, my dear!" The Countess of Acton laughed. "I have never personally met him before, of course. But I have two sons who have been known to decorate the *ton* with their talents. And a husband who isn't averse to visiting the gaming dens when we're in town. Mr. Campbell's a very high flyer, I understand."

"It's not a connection in which I take pride, Felicity, but I believe I have done my duty—more than my duty. And although I don't acknowledge him in town, he is Diana's half-brother and always allowed to visit Hawksley."

"Such a handsome young man," sighed Lady Acton,

though she still seemed closer to laughter. "He's very like Gerald as I remember him. And like his father, if all accounts are true, he's taken to reckless gaming and vice. His situation is most unfortunate, of course, but one would think there are any number of respectable trades in which he could engage."

"I am forced to admit that I believe him entirely profligate," said Lady Augusta sternly.

"How can you say so, Mama?" asked Diana, who was suffering from a rising indignation. "You know it's not true!" And then she blushed scarlet as the two countesses fixed her with their gaze.

"Diana, you know nothing at all of the matter. He was a charming child, of course. But now he throws away his life on the most worthless of pursuits. I do not deny you your relationship with your half-brother. And when we are in the country and our kind neighbor sees fit to entertain him and his friend, Mr.—what was his name . . . ?"

"The Honorable Mr. Feveril Downe, Mama," breathed Diana.

"Yes, Mr. Downe. When we are in the country, I say, I see no harm in it, but you must begin to distance yourself from your brother. Lord Ranking will not expect Mr. Campbell to come calling at May Castle."

"Yes, Mama." And Diana looked in dismay at Eleanor who had sat quietly beside her on the ottoman during the entire conversation, thinking how extremely awkward it was going to be when the handsome Mr. Leander Campbell came calling again.

The carriage splashed through the night toward Deerfield. Mr. Campbell lounged comfortably in one corner, with his booted feet on the opposite seat. An observer might have judged him simply bored, but in fact his fertile brain was thinking very seriously about the Actons. For one moment at the inn he had mistakenly believed that Eleanor was the

Lady Acton that Barnes had meant, but of course that was absurd. It was her mother, the countess. But what on earth could be that lady's connection with Manton Barnes and blackmail? And why was Lady Acton in Norfolk? After a while he looked across at his yellow-headed companion.

"If you sigh one more time, Downe, I shall simply slaughter you in your seat."

"She does care for me, doesn't she? You're her brother, has she told you anything?"

"She doesn't have to. You look at each other like paupers staring into a gingerbread stall. But our Diana's very much under her mama's thumb, I'm afraid. If you were not both such pillars of respectability, the answer would be simple, of course."

"You mean elope with her! Are you really so lost to everything, sir?"

Leander Campbell laughed. "Of course."

Walter looked away and frowned. "I'm sorry, old chap. Of course my affairs are no problem of yours. What were you thinking about?"

The violet gaze was almost black in the dark carriage. "As a matter of fact, about how I shall tell Major Crabtree that his nephew Manton Barnes is dead."

"Did he care for him?"

"Very little, I should think."

"Will you tell him it was suicide—about the blackmail?"

"Certainly not." Lee leaned back again and closed his eyes. Walter thought it the end of the conversation when suddenly his friend spoke again. "No, I am more interested in what St. John Crabtree might be able to tell me about Barnes and his connections. But right now what I should really like to know is: What the devil are the Actons doing here?"

"Visiting old friends, of course. Diana and Lady Eleanor were at the same school. It's odd, isn't it, that Lady Acton is such an outstanding beauty when her daughter's so ordinary?"

Lee sat up and fixed his gaze on his friend. "Why do you think so?"

"Why do I think her ordinary? Good Lord, Lee! I thought appreciating the finer points of the fair sex more up your alley than mine. All that straight brown hair for a start . . ."

And suddenly it seemed as if the self-possessed Mr. Campbell was truly exasperated. "For God's sake! Why must a woman be colored like either a buttercup or a crow to be considered worthy of notice? Lady Eleanor has remarkable eyes, perfect skin, and the spirit of a firebrand. I don't consider her in the least ordinary."

"Don't say you admire her?"

The answer was heavy with sarcasm. "I offer my expert judgment, that's all."

"Well, she certainly seems to have taken you in dislike," said Walter. "She would hardly shake hands when we left."

"With good reason," replied Lee, and laughed. "I met her at the Three Feathers at my most bloody-minded. I was three sheets to the wind, of course."

"I remember," said Walter dryly. "I went to bed and left you with several bottles of the best brandy in our private parlor. And Lady Eleanor was at the inn? On her way here too, I suppose. Did you run her down in the hallway?"

The obviously exaggerated sarcasm was unrelenting. "No, I threatened to ravish her, of course. And being so remarkably lost to myself, I forgot that the Actons have only one name."

"And?"

"So that to a drunkard the countess and her daughter were both Lady Acton."

"You have entirely lost me, sir."

"Forget it," said Lee. "I entirely lost myself a long time ago."

* * *

The next morning broke fine and clear. A light breeze ran through the grounds of Hawksley Park and sent little waves racing across the ornamental lake before dissipating itself in a shimmering array of tree-shaded daffodils. Three elegant ladies were strolling beside the water. Lady Diana had her arm through Eleanor's and Lady Acton walked beside them. That the countess intended to partake in such unsuitable exercise had caused a scandalized lift of Lady Hawksley's superior brow at breakfast.

"Surely you won't go walking with the girls, Felicity? I cannot approve. There is a stiff wind!"

Lady Acton had glanced casually with her beautiful black eyes at her hostess. "Why ever should you think I would care about your approval, Augusta? Do you find it beneath the dignity of a countess to use her own feet? I happen to love country walking, do I not, Eleanor?"

Eleanor, who up until that moment had never heard her mother express such a sentiment, looked up in surprise. Lady Acton was far more likely to be amused by an elegant promenade past the shops in Bond Street! But she assented willingly enough. The presence of Lady Acton would prevent further intimacy with Diana for a moment. Eleanor wasn't sure she wanted to have to hear more from her friend about the perfection of the Honorable Mr. Feveril Downe, though she had liked him immediately when they had briefly met the previous evening. Instead she wanted to think about the dastardly Mr. Campbell, for though she had determined that she would ask Diana nothing about him, she couldn't get him out of her mind.

Diana seemed to worship him. Though Lee had been sent away to school, he had spent the rest of his childhood here at Hawksley. It must have been difficult to grow up in a beautiful place like this and know that you had no right to any of it. Perhaps he was bitter about it. Eleanor's own childhood had not been particularly warm except for the love of her older brothers—but to know that your father had so cruelly abandoned both you and your mother! As the by-blow of such a man, no wonder he was irresponsible. Even her mother had heard of his reputation.

She wasn't to have the opportunity for further reflection. The ladies had barely entered the woods when three gentlemen in stylish jackets and tall boots could be seen striding toward them. Eleanor's attention was immediately caught by the object of her musing. The breeze tossed his dark hair about his forehead and sunlight glanced from the planes of his face as he made some comment to Walter. For heaven's sake, she said to herself, to have such stunning good looks hasn't helped either. No wonder he's become a profligate! He probably never did a worthwhile thing in his life. She forced herself to look away from Mr. Campbell and studied with frank curiosity the distinctly military gentleman who accompanied Mr. Campbell and Mr. Downe. His graying hair betrayed him to be a generation older, but he seemed to be hard and fit, and his vigorous stride was no slower than theirs. A splendid mustache dominated his face.

"Sir Robert!" exclaimed Lady Acton, holding out her hand as bows and nods were exchanged. "So delightful to see you again! My daughter Eleanor and I had the pleasure to meet Mr. Downe and Mr. Campbell last night."

Eleanor's hand was briefly taken by Sir Robert. He had already bowed very low over her mother's hand. It had even seemed that Lady Acton was in no particular hurry to remove her fingers from his and was blushing a little, but then the countess was an accomplished flirt and the major was an extremely distinguished-looking escort.

"Do the young gentlemen stay with you long, sir?" asked Lady Acton as she took the major's arm and they began to stroll forward.

Eleanor immediately attached herself to her mother and the major, and allowed Mr. Campbell to walk with his sister and friend.

"They come to look at some old books I have found for

sale, ma'am. Your ladyship might not know that Mr. Campbell is considered quite an authority on early editions."

"Oh, everyone in London has heard about Mr. Campbell's collection, Sir Robert. Lord Acton wished to purchase part of it for the library at King's Acton, but I understand that Mr. Campbell was not in a selling mood."

"He is never in a selling mood, my lady," laughed the major. "He only collects, he doesn't trade. And besides, I believe he loves the books like children."

Eleanor had to choke back her reaction to this surprising revelation, and with an effort she forced herself not to look at the rake and gambler who apparently spent his winnings on old books. It ought to have been simple to ignore him, but it took a great deal of resolution not to watch the dark head and listen to the infectious laugh as he walked ahead of her with Diana and Walter. Then in the next moment, she was forced to acknowledge him. They had reached a stile and Walter was helping Diana to climb it. At the same moment, her mother and the major hung back so that she was face-to-face with Mr. Campbell. She had the infuriating feeling that he was laughing at her.

"May I assist you, Lady Eleanor?" he asked politely.

"No thank you, sir. I am perfectly capable of stepping over a stile by myself."

"Then you are more cruel than I thought."

"I can't think what you mean, Mr. Campbell."

It was impossible to know if he was serious. "You rob me of the opportunity to act like a gentleman, of course. It is common practice, isn't it, for gentlemen to assist the ladies with such small obstacles when walking?"

"But I thought we had determined that you don't belong to that class of males."

"And you condemn me to remain there, like Hercules in the Underworld. Very well. By all means climb the stile by yourself." To her dismay, Eleanor saw that Diana and Walter had disappeared up the path ahead of them, and that her mother and Sir Robert seemed to have turned back to admire a patch of violets in the hedgerow. As she watched, they stepped through a gap in the hedge and were gone. Leander Campbell leaned against the stile and crossed his arms. "Only you will have to pass by me to do so," he added very gravely.

"Do you take pride in being impossible, sir?"

Lee laughed. It made the tiniest crinkles at the corners of his blue eyes. "I assure you, my lady, that I can be a great deal more impossible than this."

Eleanor refused to look away. "What do you want?"

"I want to know why Lady Acton is here in Norfolk when most of the *beau monde* are hastening to town."

"She came to visit the dowager countess, of course."

"Did she?" said Lee. "I can't think why. They are no more than social acquaintances, and Lady Augusta is one of the most unpleasant people I could think of choosing to visit. Your mother is a renowned beauty and sought after by every London hostess, yet she buries herself in East Anglia with beauty and the beast. The *ton* will be lost without her."

"I suppose Lady Augusta is the beast?"

"And Diana the beauty, of course."

"Then why aren't they too hastening to London?"

"Because Lord Ranking will stop here and escort them very shortly, and my stepmother hopes he will propose in the hall as soon as he arrives and make Diana the future Duchess of May."

"And will he?"

"Very probably."

"Diana will never accept him."

"Ah," said Mr. Campbell. "Because she's in love with Walter Downe. Quite the quandary."

"You seem to think they should elope, which you must know perfectly well Diana would never do. What can you possibly hope to gain by such advice?"

The violet eyes were looking at her quite guilelessly. "I rather hoped she would take it."

"And have Lady Augusta disown her and make you heir to Hawksley?"

He seemed to find the idea extremely amusing. "For God's sake, Lady Eleanor, that's absurd and impossible!"

"Is it? I find it despicable that you should try to use them for your own ends. You seem to me to be entirely selfish and ruthless. How can you make light of their distress? Diana will never love again like this!"

"Thus speaks the schoolgirl. Yet I fear you may be right. Walter is certainly besotted enough. But what can you know of love between men and women, brown hen?"

"Nothing, of course. Though I imagine you're an expert— on seduction, if not on love."

He laughed. "Really? For such an infamous libertine, I'm not doing very well with you, am I? You seem strangely immune to all my renowned and deadly charm when the loveliest ladies in London are at my feet whenever I beckon. But no doubt you have more romantic ideas about love than the depraved notions of a rake."

She glared at him. "I don't think I wallow in absurd sentiment, Mr. Campbell. But I do see what my brother and his wife share together, which is the most beautiful thing I have ever witnessed."

"I'm very glad to hear it." To Eleanor's immense surprise, it sounded as if he meant it. "Now," he said after a moment. "I wish you would let me hand you across this stile."

Eleanor was very angry, though she wasn't sure why. She would never allow him to so much as take her hand again! "If you will kindly stand aside, sir?"

"I'm not a monster, you know," said Mr. Campbell suddenly. "I am quite capable of giving you my hand without ravishing you."

"Or even kissing me?"

"Of course. Unless you should wish it?"

Eleanor almost stamped her foot. "I don't wish it. But perhaps I should feel better about the entire situation if you would just once apologize for your behavior at the Three Feathers."

"Now that," said Leander Campbell, with a sudden genuine grin, "I can't do."

"Why not?"

"Because only a gentleman would admit that he was sorry. A profligate like me would take pride in stealing a lady's kiss and feel no remorse at all, don't you think?" He stepped aside and made her a small bow. "By all means, climb the stile, Lady Eleanor."

Eleanor gathered her skirts in one hand. The other was occupied with her parasol, which left her no free hand to grasp the top of the little wooden obstacle. Blushing with chagrin under his merciless gaze, she awkwardly managed to mount the step and put one foot over the top.

"You have the most elegant petticoats, ma'am," said Mr. Campbell. Eleanor instantly dropped her skirts. But that left her in danger of tripping over them. So she set her parasol down in the hedge and grasped the top of the stile with both hands as she jumped down the other side. "And a very neat ankle," he continued.

Blushing to her eyebrows, Eleanor ignored him, took up her parasol, and marched away up the path.

Leander Campbell sat on top of the stile and watched her retreat. "Damnation," he said suddenly to himself and laughed. And then, as if only for his own amusement, for there seemed to be no one to hear, he began to quote aloud from Hamlet:

" 'But, you may say . . . he's very wild; / . . . And there put on him / What forgeries you please; marry, none so rank / As may dishonor him; take heed of that; / But, sir, such wanton, wild, and usual slips / As are companions noted and most known . . . to youth and liberty.' "

A soft voice behind him filled in Reynaldo's response: " 'As gaming, my lord.' "

Lee looked around to meet the arch smile of the Countess of Acton. Without hesitation, he quoted Polonius's answer: " 'Ay, or drinking, fencing, swearing, quarreling, / drabbing: you may go so far.' " The countess had the grace to blush. Though the Elizabethan expression for harlotry had gone out of use, she understood its meaning perfectly well. "I wish you good day, my lady," continued the lawless Mr. Campbell. "Have you lost the major? Oh, no, I see he's coming. And he brings violets—the symbol of Napoleon. How very quaint!"

Four

The path came out into an open meadow. There was no sign of Diana and Walter. Eleanor started across the grass and saw that there were three possible ways out of the field. In one corner two stones stood upright with just enough room between them for a person to slip through sideways while not allowing passage to a cow—an obstacle locally known as a "lady-squeezer." Further along the hedgerow, a wooden stile gave entrance to a small birch spinney. And to her left, a five-barred gate led into a lane. Any exit would leave her equally lost. To her relief she noticed that there was a rustic in leather gaiters and a sturdy smock walking up the lane. Eleanor ran over to the gate.

"Excuse me," she said, leaning on the top bar. "Have you seen a lady and gentleman pass by?"

The man shifted the pruning hook on his shoulder and looked at her. "Oh aye," he said. "Lady Diana and that young gentleman as came with Mr. Campbell, making for Little Tanning by way of the footpath. And who might you be, ma'am?"

"I'm a friend of Lady Diana's, Lady Eleanor Acton."

The rustic was chewing slowly on a briar pipe. The breeze blew the smoke away in thin eddies past his hat. "And what might have become of Mr. Campbell, then? The gentlemen all went a-calling this morning together."

The shrewd Norfolk gaze gave her no quarter. "I have no idea," she said, trying to sound dignified.

"I'd like to see him and have my say, my lady. Perhaps you could convey a message, like?"

What on earth could this honest old fellow possibly have to say to Leander Campbell? "I can't be sure to do so, sir," said Eleanor kindly. "But I will try. Is it urgent?"

The bland eyes were still fixed steadily on her face. "You might tell him from Frank Garth that the extra coal and the flannel petticoat for our Betsy was like to have saved her from being carried off this winter."

Eleanor felt herself swallow in amazement. "Flannel petticoat?"

"Aye, best red flannel—stopped the cold getting on her chest. Always very delicate about the chest, our Betsy. And Mrs. Pottage would think it a kindness to kiss his hand for the purchase of her new cow when the old one took up and died."

"Mrs. Pottage's cow?"

"Aye, and then there's the little matter of our roof."

"You mean Mr. Campbell repaired your roof?" Eleanor felt completely at a loss.

"Sent for it to be done, like. We had the rain down the wall beside the chimney and it's been a hard winter, quite froze out my rosemary. We'd many of us at Little Tanning be closer to our graves if it wasn't for Mr. Campbell."

"But Little Tanning is part of Hawksley, isn't it?" asked Eleanor. "Doesn't Lady Hawksley pay for fixing your roof?"

"The dowager countess's steward keeps a tight purse, beggin' your pardon, ma'am, though the old biddy means no harm."

"You mean Leander Campbell sends money to the tenants and sees to repairs? But it's not his estate," said Eleanor a little desperately.

"More's the pity, ma'am. He'd be a fine master, all right. Lee Campbell always looks like the devil's in his pocket, but it'd be hard on folks hereabouts if it weren't for him. He helps us from his own purse and his own kind heart; the lad doesn't get a penny from the land. As you said, it's not his. All the years we watched him growing up, there was grief he'd never be master of Hawksley Park. But no doubt little Lady Diana will marry a good man who'll see to things. Perhaps the fine young fellow she was walking with?" he added hopefully. Then when Eleanor didn't reply, Frank Garth touched his cap and turned to move away up the lane. "Through the lady-squeezer, ma'am," he said. "Another half mile will take you to the village."

"Thank you," said Eleanor to his retreating back, and then she felt herself flush with color, though she had no idea why. She had accused Leander Campbell of being entirely selfish and ruthless. After all, he had told her himself he made his living at gambling and he had kissed her without mercy or compunction—surely the behavior of a careless rake? So why was he helping the tenants at Hawksley? And he collected old books, apparently just for the love of them—an extremely odd passion for a worthless blackmailer. However was she to reconcile this with everything else she felt she knew about him?

Lady Acton looked thoughtfully at the handsome face and the fathomless violet eyes.

"Do you always, Mr. Campbell," she said acidly, "do your best to make enemies?"

"On the contrary, Lady Acton, I value friends. Though now I have one less than I did. I miss the blameless company of poor Manton Barnes, for instance, though doubtless he's as well off where he is now, as he was in the merciless streets of London."

"Manton Barnes?" repeated Lady Acton seriously. "I know the name, but I don't believe I ever had the pleasure of his acquaintance, sir."

"Your ladyship will never have it now. He's dead."

"I'm so very sorry. Was it sudden?"

"Very sudden. A gun accident."

"And you have taken it rather hard, haven't you?" The countess's beautiful black eyes looked unflinchingly into his. "I wish I had known the man who could inspire your friendship, Mr. Campbell. I have the feeling it might be rather a precious commodity, after all."

"The odd thing is," continued Lee without blinking, "that Barnes seemed to know you."

"Did he? How very extraordinary, for I'm sure I never met him. But then, I'm rather well celebrated in town, sir. Perhaps he knew of me by reputation?"

"Perhaps," said Lee, and smiled. It was a captivating smile, of genuine apology and even relief. For he was convinced, though he couldn't prove it, that the countess was telling the truth. She had not known Barnes and that was some small compensation. He very much wanted to know that the Actons were not involved in the blackmail of his friend. But then, who was? And what had Manton Barnes meant when he said that Lady Acton would know about the punishment of Prometheus?

But the Countess of Acton had turned away from him and held out her hand to the gentleman who was now joining them. Major St. John Crabtree of the splendid mustaches gave her a charming smile, a military bow, and the violets. She made no objection when both gentlemen helped her over the stile.

Lady Diana Hart and Mr. Feveril Downe were sitting side by side on some slabs of sawed wood outside the Norman church of Little Tanning when Eleanor caught up with them. As in many Norfolk villages, the church was bigger than all the little cluster of houses put together.

"Where's Lee?" asked Diana.

"I'm not sure," said Eleanor, dropping down beside Walter. "But I have a rather odd message for him from an old man I saw in the lane."

"A message?" asked Mr. Downe.

Eleanor laughed. "Yes, about red flannel petticoats and a cow. Oh, yes, and some roof repair as well. His name was Frank Garth."

"Oh, old Garth's been here forever. That's his cottage, at the end of the row," said Diana, pointing. "His wife was taken ill last winter. I took her some food and did what I could. Lee probably sent them some funds."

"Did he, by Jove?" said Walter. "I didn't know Leander Campbell was given to rustic charity, though I'm not surprised."

"Well, I am," said Eleanor.

Diana looked at her in genuine astonishment. "Lee's known folk like Garth all his life. If they have trouble they always turn to him because they know I don't have any funds of my own and he's always sure to help if he can."

"But he's a gambler, isn't he? And a libertine? I'm sorry, Di, I know you love your brother, but it seems very odd to me."

"You're too harsh, Lady Eleanor," said Walter very seriously. "Lee told me he bumped into you at the Three Feathers, in the corridor or something, and he was rude, wasn't he? He was pretty foxed, I imagine. Well, he'd just found a good friend killed and he wanted to forget about it. In normal circumstances he's never a deep drinker, believe me."

"Killed?" cried Diana. "How very dreadful!"

"It was Manton Barnes—Sir Robert's nephew, as a matter of fact. Had an accident cleaning his gun." Walter Downe flushed deeply at the necessity to lie to his beloved.

"Oh, this is awful," said Diana. "Poor Sir Robert—and how terrible for Lee! If my brother was offhand when he met you, Eleanor, surely you can forgive him?"

Eleanor said nothing. The sad death of this Manton Barnes might explain why Leander Campbell chose to get foxed,

but it certainly didn't excuse him kissing her so ruthlessly
or trying to blackmail her! But for Diana's sake, she would
try to be friendly to Mr. Campbell. After all, once this visit
was over, she would very probably never see him again. It
might be unexceptionable to be in his company in the country, but the profligate by-blow of the late Earl of Hawksley
was hardly the kind of person her mother would encourage
to come calling at Acton House on Park Lane.

Lady Acton, accompanied by Sir Robert and Lee, came
strolling from amongst the birches. The breeze whipped at
her elegant skirts and brought a flush of color to her perfect
cheeks. She looked exquisite.

"Dear children," she said, as they came up. "Sir Robert
is going to show me the brasses in the church, but by all
means go on if you wish. You will escort my daughter, won't
you, Mr. Campbell?"

"With pleasure, my lady." Lee gave her an exact bow.

"I have some bread for the ducks," said Diana, leaping to
her feet as the major and the countess disappeared in the
direction of the church. "Let's go down to the pond."

Eleanor walked beside Lee as Diana led Walter across the
green toward the duck pond, which reflected in its choppy
surface broken images of the flint-and-brick laborers' cottages. A small tree-shaded stream fed the pond and then gur-
gled away under a solid low stone bridge. The hamlet of
Little Tanning was entirely enclosed by the Hawksley estate
and every house in it was the property of the dowager countess. Thus most of the inhabitants, including the children,
were out somewhere on the farms.

"I met a certain Frank Garth," Eleanor said, clutching at
her parasol as they met the full force of the wind whipping
across the open green.

"Did you?" said Lee.

"You're to be thanked for a red flannel petticoat."

"Good heavens." He had taken off his hat and tucked it under one arm. The wind tossed his dark hair wildly about his face.

Eleanor began to try and fold her parasol, since it now threatened to turn inside out. "And a roof."

"This Mr. Garth is a doited old gaffer, no doubt."

"And a cow for one Mrs. Pottage. Does she have windmills in her head as well?"

"Without question," said Lee perfectly seriously.

"It seemed to me, sir, that Mr. Frank Garth was entirely in possession of his wits, and if the lady who is waving her apron at you from that doorway is the same Mrs. Pottage, she would seem to be a stout sensible country woman, not in the least given to wild fancies."

"Indeed," said Lee, waving back to the dairy-woman who smiled and nodded from one of the cottages. "Then perhaps I'm the one with wild flights of folly, Lady Eleanor?"

"If you try to tell me that you send charity to these people because you suffer fits of madness, Mr. Campbell, I shall only think you lacking in the wit to come up with a better explanation."

"Like the Norfolk men staring at the moon's reflection in a pond?" he said, smiling down at her. "I think the only question that arises is why four otherwise perfectly sensible people are fighting gale-force winds in order to feed some ducks. The birds are dabbling quite happily without us, although large waves are now racing through the water and our gentle spring breeze is rapidly threatening to carry us off."

"Whatever the wind, I hope my feet at least are firmly planted on the ground. Oh, no!" cried Eleanor. She burst out laughing. "There goes Diana's best bonnet!"

As she spoke, the wind also caught Eleanor's parasol, which sprang open and was torn from her grasp. It sailed wildly after the devastating little straw-chip bonnet with the blue ribbons that Lady Diana had selected with such care that morning. The truant hat whisked off across the duck pond. It seemed to hesitate for a moment above the water, then a fresh gust caught it and it went racing away into Little Tanning. The parasol, now floating like a giant dandelion seed, danced after it.

"Tally ho—the fox is away!" cried Walter. "Come on, Lee! Let's after the quarry!"

"Have you nerve to face your jumps, ma'am?" said Lee. Diana and Walter were already racing around the pond after the bonnet.

"I've ridden to hounds with my brothers, sir," laughed Eleanor, picking up her skirts in both hands and running after them. "I hope I'm game for anything!"

The bonnet was now bowling fast down the dirt lane that served Little Tanning for a main street. Walter ran full tilt after it, while Diana chased in his wake. Meanwhile the parasol had soared over their heads and lodged for a moment in the faintly greening branches of an oak tree. Eleanor and Lee raced over the bridge and without hesitation, Lee tossed aside his hat and began to climb the tree.

"For heaven's sake, be careful, Mr. Campbell!" cried Eleanor. "The parasol is of no account whatsoever!"

Her only reply was a shower of twigs as he rapidly ascended the trunk. He had almost reached the offending parasol, when another gust caught it and sent it tumbling onto the rooftops of the cottages where it proceeded to bowl along the ridge cap. Lee gave Eleanor a wink, then he let go of the tree and leapt. She felt her breath stop in her throat, then come back in a rush as he landed safely beside a softly smoking brick chimney. Instantly, he was on his feet and running lightly after the parasol. The silk fringe flapped wildly as it danced ahead of him and he leapt from one roof to the next.

"I suppose I should be grateful, Lady Eleanor," she heard him say before the wind blew away the words, "that old Frank Garth repaired his roof!"

Eleanor picked up his hat and ran along behind the cottages as Lee traced the ridges of one after another. But the parasol skipped beyond them and Lee stopped at the edge of the last roof. The quarry had spun up again out of reach. It was now rolling across the high peak of Mrs. Pottage's dairy barn. A little loop of leather hanging from its handle trailed behind it. Then with another burst of wind, it jumped up off the pantiles and the loop caught in the spinning tine of a weather-vane. Solidly captured by the highest perch in the village except for the church tower, Eleanor's parasol danced a jig in the wind as if mocking its pursuer. The space between the buildings was much too far to jump and the barn roof was some feet higher than the cottages. Yet Mr. Campbell tugged off his jacket and tossed it to Eleanor, leaving him clad in his elegant maroon waistcoat and buff breeches. The wind instantly flattened his white shirt against the strong clean muscling of his arms.

"If your ladyship would be so kind as to pass me that washing pole?" he said, as casually as if he were asking for more wine at dinner, rather than being balanced precariously on a rooftop.

Eleanor was breathless with running. "But what are you going to do?"

"Do not gainsay me, ma'am! The pole, if you please!"

Eleanor took the long forked stick that the cottagers used to prop up their laundry lines and flung it to him like a javelin. He caught it in one hand and bowed his thanks. "Where on earth," he said, as he tested the stick, "did you learn to throw like that?"

"You know I have two older brothers. We played together every summer at Acton Mead and I had to keep up, you know."

"And become an Amazon? You leave me trembling in awe of your prowess." He didn't seem to be trembling in the least, unless it was with laughter. "Now, for the parasol!"

In spite of herself, Eleanor was also laughing. "Pray, don't do anything more, sir! It's not worth it, truly!"

"I think, brown hen," he said, suddenly serious, "that it's worth a great deal to see you laugh."

"What?" said Eleanor, staring up at him.

"In all my wicked experience, ma'am," he continued with a wink, "I can't think when I have seen a more beautiful laugh, nor more beautiful eyes."

Eleanor stopped dead in her tracks. "Are you trying to court me, sir?"

But Lee was no longer looking at her. He had backed up several paces and was coiled like a spring. The smooth muscles of his back were as lithe as a cheetah's. As she watched, he took a short run and, using the washing pole, vaulted cleanly to the barn roof. Abandoned, the pole fell bouncing from the cottage roof to the ground. Lee ran along the pantiles and caught up the parasol. He flourished it in triumph.

"Don't be ridiculous, brown hen," he said lightly, as if there had been no interruption. "You're an earl's daughter, and I seem to be the most notorious rake in London. I'm certainly without birth, position, or prospects. I'd be lucky to marry a City chit with a large enough portion to support my dissolute career. In the meantime, pray don't refuse me the harmless pastime of practicing compliments."

Eleanor gazed up at him. There was an odd constriction around her heart. "For heaven's sake!" she said. "I don't want your professional compliments! Supposing they were to turn my foolish schoolgirl's head? Don't you have a conscience?"

"Of course. Even a hardened rake has some shreds of conscience when in the presence of a lady with so skillful a throwing arm. But I promise I'll keep my observations to myself in future. 'Thus conscience does make cowards of us all, / And thus the native hue of resolution / is sicklied o'er with the pale cast of thought,' " he quoted freely. "But you can't stop me thinking . . ."

With a sudden clatter, some rotten tiles gave way beneath him.

"Good Lord! The roof's giving way!" cried Eleanor.

He laughed again. Eleanor found herself filled with some indefinable emotion that she knew she'd never experienced before.

" 'And enterprises of great pith and moment,' " he continued to quote, as he edged along the ridge, " 'With this regard, their currents turn awry, / And lose the name of action.' " There was another fall of tile, and Lee watched for a moment as the pieces hit the ground and shattered. "Alas, poor Hamlet! I should have sent funds for the barn roof, too!" he said with exaggerated regret. "I'm very afraid my enterprise of great pith and moment is going to end in absurdity!"

In the next instant, Lady Eleanor Acton's heart thudded into her ribs and sent the breath from her body as a whole section of tile was dislodged and rattled down off the roof. Mr. Leander Campbell, the ground stolen from under his booted feet and his hands occupied with the parasol, slipped out of sight and began to roll off the far side of the building where it was a good twenty feet to the ground.

Five

Dropping both coat and hat, Eleanor rushed around the barn. She had a terrible vision of finding the impossible Leander Campbell shattered on the ground like the pantiles. Although she was thoroughly confused about him, she couldn't bear to think of that lithe and beautiful body being damaged. How could he behave so recklessly? He might even be dead!

Instead she found him sprawled on his back in a haystack, obviously unhurt, the parasol still grasped in one hand. Pieces of tile lay in a tumbled heap at the base of the stack where they had shot to the ground. It was not that, however, that made Eleanor's fear turn instantly to anger. It was Lee himself. Far from being suitably chastened by the dreadful results of his own wild behavior, he seemed helpless with laughter.

"How could you?" she almost shouted. "How could you be so entirely and outrageously irresponsible? You might have killed yourself!"

He sat up and began to pick straw from his shirt and hair. "My dear Lady Eleanor," he said, still smiling, "you're supposed to be impressed with my derring-do, not berating me like an irate nanny." He slipped smoothly off the side of the hay and gave her a bow. "Your parasol, my lady."

Eleanor was forced to take it. "You have ruined the barn roof!"

Lee looked around at the scattering of pantiles and smiled. "Why, so I have. I hadn't noticed."

"Of course you noticed! How can you be so ridiculous?"

"I thought I was merely irresponsible. Now I'm ridiculous as well?"

"Do you take nothing in life seriously, sir?"

"Only what warrants it, which is not very much, I find. Don't tell me you were worried about me, brown hen?"

"Not for one moment," Eleanor lied. "What happens to you leaves me perfectly indifferent. If it weren't for Diana, I wouldn't be with you at all!"

"Now that would be a shame. For I'm enjoying your company a great deal."

"Then you have a very odd sense of pleasure, sir! Most people only want to stay where they're welcome."

"But my hide is well thickened and your manners so delicate and well bred that I haven't felt unwelcome."

Eleanor colored. She was behaving more disgracefully than he! Did he think that she too held his birth against him? Anywhere he went, he probably met rejection and prejudice. Yet a lady should be gracious to anyone. Her mother certainly could put anyone at their ease if she wished. And he was Diana's brother!

"I'm sorry if I was ungracious," she said stiffly. "You were most kind to retrieve my parasol, sir."

At which Leander Campbell seemed to want to burst out laughing again. He suppressed it, but Eleanor was infuriated all the same. Violet lights danced in his eyes as he bowed formally and spoke as seriously as he might to an aged aunt.

"You are most welcome, my lady. Now, shall we find the others?"

He held out his arm and Eleanor was forced to take it. They came around the barn where Lee retrieved his discarded clothing. The wind had now died away as suddenly as it had arisen. He shrugged into his coat and ran one hand carelessly back through his hair before putting on his hat. As soon as he released Eleanor, she very deliberately left him and went to pick up the laundry pole where it had fallen. She put it back where she had found it. But Lee wasn't left standing, shamed by her action. He had crossed the yard and knocked at one of the cottage doors. Mrs. Pottage came out and they talked together. Eleanor noticed that far from being furious at the destruction of her barn, Mrs. Pottage seemed only delighted that Mr. Campbell would deign to stop and talk with her. *He thinks he can do whatever he likes and charm his way out of the consequences!* thought Eleanor. *Well, not with me!* Then she looked away from him as Diana and Walter came running up from behind the cottages.

"Oh, Eleanor!" called Diana in genuine distress. "Come quickly! Your mother's been taken ill!"

All thoughts of the infuriating Mr. Campbell took instant flight. Eleanor and her mother weren't close. The Countess of Acton was too elegant, too clever, and too beautiful to have ever made a particularly warm mama, but Eleanor loved her and even felt an odd sense of wanting to protect her. Her husband was a harsh man. They had been married to each other because it had made a brilliant match, not because of any empathy or love, and they had almost nothing in common. Lady Acton wasn't able to take refuge in her children, though in a distant way she wanted them to be happy. Instead she had thrown herself into the giddy delights of high society and become a social butterfly. Yet though the countess might look fragile and delicate, she was never ill. Eleanor's concern was genuine as she ran after Diana.

Lady Acton was sitting on the firewood outside the church. The major hovered over her in obvious distress.

"What is it, Mama?" asked Eleanor as she hurried up.

"Nothing, really! Pray don't refine so, everyone. I just felt a little faint while in the church, that's all. The fresh air has me quite revived."

"Let me go for the carriage, my lady," said Lee, who had

followed Walter and the girls. "You shouldn't walk back to Hawksley."

Eleanor sat beside her mother and took her hand. Lady Acton's pulse was a little fast and her skin seemed pale and clammy. "You are so kind, Mr. Campbell. Will you go?" the countess asked, looking up at him.

He bowed. "Nothing would bring me more pleasure."

"I saw a cob in the pasture behind the church," said Walter. "Come, I'll help you get him."

As Eleanor watched, the two young men ran off to fetch the horse. Moments later she saw Lee, riding bareback and with just a halter, set the horse into a canter in the direction of Hawksley Park. He seemed to personify the power and grace of a centaur. Walter came puffing back up to them.

"He'll have the carriage here in two shakes," he said earnestly. "And the doctor will be summoned. I insisted on it." His honest eyes searched Lady Acton's face. She already seemed much recovered. Perhaps Lee had been right.

"You'll send for a doctor, won't you?" Walter had asked as Lee caught up the surprised nag.

The blue eyes had looked back at him with a faint derision. "Do you think one necessary?"

Mr. Downe was used to his friend's manner, but this really annoyed him. "For heaven's sake, Campbell!" he replied. "Lady Acton looks as if she'd seen a ghost."

Lee leapt onto the horse's back, then smiled down at his friend. "Precisely," he said. "Lady Acton isn't sick. She's had a shock. Something has happened to frighten her. Now what, do you suppose?"

"Frighten her? In a church? What could have scared her in there?"

"No so much what—as who, dear Walter."

Which had left the Honorable Mr. Downe more puzzled than ever. For Lady Acton's only companion in the church was the straightforward major who was proving such a good host at Deerfield. Sir Robert St. John Crabtree hardly seemed the type to frighten a woman. Indeed, Walter would have said that if the major had any feelings for Lady Acton, they took the form of doting admiration. His thinking stopped there. It was only Lee whose perceptive gaze went so much further. The judgment that resulted, however, he would obviously keep to himself.

By the time the curricle arrived, driven by the Hawksley coachman, Lady Acton was indeed quite recovered—at least from physical ill-effects. Lee had ridden back on the cob. It didn't seem to have bothered him in the least to ride fast with no saddle, and he slipped easily from his mount's back and gave it a pat. While Walter held the horse by the halter, Lady Acton laughed charmingly at Lee and the major, and allowed them to help her into the carriage. Eleanor and Diana climbed in beside her. The gentlemen would walk back to Deerfield and send inquiries later.

As the carriage bowled away, Eleanor refused to look back. Had she done so, she wouldn't have been able to read anything from Mr. Campbell's expression, for that gentleman was already in conversation with Manton Barnes's uncle, Major Crabtree, and appeared to have forgotten her. Lee didn't look once at the retreating hats and colorful dresses, nor at the parasol which had cost him so much effort. It was only Eleanor who had to face the strange and disturbing emotions the sight of her own sunshade seemed destined to bring her. Firmly she thrust them out of her mind, and concentrated instead on a question that seemed less troubling: what on earth had happened to her mother in the church?

Lady Augusta was in alt that evening as they all sat at dinner. She turned to Lady Acton with considerable satisfaction.

"I thought it could not be suitable, Felicity, for you to tramp through the lanes as if you were a mere nobody. Look at the result! You had to be brought back in the carriage, as

white as a sheet! It causes distress among the tenants when
we do what is inappropriate. Nothing is more important than
to maintain the distinctions and dignity of our station. Pride
of birth, of rank—social position is everything. Society
would be overthrown without it."

Eleanor glanced at her mother. Something was still wrong.
Lady Acton had recovered her color and poise, but there was
a tension in her that Eleanor couldn't remember ever having
noticed before. What could have happened?

"No doubt we shall have revolution if countesses walk
too often," replied Lady Acton acidly. "But since Acton is
an older title than Hawksley, I don't think it is your place,
Augusta, to criticize what I choose to do. I was a little faint
from the wind, nothing else! It is hardly enough to cause
scandal!"

Lady Augusta gave one lift of the eyebrows. It would always rankle that the Countess of Acton enjoyed precedence
over the Countess of Hawksley, due to an accident of history.
It was also frustrating that Lady Acton was such an accepted
arbiter of taste. Scandal had never been attached to her name,
in spite of her beauty and fortune. Lady Augusta sniffed and
relapsed into silence. Felicity might have more social standing, but the Hawksley name was among the greatest in the
land. No one should ever take that from her.

Sir Robert came that evening in person and by himself to
inquire after Lady Acton's health. Eleanor had retreated into
the library where she found a wonderful selection of old
books. Choosing one from the shelf, she curled herself into
a large old-fashioned settle by the fire. The tall wooden
wings left her entirely hidden from anyone who might come
into the room. Diana and the dowager countess were playing
cards together and Lady Acton had retired. Eleanor really
should have made up a third hand or played for her hostess
at the pianoforte, but she had excused herself also and es-

caped into this lovely room with its rich old paneling and shelf upon shelf of books. There was nothing she particularly needed to think about, but her emotions felt oddly fragile and she wanted to be alone. When she heard the door open, she began to stand up and make herself known, then in the next breath, she was frozen where she sat.

"Robert, thank God! In here—we can be alone. Do you know any more?" It was Lady Acton's voice.

"Sweetheart, are you recovered, truly? I felt like a brute to give you such news in the church, but what else could I have done?"

Eleanor shrank back into her settle. For heaven's sake! The major was calling her mother "sweetheart"?

"No, you did right, of course. I had to know immediately and it was private there. No doubt I shall get my own request soon enough. You have given me some warning and for that I'm grateful. Better to feel faint in Little Tanning than pass out beneath the breakfast table at Hawksley."

"But such news! It tears out my heart to see you so distressed."

Lady Acton gave a bitter little laugh. "I would I had not been so foolish as to write to you. How could you keep my letters when I instructed you to burn them, as I did yours?"

The major's voice dropped. "I couldn't bring myself to do it. Your sweet words were all I had. I have read and reread them—I know them by heart, my dear."

"Then I wish you could have relied on your memory, since it's so perfect! Now this unknown person has them. Stolen, you say, from Deerfield?"

"I am more than mortified, Felicity. If I could get the letters back by cutting off my right hand, I would do so."

"I imagine that gold will be more to our tormentor's taste than your flesh, Sir Robert, however nobly given. How much is he asking?"

The answer seemed wrung from him. "More than I have."

"But not, probably, more than I have. Very well. I am

prepared to be bled dry. I have my own fortune. The earl shall never know—indeed, he must never know or I shall be ruined."

"I am so angry and so humiliated," said the major. "Yet I cannot find it in my heart to regret our love, Felicity. You are more to me than the earth."

"Oh, spare me, sir! We are adults. We know quite well what we have meant to each other. Pray, don't make it more than it is. You may regret nothing, but I regret everything very bitterly. Had you done as I asked and burned my letters, I wouldn't now be considering the pleasures of being black-mailed."

"Forgive me, my dear. I'll move heaven and earth to find the villain who stole the letters, believe me."

"He's picked a good target, hasn't he?" said Lady Acton. Eleanor could imagine the look of irony on her mother's beautiful face. "The Countess of Acton! This rogue is going to become a very rich man. Now, leave me, sir. Tomorrow will be soon enough for me to begin to decide which jewels I shall have to sell."

The door opened and closed again. The major had gone. Eleanor sat where she was and listened for her mother to also leave the room. She now understood very exactly why the countess had looked so ill when she came out of the church. Eleanor felt a little pale and clammy herself. It might be a shock for Lady Acton to learn that her indiscreet letters had been stolen and were in the hands of a blackmailer, but it was perhaps more of a shock for her eighteen-year-old daughter to learn that her lovely mother had been having an affair.

Yet could she blame her? The major was very good-look-ing and made witty enough company. Compared to her fa-ther, who looked and behaved something like Henry VIII with the headache, he must have seemed charming indeed. It was only natural that the countess had looked outside of her barren marriage for a little solace. But this business of the letters was a disaster! If it ever came out, the earl would demand a divorce. Lady Acton, who lived only for society, would find herself an outcast. No wonder she was prepared to sell her jewelry. Eleanor put her head in her hands. What crime was more despicable than blackmail? Her mother had never harmed a soul. Did a moment of human weakness deserve a lifetime of punishment? Who could possibly have stolen the letters? And then unbidden it came to her:

"First you must tell me what you know about blackmail, brown hen."

Lee! When they had first met at the Three Feathers, he had said that. She had thought he meant to blackmail her over the kiss, but he knew the major, he was staying at Deerfield, and he gambled for a living—he must be in constant need of money. Opportunity and motive, both were there. She had thought him arrogant and infuriating, but not really so completely despicable! Now why should that realization hurt so very much?

"How much did you hear?"

Eleanor was so lost in her own misery, she didn't respond until Lady Acton sat beside her and repeated the question. "How much did you hear, Eleanor?"

She looked up to meet the countess's gaze. "I didn't mean to eavesdrop, truly, but how could I make myself known with the major there? Oh, Mama, I'm so terribly sorry. No wonder you felt ill!"

"Oh, it was nothing. I admit I was upset when I first heard, my dear, but it's not the end of the world. Why, I think being blackmailed might add a little spice to life. It's never happened to me before!"

"But to sell your jewels! Papa will notice."

"Dear child, I have a fortune of my own, as no doubt the blackmailer is aware. It'll be a while before the diamonds must go to be cleaned, believe me. Do you hate me?"

Eleanor looked into the lovely black eyes. "Hate you? Why?"

"For not being faithful to your father."

"No, of course not! How could l? You didn't choose him!"

At which Lady Acton threw back her lovely head and laughed. "No, my father did and at the time it broke my heart. I thought I was in love with a young man, you see, who was entirely unsuitable. But he married someone else, and your father and I rub along well enough. Lord Acton's a good man at heart, Eleanor; I wouldn't hurt him for the world. He must never know about this."

"He won't learn it from me!"

"I know he won't. And no doubt Major Crabtree will recover my letters and he won't learn from the blackmailer either."

"Do you have any idea who the villain is?"

"None. But he'll reveal himself eventually and then Robert will shoot him. Now, in the meantime, I want you to put it out of your head. Promise me that you will?"

Eleanor shook her head. That was the one thing she couldn't promise. If Leander Campbell was blackmailing the major and her mother, she would do her best to stop him. In the meantime, she had no proof and she had better keep her suspicions to herself. Lady Acton chucked her gently under the chin.

"Never mind, Eleanor. You're a remarkable child and so are your siblings. If there's one thing I shall never fathom, it's how your father and I produced such a splendid brood. And yes, you are all your father's children; don't worry."

With that, she rose gracefully to her feet and winked. Eleanor smiled back. Lady Acton might have been a little indiscreet, but she wasn't foolish. Eleanor knew that her reassurance was true. In fact if her mother hadn't mentioned it, she wouldn't have given such a thought the time of day.

"We all look just like different bits of the two of you, except me," she said with a grin. "Look at Richard: he has your eyes and Papa's hair. But I've seen the portraits of Papa's mother, and she and I might have come out of the same plain brown pod. Actually, I wouldn't mind in the least having a different father, but there you are. We don't choose our parents."

"Nor do we choose our children," said Lady Acton with mock severity. Then she turned with a last shared smile and left the room.

Eleanor stared into the fire. Mr. Leander Campbell! An image of him carelessly running along the rooftops and athletically controlling the bareback horse danced in the flames. He was so very handsome and undeniably charming, she had been in danger of being dazzled for a moment. Well, she shouldn't blame herself too much if her head had been turned a little—she had spent most of her life so far in complete shelter at Miss Able's Select Academy for Young Ladies. What did she know about rogues like Mr. Campbell? Her brothers were selfless men of impeccable honor. Though she didn't know all the details, she had gathered from Helena that Richard had recently risked his life in Paris trying to save innocent girls from ruin. Harry too would move heaven and earth to do what was right. Men like her brothers lived and were prepared to die by their personal codes of honor, however much they might delight in a careless appearance.

Meanwhile Leander Campbell appeared to be entirely ruthless. He hadn't thought twice about threatening her at the inn. He was trying to get Diana to elope with Walter. No doubt it was somehow a way to steal his sister's inheritance. And now it seemed that he had stolen Lady Acton's letters and was blackmailing her and the major about it. Mr. Campbell might be Diana's half-brother and used to the blind adoration of females, but he hadn't met Acton determination before. What he didn't know was that Lady Eleanor Acton was onto his game. *Virtus Actonorum in Actione Consistit.* It was the Acton motto: Action is the Acton virtue. If he thought of blackmailing an Acton, the arrogant Leander Campbell was going to find out very soon that he had at last met his match!

Six

At that moment the arrogant Leander Campbell was indeed thinking about blackmail. He and Walter Downe were sitting comfortably before the fire at Deerfield. Each man sipped gently at a glass of the finest brandy from the major's superb cellar. Lee held his up for a moment to the light and watched the seductive change in its color.

"Have you learned anything, Lee?" Walter was asking him.

"About Manton Barnes? No, I haven't. Sir Robert was never close to his nephew. Certainly, he was rarely here as a child. We met for the first time at Eton. Sir Robert claims to know very little about Manton's private life and to take little interest."

"Then Barnes kept his secret from his uncle?"

Lee looked thoughtfully into the hearth. "It would appear so. Sir Robert said all the correct things when he learned of our friend's death, but I don't think it touched him at all. But then he's never been a man to show much genuine emotion, I think."

"He wouldn't suspect suicide?"

"Why should he? There's no reason to think he knew Barnes might be facing the gallows. No, someone else knew and I suspect it was Blanche who told him."

"Miss Blanche Haricot?"

"Who else? She was devastated when Barnes broke off their engagement. I suggested he make some excuse, but perhaps he told her the truth and in her distress she went to someone else for help—someone who then used that knowledge for blackmail."

"You suggested he break off the engagement? I didn't know you had a hand in it."

Lee stood up and strode to the sideboard. He refilled his glass. In the flickering light from the candles, his features looked stark. "May God forgive me! It's too easy, isn't it, to give advice? When Barnes told me he'd proposed to Miss Haricot, I gave him the worst dressing-down he'd ever received in his life! Poor fellow! He hoped marriage would be a cover for him, but he'd never thought of Blanche. I couldn't stand aside and let him ruin her life! I would do it again, even knowing the consequences, but as it turned out, one might lay Barnes's death at my door, I suppose."

"That's nonsense, Lee, and you know it. If he hadn't been blackmailed, he'd never have taken his own life."

"And if I hadn't interfered, he'd have married and kept his secret for ever. There'd have been no blackmail."

"No, you did the right thing—to save Miss Haricot. But if you think she told someone the truth, why don't you ask her? Where is she now?"

"In America," said Lee with a wry smile. "And no one knows where."

"Then there's no way to find out anything at all?"

"Not from her, certainly. And I have no other leads. Yet . . ." He stopped.

"Yet, what?" asked Walter.

"Yet Major Sir Robert St. John Crabtree isn't telling me the truth. God knows why. I've known the man since I was five years old and I've always respected him. Of course, I've seen little of him these last few years, but I thought he was even fond of me. He's holding something back, I can sense it." He turned again and strode across the room to the window. Pulling aside the drape he looked out into the dark night. In the light of the flambeaux, a solitary horseman rode up the drive. "No doubt it's not important," he said calmly. "The major returns. I hope he found Lady Acton recovered— and that she's not chained to a rock while vultures devour her alive."

Walter looked sharply at his friend. What was he talking about? Then he sighed. Leander Campbell always saw more than anyone else. It was one of the things that made his friendship so attractive and yet so infuriating. How could brother and sister be so different? For Lady Diana was as open and uncomplicated as a daisy. Walter sighed more deeply. In the next moment he forgot all about the problem of Manton Barnes and the mystery surrounding him, and instead began to think about Diana. Thus when Major Crab-tree entered the room, he found both his guests looking re-laxed and happy. It was only with Walter, of course, that the expression reflected the true state of mind.

Eleanor had made up her mind with great resolution, but she had no idea how she could put it into practice. Obviously she couldn't just march up to Leander Campbell and accuse him of blackmailing her mother. He would merely laugh and deny it, and then carry right on with his nefarious scheme. Somehow she would have to get proof. Yet she was just a young woman in a world where only men had any freedom of action. She had never really resented it before, but she did now. Nevertheless, she would do what she could, so when Diana suggested the next morning that they walk over to Deerfield, Eleanor agreed instantly. It would put her into Mr. Campbell's unsettling company, of course, but that was the price she was going to have to pay if she was to rescue Lady Acton.

They took the path which lead through Little Tanning, but not by way of the footpath and the stile. Instead the two girls followed the lane where Eleanor had seen Frank Garth the day before. As they came up to the village, they were greeted by the sound of hammering.

"Oh, good! Lee's having the barn roof repaired at last," said Diana. "Mrs. Pottage will be so pleased. She's been after Mama to fix it for so long, but our agent always encourages us to wait until the last minute and the tenants have a dreadful time of it."

"Well, I should think he ought to do it," said Eleanor indignantly.

"Why? It's outrageously generous of him. He only does it because he's fond of the people here."

"After he brought down half the pantiles yesterday, of course he must do it. And he has a very odd way of demonstrating fondness for people, since he almost destroyed their barn. He's lucky the roofers were able to get here so fast, or Mrs. Pottage might not be smiling so kindly the next time she saw him."

Diana gave her a puzzled look. "Oh, no, he's had it arranged to get this roof done for ages. There was a delay in getting the workmen free, that's all. Good heavens, Mrs. Pottage said the thing was positively dangerous and the next storm would have half the tile into her haystacks."

Eleanor took her friend by the arm. "Are you trying to tell me that your brother knew this roof was unsafe and had already arranged for the men to come today? That he knew all that yesterday?"

Diana gave her an exasperated grin. "That's exactly what I'm saying."

"Then he's an impossible, deceitful, manipulative—"

Diana interrupted her. "Why on earth must you fly into the boughs about it? Eleanor, I wish you'd be nice to Lee. He has the hardest time of it and he's the most generous, most honorable, best person in the world! There's no one to match him, you know."

Eleanor looked down and bit her tongue as Diana stalked away. Mr. Campbell must be mad! He had gone running after her parasol even though he knew that the roof might give way beneath him. It was splendidly dashing, of course, and it meant that he knew that it didn't matter if the roof was damaged by his boots, but didn't danger mean anything to him? She remembered how he had looked as he leapt to the barn from the top of the cottages. No, he had liked it! The man enjoyed a physical challenge and had the most conceited faith in his own athletic ability. He'd never believed for a moment that he might be hurt. *Nor did he care if I was worried,* she thought fiercely. Then she shook her head. It seemed that ever since she had met Mr. Campbell, she must constantly find herself lost in confusion about him. Only one thing seemed clear. She felt angry and it was his fault.

"Good day, my lady."

Eleanor looked up. Old Frank Garth stood at her elbow and had just doffed his cap. Lady Diana had gone over to the cottages and was talking with Mrs. Pottage.

"Why, good day, Mr. Garth," she replied with a smile. "Are you just returning from hedging?"

"Aye, I am that. Did you see Mr. Campbell and give him my message?"

"Yes, I did. Why didn't he come to see you himself?"

The old countryman and the young lady fell into step together and began to walk into Little Tanning. "Well, he will, no doubt, before he leaves," said Mr. Garth. "He did pay his compliments to the missus already. But he's a lot on his plate, that young man, besides visiting with an old gaffer, and I've been out in the lanes, not so easy to find."

"You've known him since he was a boy, haven't you, Mr. Garth?"

"Aye. He was always a good lad—a bit wild, but a heart of gold."

How could Lee have been so deceptive that none of these simple people had seen through him? "And were you always a hedger?"

They had stopped where they could watch the workmen

putting up the pantiles. Eleanor found she always took pleasure in seeing any such display of skill. Frank Garth had narrowed his eyes and was also admiring the men as they neatly and swiftly replaced the roof.

"Oh aye. I never amounted to very much, my lady. But my brother was a carpenter. If he were alive he'd have been happy to have helped us out with repairs. Though he was a fine finish carpenter, mind you. He could build cabinets and furniture and such like, as pretty as a picture. He went for a 'prentice to Norwich and never worked around here, except for that little project for the major."

Eleanor was paying only scant attention, for her mind was still filled with her indignation about Leander Campbell. She smiled and asked a polite question about the brother's work.

"Well, the major wanted some little secret chambers put in, behind the paneling in the library at Deerfield. My brother told me about it; he was proud as a peacock about his work. You'd never know the places were there, he told me, until you twisted the rose-bosses. Then the panels slide back and there's your cupboard, as neat as a pin."

And suddenly Eleanor was passionately interested. There were secret cupboards at Deerfield, where a person could hide things—like letters! "Did Leander Campbell know of these secret cupboards, Mr. Garth?"

"Oh aye, I'm sure he must have done. Though he was just a lad, he liked to learn from my brother, or any of us. Lee Campbell could weave down or trim out a capital piece of hedgerow if he'd a mind to it, I dare say!"

Then the old man tipped his hat and walked off, leaving Eleanor with her heart in her mouth, standing in the lane. If Mr. Campbell had stolen her mother's letters from the major, they might well lie hidden in one of the secret compartments in the library at Deerfield. What if she could recover the letters? That would put a spoke in Mr. Campbell's wheel! Moments later, Diana rejoined her and slipped her arm into Eleanor's. Diana could never hold a grudge for long. She had already forgiven her friend for saying such odd things about Lee.

"Old Frank Garth's taken a liking to you," she said with a laugh. "He's pretty close as a rule with his affection, but the fellow's a great judge of character."

Except where it comes to Lee! thought Eleanor. *He's got even the honest old farm worker wrapped around his little finger. Mr. Campbell is a despicable rogue! If it weren't for my mother, I'd never give him the time of day again.* But an idea had already taken hold in Eleanor's active imagination. *Virtus Actonorum in Actione Consistit,* indeed. As soon as the opportunity presented itself, she would act.

Deerfield lay in a pretty little park. It seemed that no expense had been spared to make it into an idyllic gentleman's country seat. The gardens were extensively landscaped in the modern style and an army of gardeners were in invisible residence. Their ceaseless labor maintained the appearance of an untamed wilderness suitable for ladies and gentlemen to admire. There was also a Greek temple, an orangery, and an impeccably kept stable. Diana led the way through the home wood toward the back of the house.

It was totally unexceptionable that they should call. Lady Acton preferred to remain indoors today, but she was much recovered and sent her sincerest thanks for the gentlemen's concern, as expressed by the major the previous evening. Diana and Eleanor could assure them that Lady Acton had taken no permanent ill-effects from her faintness in the church. At least, that was what they would say; though Eleanor thought very bitterly that her mother might well have a permanent problem, unless her own plan worked, and it might be some time before she would get the chance to put it into action. Meanwhile she would have to try to be polite to the detested Mr. Campbell. How was she to manage when she saw him?

The girls reached the edge of the woods; the charming brick house seemed to smile at them over its lawns. And it was then that Eleanor discovered that in spite of all her firm resolutions, she was far from indifferent to Leander Campbell's charisma. The long patch of sward that lay behind Deerfield had been set up as a cavalry exercise ground. While Walter Feveril Downe cheered from the sidelines, Major Crabtree and Lee were practicing their horsemanship. Eleanor had never seen anything like it.

Lee was mounted on a huge black charger, very different from the simple old cob he had ridden bareback the previous day. The horse rippled with muscle. His shining coat was already dark with sweat and flecked with little beads of foam from his mouth. The major was similarly mounted on a large bay. Each man held a lance and, as Walter threw out inflated pigskins, they took turns galloping like Apaches down the field and impaling the innocent objects on their spears. The major was accurate, fast, and solid. But Lee rode with a dash and flair that sent Eleanor's heart into wild palpitations. At the side of the field, a series of poles had been set up to make an elaborate obstacle course. With his lance in one hand and the reins in the other, Lee set his mount at the poles and cleared them all in a blurring display of agility. He was laughing.

"Come, Major!" he cried. "I'll wager you five guineas you'll not make it through one more time!"

"Damn you, Campbell! You'll never beat me at my own game, sir!"

The major spun his bay and rode after the younger man. His face was red and the mouth was set into a grim line under the splendid mustaches. He managed to clear the poles, but it was clear he was laboring.

Lee merely laughed and challenged him again.

"What's he doing?" asked Eleanor. "Your brother deliberately mocks the major, Diana! How can he? It's disgraceful!"

Diana looked genuinely puzzled. "I don't know! It isn't like Lee, truly, to show up someone else. Major Crabtree is angry! Oh, Eleanor!"

Diana clutched at Eleanor's hand as Lee rode at the poles again. Walter had run out and raised the height of the last element. It was almost above his head. Without hesitation, Lee set his mount at the obstacle. Eleanor wasn't sure she could watch, but found she couldn't tear her eyes away. The black gathered its haunches and propelled itself into the air. The jump was cleared and Lee still sat the horse as carelessly as if he sat at table.

"Now, Major! Top that, if you will!"

"You're mad, sir!" cried the major.

He pulled viciously at his horse's mouth and spun the bay around. Then he raised his lance and brought it down hard across the wooden jump. The shaft shattered and sent a shower of splinters into the air.

"I'll try your swordsmanship instead, you young puppy," he shouted, and drew his blade from the scabbard.

Lee tossed his lance to Walter and galloped his horse past the major. He was also wearing a cavalry saber, but he hadn't drawn it. Major Crabtree slashed at him as he passed. Diana gave a little scream. Eleanor put her arm around Diana's waist and pulled her further back into the trees.

"Don't distract them!" she whispered. "They haven't seen us. For God's sake, I think your brother's gone insane!"

For Lee had turned his horse and was once again putting himself in the way of the major's blade. Sir Robert stood in the stirrups and struck with the entire force of his body. Lee wasn't there to receive the blow. He had dropped to one side of his saddle and the steel whistled harmlessly through the air. Once again he recovered his seat and turned his horse.

"Who on earth trained you, Sir Robert?" he mocked. "Attila the Hun?"

The major was purple with fury. "I was trained in the King's Own as an officer and a gentleman, sir! Damn the day I rescued a bastard from an Irish bog! I thought to see you raised as a member of the English gentry, but your mother was a slut and blood will out."

Lee merely laughed. "Don't let the shade of Ian Campbell of Blairmore hear you malign his pure Highland blood, sir. My mother was merely a woman. Anyway, she didn't teach me to ride and to fight—you did!"

And then he drew his own sword. Walter Downe had been standing beside the field with his jaw dropped throughout this extraordinary exchange. What on earth was the matter with Lee? Walter knew that his friend often had strange ways of going about his concerns, but this was lunatic! Someone was going to get hurt. Yet there was nothing, short of praying for a sudden downpour of rain, that he could do about it. If he tried to stop them he might well be mowed down himself, for the urbane and charming major seemed to have undergone a complete change of character. He was overwhelmed by his anger and on the verge of completely losing control. Was that what Lee wanted?

The riders clashed in the center of the field. The major's sword swung up and struck, but Lee's blade was there to meet it. "Try harder, Sir Robert," he said. "You strike no better than some soft city fellow; poor Manton Barnes could have done better."

And then Lee really had to fight for his life. The major went blind with fury. As the horses backed and spun, Sir Robert's sword hammered at Lee's defense.

"I can't bear it!" sobbed Diana. "Crabtree's going to kill him! And Lee isn't even fighting back. He could disarm the major if he wanted to! I know he could!"

But Eleanor dismissed this as the wishful thinking of a besotted sister. For Lee was retreating under the onslaught. His mount backed and backed away from the bay, until the blade flew from his hand to be lost in the grass and he was disarmed. When the major's sword slashed once again, Lee vaulted cleanly from his horse's back and onto the turf. The bay reared as Sir Robert jerked him around, and Lee was forced to drop and roll to avoid the deadly hooves. When the major also leapt from his mount, it was to raise his sword over the figure of a man spread-eagled and apparently helpless on his back. The loose horses galloped toward the stables, where the major's expensively liveried grooms caught them up. Diana tore from Eleanor's arms and ran out onto the field.

Walter's astonishment and distress when he saw Diana was obvious. He raced to intercept her. Meanwhile Eleanor could not take her eyes from the figures on the grass. She could no longer hear what they were saying, for the exchange seemed to be taking place in hissed whispers. But while the major might think he had Lee at his mercy, in his blind fury he hadn't seen what she had: Lee's outstretched hand was lying on the hilt of his weapon where it had fallen into the grass. If the major tried to thrust home his saber, Lee would be able to intercept the blow. He might appear to be beaten, but the defeat was voluntary. It's all a game to him! she thought wildly: people's emotions, people's lives—even his own. Diana's brother is a consummate rogue!

And at that moment, Lee saw them: Diana and Walter— and Lady Eleanor Acton, standing white-faced in the trees.

"I yield, Sir Robert," he said instantly. "Forgive my ill-humor and worse tongue. You're a damned fine swordsman, sir! And a true gentleman. Too true no doubt to butcher me as I deserve."

At which Sir Robert slowly straightened and put away his blade. "No harm done, Campbell!" he said with bluff good humor. Eleanor could tell what an effort it cost him to swallow his anger. "You gave me a damned fine workout, sir! Made me feel young again. Now what do you say to some refreshment?"

Lee sat up. The thin April sunshine danced across the planes of his face and caught dark highlights in his disordered hair. He was smiling, but not as if with genuine satisfaction. "As you have noticed, we have female company to grace your drawing room, Major. No doubt Lady Eleanor and my sister would like some tea after witnessing our shocking display. Lady Eleanor looks pale as a ghost."

Sir Robert glanced at her and bowed. He was still breathing hard and there was a strange glitter in his eyes. Eleanor thought that surely the major would come and escort the ladies into the house, but it was as if he still couldn't be certain of his control over his emotions. Instead he merely called out that he would go in and have the servants prepare tea. Meanwhile Walter had taken Diana's hand and was leading her in through the French windows, which left Eleanor facing Lee alone on the grass.

He met her gaze frankly enough, but the violet eyes were unreadable.

" 'Why, what should be the fear?' " he quoted softly. " 'I do not set my life at a pin's fee.' "

Seven

"I was not afraid!" said Eleanor indignantly.

Lee stood up. Then he bent to catch up the saber and thrust it into the scabbard. "No, because you knew I was in no danger, didn't you?"

"I don't give a tinker's whistle whether you live or die, Mr. Campbell! Why were you baiting the poor major like that? I never saw such a mean, ungentlemanly display in all my life."

"You are right, of course. I have no excuse."

"But you must have had a reason!"

He sighed. "If I did, it wasn't good enough. I achieved precisely nothing and wish very fervently that ladies hadn't had to witness it."

"Diana was very upset!"

"She'll no doubt forgive me."

"Yes, because she loves you. You trade on that quite a bit, don't you? Other people's love and honor. Like the major's. In spite of his anger, he'd never have harmed you. He rescued you from the convent!"

The violet eyes flashed. "And lives to regret it? Good God, Lady Eleanor, you are very quick to take sides, aren't you? But then you think honor and loyalty are involved. I won't deny it. I owe the major more than I can say. He did indeed bring me back from Ireland. He had no reason that I can fathom for so doing. When I was a boy, he even taught me to ride and shoot. I thought him the very model of a gentleman. There can be no reason at all for me to bait him, can there, except for my own perverse ingratitude?"

"I don't know," said Eleanor desperately. She couldn't account for her own feelings when she faced Leander Campbell. She could easily build him up into a monster in her imagination, but when they were together it was as if a clamor of other voices jumbled together in her mind to confuse her judgment. *It's because he's so beautiful,* she told herself. *That's why he gets away with it. Because no one can believe that such a face and such a body could hide nefarious intent. Wasn't the devil always supposed to be attractive? And to so abuse the poor major, after creating this predicament over her mother's letters! It was unconscionable.*

"I wish it could be different, my lady," said Lee suddenly. Then he grinned, as if it cost him no effort at all. "Just don't forget that I'm a bastard. You don't need to find reasons for my behavior, they're all bad ones. And I'm not even foxed this time."

As he had claimed to be when he kissed her? Eleanor was furious to feel herself blush. "Nor were you yesterday when you pretended not to know that the roof was unsafe!"

"Only a slight error of judgment," he said. "I had ordered it repaired, but I had no idea it was in imminent danger of collapse."

"You must have done."

He shrugged. " 'Mad let us grant him, then,' " he quoted.

"You *must* be mad!" said Eleanor. "Now I think I shall go and get some tea."

She whirled away and dashed up to the house in a flurry of muslin. Lee watched her go. Then he sat back down on the grass and put his head in his hands.

"You're a damned idiot, Leander Campbell," he said to himself after a moment. "Let her hate you! You can never have her and it's far kinder this way." He dropped his hands and looked up at the sky. His voice had dropped to a whisper, but it was still full of self-mockery. "Damn it all! You've enough debts of honor! What's one more you owe to yourself and to her, you fool? For God's sake, she's entirely, irrevocably and always beyond you. And she's just a schoolgirl, remember?"

His pain so distracted him that he thought no more about what he might have discovered from Major Crabtree. He had intended to get the major angry enough that he would let down his guard and allow something, anything, to slip. It hadn't happened. Or had it? There must be something that had made the major so very angry when Lee had mentioned Manton Barnes, but God knew what. Lee stood up and walked deliberately into the house. He carefully put away the saber—it belonged to the major—and washed his face in cold water. When he finally joined the company in the drawing room, he was as charming, as wickedly inventive, and as impossible as ever.

Eleanor refused to allow herself to notice him. If she did she would never maintain her hard-won indifference, nor her determination to believe the worst of him. Instead she glanced around the room. The drawing room gave onto a hallway. Where was the library?

"Do you love books, Sir Robert?" she asked as soon as the chance presented itself. "Is that something else Mr. Campbell has learned from you?"

"I have a fine collection, Lady Eleanor. But it doesn't match Mr. Campbell's. His London library is famous."

She allowed herself to sparkle just a little. "Oh, I do love libraries! Is there a large one here at Deerfield?"

"Let me show you," said the major instantly. "It's just on the other side of the hall."

Eleanor was delighted that it was so easy to be a detective, but it was a great deal more difficult to act like a spy. There was the paneling, just as Frank Garth had described it, and there were the bosses shaped like Tudor roses. Yet she could think of no earthly reason why she should be left alone in Major Crabtree's library. In fact, Walter and Diana had followed them through and were also admiring the books. Lee lounged carelessly in the doorway and watched them.

"Did you ever find a copy of that Latin bestiary we were hunting for, Sir Robert?" he asked after awhile.

"Indeed, sir!" The major turned and smiled at the younger man. He seemed to have entirely forgotten the episode in the park. *It just goes to show what a thorough gentleman he is,* thought Eleanor. *No wonder Mama made him a special friend.* "In fact, the bookseller in Red Lion Street in Norwich has a copy now, and I believe I have almost persuaded him to part with it for something less than the fortune it's worth."

"Then let's go there," said Lee instantly.

"If you wish it," smiled the major. "We'll show your friend Mr. Downe our fine city."

"Norwich?" said Diana in some dismay. "You'd be gone overnight."

"Indeed, my lady," said the major. "What do you say, Mr. Downe?"

"Well, if Lee wishes it . . ." began Walter.

"I can't wait," said Lee. "If it's a fine enough copy of the bestiary, I'll get it out of the man if I have to hang him by his toes."

Eleanor turned to him, eyes blazing. "No doubt you would," she snapped.

Lee's violet gaze seemed only to mock her. "I'd even roast him alive, Lady Eleanor," he said.

Diana giggled. "Lee! How can you say such things?"

"No doubt your purse will be sufficient inducement, Mr. Campbell, without having to revert to savagery," said Eleanor. Indeed, if her suspicions were correct, his purse would soon be overflowing with her mother's money.

"You say so only because you're not a collector," replied Lee. "You may have an interest in libraries, but you can have no idea of the passions of the chase felt by the true fanatic on the scent of a rare volume."

"Then when do we leave?" asked Walter, who was far too

polite to demur when a plan so important to his friend was proposed for his entertainment, even if it would take him away from Diana.

Lee smiled at his friend as if he were too dense to notice Walter's reluctance. "What's wrong with tomorrow?"

"Tomorrow it shall be, then," said the major. "I can put other things on hold for two days. Now, ladies, may I call out my carriage for you?"

"Thank you, Major, but there's no need, really," replied Diana with a pretty smile. "Eleanor and I like to walk, and maybe the young gentlemen may escort us back?"

"With pleasure—" began Walter, but Lee interrupted him.

"No, take the carriage, dear Di. Major Crabtree is drowning in urgent business, and Mr. Downe and I must also prepare for our venture to Norwich. No doubt we'll see you in a few days when we return."

Must he always have his way? thought Eleanor angrily— *even when it inconveniences everybody else?* Lee gave her a small wink and left the room. Eleanor turned to the major, who stood at her elbow. "You are very forbearing, Sir Robert. It would seem that Mr. Campbell takes flagrant advantage of your goodwill."

"He means no harm at all," said the major with a small sigh. "But I admit it's not easy to see a lad that you've led on his first pony take such pleasure in being headstrong and irresponsible, but there you are. He likes to goad. But someone who's known him as long as I have must find forgiveness in his heart for the excesses of youth."

Which only goes to show once again, thought Eleanor, *that Mr. Campbell doesn't deserve the kindness of someone like Major Crabtree.*

Not five minutes later, she and Diana were seated in Sir Robert's carriage and being driven back to Hawksley by his coachman. She had had no desire whatsoever to have been escorted on so long a walk by the infuriating and wicked Leander Campbell. So she had no real excuse for her annoyance. And besides, events were falling out more perfectly than she could have planned. All three gentlemen were leaving for Norwich, and they would be gone several days. Deerfield would be inhabited only by servants. Such a chance might never come again and she would seize it.

Eleanor had never been out alone after dark before. The walk was all of three miles, but it was a fine night with a bright spring moon shining above the treetops. As she marched bravely up the lane toward Deerfield, she felt nothing but the thrill of adventure and excitement. Occasionally a bat flitted by overhead or something rustled in the undergrowth, but she had no fear either of country creatures or country folk. It had been absurdly simple to slip unnoticed from Hawksley. She had taken one of her plainest cloaks and left it under the cushion on the settle. Once everyone was abed, she had slipped downstairs, retrieved the cloak, and climbed out of the library window. The walk should take her less than an hour, so by midnight she expected to be back in her bed. With any luck, she would have her mother's letters with her.

As Deerfield loomed up in the darkness, she hesitated for a moment. Perhaps there would be dogs? But if so, they would probably be tied near the stables. She had made careful note of the layout of the place, so she gave the stables a wide berth and came softly up to the side of the house. She tried one of the doors. It was locked. Surely there must be a window cracked somewhere? She went on around the house, trying all the sashes. To her amazement, there was not only an open window, but one leading directly into the library. It slid up silently in well-waxed tracks and Eleanor was inside.

Now for the first time, she began to feel afraid. Her heart was pounding heavily in her breast and she could feel her skin getting cold. *Fiddlesticks!* she said to herself. *There's no one here but the servants; even if they catch you they can't do anything.* She stumbled blindly up to the mantel where she had noticed some candles when she inspected the room the previous day and lit one. The light flickered up and danced over the room. Instantly the far corners sank into even deeper shadow. Taking the candle in her hand, Eleanor began to try the Tudor roses. There were scores of them: running around the chair rail, accenting the sides of the fireplace, even gracing the plaster ceiling far above her head.

She had gone nearly two-thirds of the way around the room. Those parts of the wall actually occupied by bookcases had no roses, so it took less time than she had feared. At last, as she tugged and turned at one of the roses beside the fireplace, a piece of the paneling slid aside to reveal a dark cavity in the wall. Bless Frank Garth and his carpenter brother, she breathed silently. Heart beating wildly, she held up the candle and peered into the hole. There was a bundle of papers inside, tied up in a ribbon. Her mother's letters! It had been so easy!

"I should like to see your face, Mr. Leander Campbell," she said softly to herself, "when you discover these are gone!"

"If you like," replied an amused whisper, "you may see it now."

Eleanor screamed. It wasn't a particularly loud or piercing scream, more of a sudden gasp of breath, but the bundle of papers slipped from her hand and scattered over the floor.

"Shall we have more candles?" said Lee. "It's so uncomfortable to converse in the dark."

"You didn't think so at the Three Feathers!" Eleanor defiantly shot back.

"Alas, now I am starkly sober. Far less entertaining, but it puts you more closely in touch with reality."

Lee calmly struck a light. In moments the flame from several branches of candles warmed the room. He turned and stood with his back to the hearth, making no attempt to approach her.

Eleanor knelt and frantically gathered up the bundle and clutched it to her breast. "What are you doing here? You were supposed to be in Norwich!"

"Yes, I'm a disgracefully unreliable person. We did start out, the major and Mr. Downe and myself, but then I made a simple excuse to return and rejoin them there on the morrow."

"Why?"

"Because I wanted to find out what so interested you here in the library, Lady Eleanor, and you'd never have told me if I'd asked, would you?"

"How did you know I would come here?" Then she blushed. She could remember how those violet eyes had watched when she had made her excuses to have the major show her the library. He had seen right through her. She must be the most dreadful actress imaginable.

"No, you did very well," he said, reading her thoughts. "The major and Mr. Downe suspect nothing. It is only my devious mind that wondered at your sudden interest in the paneling at Deerfield. Meanwhile you seem to have found what you wanted. May I see?"

"No, you may not! How can you be so despicable? You know perfectly well these are my mother's letters to Major Crabtree. If you try to take them from me, I'll scream in earnest and wake up the major's servants."

"My dear Lady Eleanor, I shouldn't dream of taking those papers. If they're what you say, they're no earthly business of mine."

Eleanor dropped onto the sofa opposite him, for she found suddenly that her legs would no longer hold her. He didn't seem surprised that her mother had been writing to Major Crabtree. That confirmed everything, didn't it? "You're a liar, sir," she said. "You stole them and are trying to blackmail the major and Lady Acton. When he told her in the church at Little Tanning that the letters were missing and in the hands of a rogue, she almost fainted away. You know very well that if you published these letters, it would ruin her. What has she ever done to you? For God's sake, how could you be so cruel?"

The violet eyes closed for a moment. Lee could still see that desperate scrawl in the note left in Ryder Street: *I am bled dry. Once he has his claws into you, it's worse than the punishment of Prometheus. Ask Lady Acton.* So that's what he meant! Manton Barnes had somehow known that the countess was also about to become a victim.

"Your mother is being blackmailed?" he asked, very deliberately.

"You mean to stand there and tell me this wasn't your doing?"

And that was when he turned and walked away. "It is like the punishment of Prometheus to be blackmailed," he said suddenly. "While you stand chained by Zeus to a rock, the vultures come and tear at your liver, but the next day you are still alive and they come, still hungry, again. And all because you wanted to steal fire." Then he spun on his heel and faced her again. "You may believe what you will, my lady. I shan't gainsay it."

Eleanor stared at him, her heart in her mouth. There was nothing he could have said that was more likely to make her doubt her suspicions. Had he spluttered denials, that would have confirmed his guilt as surely as a confession. She looked down at her lap, confused. "You knew the major and my mother were in love, didn't you?"

Lee didn't even smile at the naiveté of her language. "I had guessed it," he said. But beneath the simple statement his thoughts burned like fire: *And so had Manton Barnes, the major's nephew. The blackmailer must also be someone who was privy to that information. But who? A friend of the major? A friend of Lady Acton?*

"And you knew about the secret cupboards. Frank Garth told me."

His voice held genuine, sharp curiosity. "Frank Garth?"

"His brother made them."

"I see." He had not known. But now Eleanor had given him vital information: if there was a hiding place in the library, perhaps there were others in the house. He frowned with distaste. Gentlemen did not usually rifle through other people's secret papers. Neither would Eleanor, of course, if she hadn't wanted to save her mother.

"It was you who left the window open, wasn't it?" said Eleanor. "I thought it seemed too convenient."

He smiled. "I wondered how you planned to get in."

"I didn't have a plan. I just hoped I'd be lucky."

"And you were. Now you had better take those letters back to Lady Acton, hadn't you?"

Eleanor stared at him. "You're going to let me win, just like that?"

"I am."

"It doesn't make any sense at all! If you knew I was coming for the letters, you could have removed them. Why wait for me in the dark, then let me go?"

"It must be my innate sense of chivalry," he said wickedly.

"Mr. Campbell, I shall never understand you. Yet I'm not a fool. You really didn't know about the hiding place?"

"No, I didn't. Admittedly, I spent a lot of time as a child here at Deerfield, but not all of it. I was away at school and I lived at Hawksley. Mr. Garth the carpenter must have done his work when I wasn't present."

"Then these papers aren't the letters." Eleanor felt devastated. But it had been too easy, hadn't it? If Leander Campbell had her mother's correspondence and was blackmailing her over it, it would have been too great a coincidence for Frank Garth to have happened to mention their hiding place. Life wasn't really so neat. If he indeed had them, Lee must have the letters hidden elsewhere. Why would he keep them at Deerfield?

"I have no idea," said Lee. "But we may assume they belong to the major and perhaps we should put them back."

"And perhaps you are bluffing me, sir," she said. After walking all this way in the dark, she would have to make certain. Eleanor went to the table and spread out the papers. In the light from the candles it was immediately apparent that they weren't Lady Acton's letters. The paper was older, for a start, and seemed to consist of a handful of documents wrapped in several blank sheets. One even seemed to be in a foreign tongue of some kind. The crabbed writing varied, but it was that of the clerks of twenty-five years before, not the beautiful copperplate in which her mother took pride. Nor was there any Acton crest in a red wax seal. Eleanor felt sick with disappointment. She began to fold up the papers when suddenly the meaning of the writing on the top sheet sunk home. She picked it up and turned to face Lee. He still stood calmly at the fireplace, watching her.

"They may belong to the major, Mr. Campbell," she said in a shaky voice, "but the content would seem to involve you." He didn't move and the violet eyes did not leave her face. Holding the documents in her hand, Eleanor went to the sofa and sat down.

"Record of Birth," she read aloud. "Born this twelfth day of February in the thirtieth year of the Reign of our Sovereign Lord George the Third by the Grace of God of Great Britain, France and Ireland, King, Defender of the Faith, and in the Year of our Lord One Thousand Seven Hundred and Ninety, at Blairmore House, in the County of Argyle, Scotland, to Moira, only daughter of Ian Campbell of Blairmore, and the Honorable Gerald Arthur Richard Hart of Hawksley Park in the County of Norfolk, England: a boy, Leander Gerald Arthur Hart." She put the paper in her lap so that he shouldn't see her hands tremble. "It's witnessed by one Janet McEwen, midwife, and Fiona Mackay, maid, who has made her mark. It's also signed by your mother, Moira Campbell—though she signs herself Moira Hart. It is you, isn't it? It's proof of your birth."

"Which is touching, but not odd," said Lee quietly. "I

have seen it before. Major Crabtree brought it from Ireland. It was one of the ways that he was able to prove to Lady Augusta that I was her husband's by-blow—apart from my troubling appearance, that is. My mother had written it, and apparently she secreted it among my clothes when I was taken from her and sent to the convent. She must have cared a great deal that the world know who my father was, yet the Irish nuns knew only Gaelic, it meant nothing to them."

"Then neither did this," said Eleanor, in a voice oddly choked with a rising panic, as she set aside the top sheet and looked at the second.

"Neither did what?" asked Lee calmly.

"This next paper." Eleanor looked up at him, her brown eyes like saucers. "She must have hidden it there, too. It's dated the third day of May, 1789, and signed by two witnesses. One of them is the same Fiona Mackay, the other is a Robbie Stewart, gamekeeper. Then there's the signature of the rector of the kirk—that's a church, isn't it?—at a place called Strathbrae. Is that near Blairmore?"

"Not far, I believe. Why?"

"Because they were married there," said Eleanor.

"My dear lady, I am completely in the dark. Who was married at Strathbrae?"

Eleanor looked up at him. She didn't understand her own emotions, but her eyes were swimming in tears.

"Your mother, Moira Campbell, and your father, of course—the future Earl of Hawksley. When they met in the year before you were born, they were married by declaration, Mr. Campbell, or should I say, my lord earl. Duly signed and witnessed by her maid, the gamekeeper, and a member of the clergy of the Church of Scotland, this would seem to be a legal copy of their marriage lines."

Eight

There was a deathly silence. "May I see now?" asked Lee at last.

Eleanor handed him the papers. The third one was unintelligible to her. It certainly was not written in English. And in any case, she felt acutely and painfully embarrassed to have stumbled upon something so intensely personal and of such moment. "You didn't know, did you?" she asked.

He read over the papers, then laid them casually on the mantel. "That they had married? No, I didn't."

"It changes everything for you, doesn't it?"

Turning away from Eleanor, he walked across the room and stared out into the dark garden for a moment. "No, I don't think it does," he said at last.

"What do you mean? Are you afraid to claim your inheritance? After so many years of being able to follow your fancy, I can imagine it'd be a burden to have to take up the duties of the earldom of Hawksley. For it does make you earl, doesn't it?"

"Yes, it does," said Lee quietly. Then he turned and the old humor was back for a moment. "So I am legitimate! How very awkward for the House of Lords for such a scandalous rogue to grace those hallowed chambers. Don't you think I should refrain from so embarrassing that august assembly?"

"My brother says they're all rogues," said Eleanor without thinking. "But you're still the heir."

His smile held nothing but irony. "Ay, there's the rub: to my father's entire estate and inheritance—his titles, his lands, everything at Hawksley Park."

"Which you've always wanted. And now that it's within your grasp, you don't have the courage!" She knew she was talking wildly, but she didn't care. This whole encounter had been too strange and his presence disturbed her too much. "Even if you don't want to be earl, think of the money! You'd have enough to waste as you choose." *And you wouldn't need to blackmail my mother,* she thought.

He came back to her, and to her surprise dropped to the couch beside her. "Eleanor," he said gently. "Hush! There is more to this than you know."

"What else can there be?" She forced sarcasm into her voice. "You're legitimate and a peer of the realm. It's like a fairy tale come true."

He took her hand, turning her fingers over in his. "Life isn't anything like a fairy tale, my dear," he said. "Now listen. I didn't know about the marriage, but I did know about the other two papers. That third paper, which you could not read, was shown to me by Major Crabtree many years ago. It's in Gaelic, but there's an English translation on the back. Had you turned it over, you would have seen it. It is a record of my mother's death. She died in the Highlands, near Loch Linnhe."

"Does it make any difference?" asked Eleanor.

"It makes a great deal of difference," he said with a wry smile. "You have just discovered that my father secretly married Moira Campbell on May 3, 1789. He married Lady Augusta on October 5, 1793—four and a half years later."

"Anyone can marry twice," said Eleanor.

"Yes, but Moira didn't die until November 1793, a month after the second wedding. So what we have proved now is that when my father married Lady Augusta, his first wife was still alive."

"Which means . . . Oh, I see!"

"Which means that Lord Hawksley's marriage to Lady Augusta wasn't valid, and that Lady Diana Hart of Hawksley isn't a Lady and doesn't belong to Hawksley at all."

Eleanor felt a lump blocking her throat. "Your mother's marriage makes Diana illegitimate?"

His eyes were dark with shadows. "Yes."

"But why did they marry secretly? What made her give you away?"

"When her father discovered that she'd fallen in love with a hated Sassenach, he went a little insane, I think. Ian Campbell had been a young child during the '45 rebellion. After Bonnie Prince Charlie was defeated at Culloden, the English reprisals on the Scots were terrible. Ian never forgot and he would never forgive his daughter her love for an Englishman. He forbade them to see each other."

"But they married anyway?"

"Obviously."

"It can't have been a very long courtship."

Lee ran his hand over his hair. "It wasn't exactly a long honeymoon. 'Nor am I loath, though pleased at heart, / Sweet Highland Girl! from thee to part.' My father came right back to England. Perhaps he was going to send for her."

"But he never did?"

"Ian Campbell wrote to him and told him Moira was dead. My father didn't question the news. Probably as soon as he came home, he regretted the marriage. When his brother was killed and he became earl, I'm sure he began to look about with some relief for a more suitable wife. Meanwhile Ian kept Moira at Blairmore until I was born. While she was still lying in, he sent me to Ireland, then he turned her from the house. I think he wanted me to disappear from the face of the earth, but even my dour grandfather hadn't the heart to murder an infant." Lee gave a wry smile. "I suppose I should be grateful."

"So you were taken to the convent? Did your mother know where you were?"

"She spent the rest of her days searching for me in the Highlands. She never tried to contact Lord Hawksley. Perhaps she hated him for abandoning her, perhaps she was too proud. Eventually she was taken in by the local people in a village near Loch Linnhe and died there. The inhabitants there were Gaelic-speaking, but they wrote a record of her death and that third paper is a copy."

"Her own father stole her baby from her? I don't know if I ever heard anything so cruel." Eleanor felt devastated. Poor Moira Campbell, whose only sin was to love the wrong man! A man whose son looked just like him.

"It's a long time ago," said Lee at last. "Though it's small comfort, isn't it?"

"How could your father not go to Blairmore and find out for himself what became of his first wife?"

The muscles of his face tightened imperceptibly. "There is nothing that can excuse my father."

Eleanor looked down. Lord Hawksley had been a bigamist and the Scots death certificate from Loch Linnhe proved it. "You speak Gaelic?"

Lee smiled. "Not a word, though it was my first language as an infant. Anyway, Irish and Scots Gaelic are quite different. Sir Robert obtained the English translation, I suppose. He had been interested to discover what happened to my mother when he found me and so he secured the record of her death. There is no question as to its authenticity."

It didn't occur to Eleanor to ask herself why she cared so very desperately about Lee's birth, nor why she should assume she had the right to question him. Since he seemed prepared to tell her the story so openly, she plunged on. "How did you learn all these details?"

"I may be a reprobate, Lady Eleanor, but allow me some natural curiosity about my mother. I would have gone to Blairmore myself, but Ian Campbell had died when I was still a child. I never met him. The local people who knew my mother hated my father—a foreigner who had seduced and abandoned one of their own. He had ruined her in their eyes. And I look just like him, remember? It would hardly have been politic to turn up in person and stir up painful memories. I hired a man in Edinburgh to go discreetly to Argyle and this is what he discovered."

"Though he never found out about the wedding in Strath-brae?"

"He did not."

"But Major Crabtree knew! He had these papers here all along."

"And must have realized what they would mean to Lady Augusta and Diana. When the major turned up here with me, Lady Augusta was a widow, seven months with child. This news would have crushed her. I never thought Sir Robert so noble, but life is full of surprises."

Eleanor felt overwhelmed by what she'd just heard. As she thought of Lee's mother, vainly searching for her baby and then dying alone among strangers, tears welled up in her eyes. "You come from a ruthless line on both sides, don't you?" she said angrily. "Who among them all cared about poor Moira?"

Lee reached up and tenderly brushed the moisture from her cheek. "Eleanor, sweet girl, don't cry."

"I am not crying!" raged Eleanor. She turned her head to hide the tears and raised both hands to brush them away.

How on earth could it then seem so natural that Leander Campbell should take her by the shoulders and softly pull her into his arms? As she struggled not to break down, he quietly held her against his own strength, while his long fingers moved through her hair, smoothing it. Against her cheek and under her palms she was aware of the edge of his jacket and the clean scent of his shirt. Beneath it, his heart beat a steady rhythm. It felt wonderful. She relaxed against him. He took her hands one at a time and gently moved them into her lap, then he tipped her face up to his. Eleanor couldn't understand the expression that darkened the violet eyes, but it seemed filled with pain and longing.

"I care, brown hen," he said gently. His voice was stripped of all sarcasm. It was a tone she had never heard him use before.

Light kisses moved across her cheeks and eyelids, taking away the tears and beguiling her into closing her eyes. She felt him brush a loose wisp of hair from her cheek and nibble gently at her ear. The sensation was exquisite. Then his lips moved down to hers, and he at last took possession of her mouth. In the next moment she forgot everything but the passion that seared between them. He kissed her until her mouth felt swollen and hot, and a shiver of delight seemed to flood through her limbs. Her arms moved unwittingly around his neck. The softness of his dark hair and the fire and strength of his skin were a strange and enticing delectation under her fingers—the most wonderful feeling she could ever remember. Eleanor knew with a burning shame that her surrender to him was absolute, and that she didn't care. She didn't want him to stop. But firm hands grasped hers as he released her mouth and pushed her away.

In the next instant he had gone to the fireplace. He leaned against the mantelpiece and put his head in his hands. It was as if he were facing some great struggle and was drawing together all of his resources. "Damn it all!" she heard him say. Then he turned to her and laughed.

"That's how it's done," he said ruthlessly. "No doubt it's how my father did it. But Moira Campbell wasn't an earl's daughter, so he faced no reprisals for his seduction. You had better be more careful in future, Lady Eleanor Acton. Rakes have few scruples."

How could she have trusted him for even a moment? Eleanor had nothing left to call on except pride. She buckled it about her like armor. "And you have none."

His face was a mask. "That's right. Nor do I want to be earl. The gutter suits me far better."

"Then return there."

The candlelight threw deep shadows under his strong jaw and chin. "I shall, with pleasure," he said calmly.

He took up the papers where they lay on the mantelpiece and looked at them one last time. The birth and death certificates he slipped into his inside pocket, but he very deliberately held the corner of the other page to the candle. Eleanor started toward him, but it was too late. The marriage papers began to blacken and curl, before they burst into flames. He held them for a moment as they flared up, then he dropped the remains into the fireplace where the ashes disintegrated into soot.

"And so ends our little melodrama," he said. "You will tell no one what you learned here tonight, of course."

"What do you take me for?" Eleanor hissed. "I hope I have sufficient honor to hold my tongue. You may have my word on it. I understand your motives very well, but I haven't forgotten what it would mean for Diana to be disinherited and disgraced. Or even Lady Augusta! Though I'm sure you don't care about her. I'm only surprised that you didn't keep the papers to hold over her head."

"And blackmail her, too? Perhaps I'm not as thorough as you think me, Lady Eleanor. It may surprise you to learn that the events of this evening have slightly disturbed my equilibrium and so I have lost a golden opportunity. Yet strangely I regret nothing."

"Well, I do!" said Eleanor with passion. "I regret that I ever met you!"

Lee knew he was close to the edge. He must hold on for Diana's sake. For God's sake, he was Earl of Hawksley! It hammered insistently at his defenses. As such he could claim rank, fortune, and privilege—and court Lady Eleanor Acton with honor. But at the cost of ruin for his sister and stepmother. He could never do it. Was anyone hurt by his sacrifice? Only himself. Eleanor cared nothing for him; ironically, he had already made sure of that himself. She would willingly forget him, so his legitimacy was irrelevant to her. There was nothing else he could do under the circumstances than make sure she continued to feel that way.

"And I you," he said without mercy. "I prefer my ladies with a little more polish and a lot more experience. Now, for God's sake, will you let me take you home?"

"I should rather die."

He raised a brow. It was the most insulting gesture Eleanor could imagine. "Dear child," he said. "We are civilized human beings in the staid and ordinary county of Norfolk. Heroines in romances would rather die. Ladies in the nineteenth century recognize that it is perfectly unexceptionable to allow a gentleman to escort them home."

"At night? Through three miles of dark lanes?"

"You think I shall ravish you under a bush? Alas, I like my creature comforts too much for anything so gothic. Now, let's go."

He went to the door and opened it. There was nothing Eleanor could do except walk through. She pulled her cloak tight to her chin and held up her head in the most superior manner taught by Miss Able. Lee followed. He made no attempt to take her arm or touch her again. He pulled back the bolts and chains that secured the front door and they stepped out onto the driveway. With Eleanor walking stiffly at his side, Lee strode away toward Hawksley in silence, but his mind was filled with clamor.

Moira Campbell, his mother, had married his father in the kirk at Strathbrae. He wasn't—had never been—a bastard. Lord Hawksley had behaved unforgivably, but he wasn't entirely wicked after all. Lee had never thought that it mattered what kind of a man his father had been, but it did, of course. When Gerald Hart went to Scotland, he had been young and foolish, and Ian Campbell had been a formidable opponent; there may even have been threats. Between them, Moira had been crushed like a shell beneath the surf. Yet it hadn't been a casual seduction. They had married, with witnesses and with the blessing of the church. The baby that Ian Campbell had torn from its mother and sent to Ireland had been his legitimate grandson. Tragedy compounds on itself, thought Lee. If Butcher Cumberland hadn't been so vicious to the Highlanders after Culloden—if Ian Campbell hadn't witnessed it—but the past couldn't be changed. Lee ruthlessly suppressed his storm of emotion. Yet when Hawksley loomed up and Eleanor marched around to the window she had left open, he was astonished to realize that they had just walked three miles without exchanging a word.

She turned to him and tossed back the hood of her cloak. "What are you going to do about my mother?" she asked bluntly.

His smile seemed perfectly relaxed. "What would you like me to do, Lady Eleanor?"

"Return the letters to her, of course."

And that was what had brought him to Norfolk in the first place, wasn't it? Blackmail. In finding out about his mother's marriage he had forgotten all about it. For someone who prided himself so much on clear thinking and competence, he hadn't managed very well tonight. As he had guessed when he saw them together, Lady Acton had come to Norfolk to pursue an affair with the major. Now he knew she had also written love letters to him and they had been stolen. She was being blackmailed over them, very probably by the same person who had blackmailed Manton Barnes. It was up to him to discover who that person was.

"The letters will be returned, Lady Eleanor," he said.

"Is that a promise?"

"Let's just say it's an intent."

"Because your word means nothing and you have no honor at all, have you? I despise you," said Lady Eleanor Acton.

Then she climbed in through the window before she should disgrace herself. For she didn't despise him at all. She didn't know what she felt, except misery. Because in spite of everything, Leander Campbell entranced her. The memory of his lips still burned on hers; she could see the way he laughed and imagine the feel of his lithe strength beneath her hands. Although his energies were devoted to mischief and destruction, his mind was brilliant and fascinating and his looks made her heart turn over whenever she saw him. How humiliating to feel a misplaced schoolgirl crush when you knew that the object of your infatuation was a wicked, unmitigated rogue.

Lee walked back to Deerfield and went straight into the library. He had ruthlessly put aside all thoughts of his birth and of Eleanor. Instead he was thinking very seriously about Manton Barnes and Lady Acton. As he had known all along, something must link them. Now he knew it was the blackmailer. There was only one clue, though it seemed too unlikely. In a deep concentration, he walked up and down. Then he came up to the sofa and dropped onto it. In spite of himself, he imagined for a moment that he was still enveloped by Eleanor's scent. Then his senses were overwhelmed by the memory of her soft skin and clear brown eyes. He bent his head into his hands and began to curse, very deliberately and very thoroughly. At last he straightened up and laughed.

"For God's sake, Leander Campbell," he said aloud. "You're no better than a smitten miss! If your gambling cronies could see you now, it would be the end of all bets on your skill!"

When Lee left very early the next morning on the road to Norwich, none of the major's servants had any idea that their guest had returned, only to go without sleep for a night, and was now leaving without breakfast. Frank Garth looked up in surprise when Mr. Campbell's black horse came trotting into Little Tanning before the farm laborers were about. The sound of the horse's hooves made a counterpoint to the voices of dozens of birds, gaily greeting the dawn.

"Good morning, Mr. Garth," said Lee, saluting the old man with his whip. "How do you and your wife do this morning?"

"Well enough, sir, and all the better for seeing you!"

"I'm glad to hear it, Mr. Garth, for I have some questions for you."

Frank Garth set aside the blade he was sharpening and looked up at the young man. He was shrewd enough to know that something was wrong, though the handsome features were schooled into indifference. Mr. Garth quietly refrained from letting his own face shown any concern. Leander Campbell had been a proud and private individual even as a lad. Frank Garth would only know what the matter was if the young gentleman chose to tell him. "Fire away, Mr. Campbell."

Lee stepped down off his horse and sat down on a stone bench in front of the cottage. He leaned back and closed his eyes, allowing the weak sunlight to play across his eyelids. "I would like to know," he said after a moment, "all about your brother. I am given to understand he was a famous carpenter?"

It was a long time before Eleanor could get to sleep. She was privy to information that could ruin Lady Augusta and Diana, and she was sworn never to reveal it. But what about Lee? Could he really be trusted? Mr. Campbell might have destroyed the critical part of the evidence, but the marriage had still taken place. Once his first shock had worn off, would he regret his impulsive action? She wished fervently that she had never gone to Deerfield. For now she had put them all in the hands of a man who was quite ruthless. Yet in spite of everything, she yearned for his company, and she couldn't seem to control her feelings for him. With determination, she turned over and closed her eyes. What she had discovered didn't change a thing. True earl or not, Leander Campbell was beneath contempt. If he decided to claim his birthright, she couldn't prevent it. But whatever else happened, Diana would never hear about it from her.

When Lee reached Norwich it was well past noon. He strode into the dining room of the Dog Inn and ordered a substantial meal. For someone who had apparently done no more than hack up from Deerfield, he seemed to have taken a profligate amount of time, and the state of his horse had caused the ostler some complaint. The black was hot and lathered; he would have to be walked out before he could be put away. The landlord had already cleared away the remains of the roast beef and left Mr. Campbell idly sipping at his claret, when Major Crabtree came in and joined him at the table.

"I'm glad to see you're here at last, sir," he said, with only a trace of reproach. "Mr. Feveril Downe has already been to the bookseller's several times in hopes of finding you there. Now he has walked to the market and is showing an honest antiquary's curiosity in the old flint guildhall. I didn't think we could interest him in anything besides Lady Diana Hart, but there you are."

"He is being polite," said Lee. "But others' affairs of the heart are not our concern, are they?"

The major's bluff face colored slightly. "I stand corrected. Meanwhile the bookseller in Red Lion Street awaits your offer."

"Excellent, Major," said Lee. "But first, I rather think you owe me an explanation."

Nine

Diana was in such a delicious state of ravaged emotion that it took all of Eleanor's energy to try and cheer up her friend.

"You do see, don't you," Diana said dramatically, "that Mama will never let me marry Walter. No one was ever so unlucky in love!"

"It's what comes of being the daughters of earls," said Eleanor with a reassuring smile. "There are only a handful of eligible bachelors in the realm. Never mind. Walter is charming and more than respectable, and at least you know what you want. It'll only be a matter of time before you get it."

Diana smiled faintly and began to extol all of Mr. Downe's many virtues in case Eleanor had missed them. But Eleanor barely listened. She had no idea what she herself wanted, did she? Thoughts of Leander Campbell haunted her day and night, yet she couldn't let herself be so weak as to have fallen for a despicable rogue just because he'd kissed her so skillfully. Meanwhile, Lady Acton laughed and talked as if nothing were wrong, but Eleanor knew that her mother had sent a banker's draft to an address in Red Lion Street in Norwich. The blackmail had begun.

The gentlemen had been gone three days when Eleanor was summoned by the butler into the blue drawing room at

Hawksley. She raced through the hall and flung open the door, and ran straight into a tall fellow with hair like gold and Lady Acton's black eyes. He caught her around the waist and kissed her soundly on the cheek.

"Richard!" gasped Eleanor as soon as she caught her breath. "Oh, you dear man! I'm so glad to see you! How is Helena? When did you arrive? How long can you stay?"

"My sweet wife is well and growing large. We're sure it'll be a daughter, just to spite Father—he so longs for us to have a son. Helena sends her dearest love to her beloved sister-in-law, and though I have just arrived, I'm leaving right away since I can't bear to be apart from her much longer."

Eleanor's brother kissed her again, then they sat together on the chaise longue and began to exchange all the family news. Richard had business in Norwich and would go on there before hurrying back to Acton Mead, his beautiful home by the Thames. Helena had made it a warm haven for the man who would one day be Earl of Acton himself. Eleanor felt a sudden pang of longing. Would any man ever love her like that and allow himself to be so loved in return?

"So much for me," he said at last. "How are you, dear child? Don't pretend everything is all right. I know you too well. You look as if something is eating you alive."

"Oh, fiddlesticks," said Eleanor. "I'm fine. Have you seen Mother?"

"The matchless Countess of Acton gave me a brief but eloquent greeting, then made some excuse that she must find Lady Augusta and inform her hostess of my untimely arrival. Our mother is playing some game, isn't she?"

Eleanor dropped her eyes away from the velvet gaze. What Leander Campbell was doing to Lady Acton was a secret she couldn't share with anyone, not even Richard. In the next moment she looked up in astonishment, as Richard mentioned the very name that haunted her thoughts.

"Lee Campbell is down here, isn't he?" he asked with a genuine smile. "I'd like to see him."

"He's gone to Norwich with Major Crabtree and Mr. Downe," said Eleanor instantly. "Do you have business with him?"

Richard laughed. "Don't say he's been behaving badly! You mention him as if he's some monster of iniquity."

"Well, he is!" Eleanor shot back.

"Now why, dear sister mine, do you think that?"

Eleanor took a deep breath. The real reason had to stay secret, but there were enough other reasons, weren't there? "Well, he's a wastrel, for a start. What has he ever done with his life? He's arrogant and conceited and irresponsible, and he'd steal Lady Diana's inheritance if he could."

"Good God," said Richard, then he threw back his head and roared with laughter. "He *has* been behaving badly. However did you get such an extraordinary idea of his character?" Then he smiled and leaned back against the curved arm of the chaise longue. "Lee has simply neglected to toot his own horn, I can see, but I would have thought his half-sister would have told you something about him."

"Diana?" Eleanor remembered how carefully she had avoided discussing Mr. Campbell with Diana. "Even if she had, it wouldn't be an unbiased opinion. She's so guileless she loves everyone. But the facts remain, don't they? The man's a worthless rake and a gambler. He doesn't deny it."

"I don't suppose he does," said Richard with delight. "Yet he hasn't had much time for this shameless career. Good heavens, we were together in the Peninsula until last summer. You must allow a man a little latitude, Eleanor, after he's been through a war. I was crazy enough myself when I came back."

"In the Peninsula?" said Eleanor. She was incredulous. Surely Leander Campbell hadn't been a soldier? He must have been some kind of hanger-on.

"Most of the last five years. He's been back on leave, of course, on and off, but hardly long enough to establish himself as a wastrel. When we finally triumphed over Boney,

Lee sold up like the rest of us and came home. He may be going to the dogs, but he's only had one winter in which to do it."

"What was he doing there? Hiding in the safety of the port while you and your men risked your lives?"

Richard suddenly looked perfectly serious. The faintest shadow of suffering darkened his eyes. He had indeed been crazy when he'd come back to England. Going without sleep because of nightmares, caring nothing for his own life, he'd married a woman he didn't know because of a debt of honor to a dead man. Thank God the woman had been Helena. She had saved him and he would always love her. Yet the scars remained. Lee Campbell was different. He was not less sensitive than Richard, but life had dealt him a harder hand since childhood and perhaps he had developed more resources to cope. Richard looked up to find Eleanor's brown eyes fixed on his face. He sighed.

"Leander Campbell was one of us: one of Wellington's secret scouts, working with the partisans behind the French lines. It was dangerous and dirty and demanding. His life was forfeit on a daily basis. I can't tell you the number of times we hid together in a ditch, or were both saved by his quick wit and matchless courage. He's also, unlike me, an outrageously good marksman, which helped."

The gentleman in the locket? Richard, Lord Lenwood, eldest son to the Earl of Acton; he's not actually a terribly good shot. Lee had told her in the Three Feathers when they'd first met that he knew Richard. Eleanor had forgotten all about it. She had never imagined for a moment that Mr. Campbell and her brother were comrades-in-arms.

"So does being good with a gun make a man honorable?"

"Lee is above reproach, Eleanor. I know him as well as any man could. You don't go through the things we experienced together without revealing your true nature. Good God, if his situation were different, I can think of no man I'd rather have . . ." He stopped.

"Have do what?"

Richard laughed. "Have marry one of my sisters, I was going to say. But it's out of the question, of course."

"Bastards don't marry earl's daughters," said Eleanor, looking down.

"Indeed, they don't. But where on earth did you get the idea that he's after Lady Diana's inheritance?"

"Because he wants her to elope with Mr. Feveril Downe; they're in love."

"I see. Lady Augusta wouldn't approve of Mr. Downe, I gather. Mother took great delight in filling me in. But that wouldn't do Lee any good, my dear. The estate is entailed to Diana as Lord Hawksley's only legitimate heir. Lady Augusta could tie up her daughter's money until she's five-and-twenty, but under no circumstances would any of it go to Lee."

Eleanor stood up and walked across the room. Why was it so difficult to think clearly when it came to the impossible Leander Campbell? Of course it made no sense that he was trying to cheat Diana out of her inheritance. She had witnessed him with her own eyes burn up the paper that would have delivered him Hawksley, lock, stock, and barrel. Now, how could he prove it? She turned back and faced her brother.

"Then why tell them to run away together?"

"Because Lee's a romantic, of course. I imagine if they took his advice, Lady Augusta would capitulate instantly to save her daughter's reputation. What else could she do?"

"That's what Mr. Campbell said."

"And it's the truth. No, I think your friend Diana may be enjoying the drama of forbidden love a little too much, or perhaps she's just scared to cross her mama."

Both of which observations were true, weren't they? "Well then, I was wrong about that part. But he's no plans for the future other than gaming and vice."

"Eleanor, I can hardly believe what I'm hearing. Lee gambles, of course; we all do. He's so damn good, in fact, that

I hear he's made a rich living these last six months and he fleeced us all regularly in Spain. God knows what he does with the money; he certainly doesn't live in any luxury. His plans, however, are quite simple. When we all sold out, we thought Bonaparte defeated and safely imprisoned on Elba, but the Corsican Monster's already escaped. He arrived back in Paris in March and the European Powers have outlawed him. There will be another terrible battle, I'm afraid, and when it happens, Lee Campbell will be there. He stays in England meanwhile because there's nothing else he can do. We're neither at peace nor at war with France right now, but Lee's a professional soldier."

As he had demonstrated in that extraordinary encounter with Major Crabtree, hadn't he? Eleanor tried to steady her voice. She knew what Lee did with some of his money: he sent it to people like Frank Garth and Mrs. Pottage. But then he had despicable ways of replacing it. "He will buy another commission?"

Richard nodded. "Once Bonaparte's finally defeated, Lee intends to spend the rest of his life in England's service, probably in India. He wrote to me about it, since I'd lived there. What other career is there for a man of his talents who has no accepted position in society and no inheritance? And in the meantime, how can you condemn Mr. Campbell if he allows himself some harmless indulgence?"

There was nothing Eleanor could say. For Mr. Campbell seemed to be allowing himself the luxury of blackmailing Lady Acton. Without admitting to Richard that their mother had been indiscreet with Sir Robert, she could never mention it.

"How dare you describe my indulgences as harmless?" said a subtle voice behind them. "It makes me sound like a schoolmarm with a bottle. For God's sake, allow me a little style at least. I already told your sister once before that I had no desire to call you out, my lord, but if you malign me so thoughtlessly, I'm damned if I won't ventilate your gizzard."

"Campbell!" said Richard, bounding to his feet and shaking the other man by the hand. "Dear fellow! I'm damned glad to see you."

"Yes, but your sister isn't," said Lee with a grin.

Eleanor had also leapt to her feet. To her fury she found that her heart was beating faster and a flush was creeping up her cheeks. She wasn't—would never be—indifferent to him. "Because I believe your indulgences are neither harmless nor stylish, Mr. Campbell. It may seem so to others, but it's not for your victims. If you'll excuse me, I think I'll leave you gentlemen to your visit."

She swept out in a flurry of skirts. Richard looked after her in amazement. "What have you been doing to my little sister?" he asked Lee. "Am I going to have to challenge you and be slaughtered after all?"

"If you like," said Lee lazily. He took a seat and stretched out his long legs, then he grinned. "I've been allowing her to think me an out-and-out rogue, which I am, of course. You wouldn't suggest that I allow her to like me, would you?"

Richard had the grace to meet the other man's gaze. "I do understand," he said after a moment. "But sometimes I think it's a damned shame that your father didn't trouble to marry your mother. For God's sake, I have been in India, you haven't! The country eats Englishmen like frogs eat flies. Any mindless idiot can die of fever in some outpost of the empire—don't interrupt me—meanwhile, England could use a man like you here at home to influence government. The need for reform cries out like a wounded animal."

"You take care of the reform. I'll become a nabob," said Lee calmly; then as Richard frowned, he laughed. "In ten years I'll be able to buy property enough to meet the franchise requirements and run for a seat in the House of Commons. Otherwise, what use am I to you? If in the meantime, fever takes me, so be it. Now, what's the latest you hear from Wellington?"

* * *

Eleanor went straight through the house. She intended to go to her room, for she didn't want to face either Lady Augusta or Diana at that moment. She was not destined to reach it. As she passed along the elegant corridor that led to the guest bedrooms at Hawksley, a door opened to reveal her mother.

"A word, Eleanor," said Lady Acton.

Eleanor followed her into the spacious chamber. There was a small fire burning in the grate, in spite of the warmth of the day. The countess glanced toward it and smiled.

"You should know, dear child," she said gaily, "that my little matter is resolved."

"The letters?" asked Eleanor.

"Are reduced to ash, there in the grate."

"Mr. Campbell brought your letters back?"

Lady Acton gave her daughter a shrewd glance. "How did you know it was Mr. Campbell?"

Eleanor blushed. "I met him downstairs. He's talking to Richard. He said nothing to me of course, but who else? No one else has visited today."

"Except Mr. Downe who is with Diana in the garden, but you are right: Mr. Campbell was my deliverer. Now, let's say no more about it."

"You forgive the blackmail, just like that?"

Lady Acton laughed. "It didn't last very long, did it? And the lesson is learned. I wash my hands of Major Crabtree; the incident is closed. But perhaps some good comes out of everything. I'm glad if we can be closer, Eleanor."

Eleanor said nothing. She knew her mother too well. Lady Acton already had a life which enthralled and delighted her. It didn't leave much room for her children. As soon as they returned to London, she would forget her noble desire to be a friend to her daughter, and plunge back into the social whirlwind. The countess went to the window and gazed out.

"He's leaving," she said idly.

Eleanor joined her and looked down into the driveway. Walter was there, already mounted and ready to depart. He was bent over Diana, who clung to his hand. Tactfully ignoring them, Leander Campbell was adjusting the tack on his black charger. He looked powerful, lithe, and self-contained. What had made him return the letters?

"Mr. Campbell is an extraordinary young man," said Lady Acton. "Sometimes I wish . . ."

"What?" said Eleanor.

"Oh, nothing. One can't change the world. Good Lord! Norfolk bores me to tears. I wonder why we ever came here? It's time we went up to town; your father will have arrived there by now. I shall order the carriage for tomorrow. Meanwhile, Richard has been kind enough to stop in to see us and we leave him trapped with Augusta in the drawing room. She will drive him to drink if we don't rescue him immediately, and when Diana comes in, wracked with despair and frustrated desire, she will need all our support. I think I'll go down and be charming. At least Richard will be amused. Eleanor, where are you going?"

Eleanor paused just long enough to grin at her mother. "To say goodbye to Mr. Downe, of course," she said.

Walter and Lee trotted along together in silence, then Lee put his mount into a canter which soon became a fast gallop. When he finally pulled up, Walter had been left several hundred yards behind.

"Devil take you!" said Walter with more good humor than his words implied, as he eventually came alongside his friend. "Can't shake off the dust of Hawksley fast enough? You might have given some thought to my sensibilities."

Lee smiled back at his friend. "I should never have brought you," he said. "I admit I thought perhaps Diana was enjoying only a passing fancy which proximity might cure, but in spite of her histrionics, I think she genuinely loves you, sir."

Walter flushed. "I'll wait for her," he said grimly. "Even if it takes five years."

"If you persist in being so honorable, you may have to."

"What about the other issue?" said Walter, deliberately turning the subject. "Did you get any satisfaction from the major?"

"About Manton Barnes? No, I didn't. And I found nothing at the house."

Walter looked at his friend in astonishment. "You searched Deerfield?"

Lee grinned. "Of course. That's why I went back there. Don't look so upset. You know I am shameless."

"I only know that you must have thought you had bloody good cause."

"I did, as a matter of fact."

There was silence for a moment. Then Walter spoke. "You're going to leave me hanging, just like that?"

The violet eyes gave him no mercy. "Yes," said Lee. Then after a moment he added, "Stay out of it, Downe. Don't speculate and don't press me. The thing is deeper than you know."

"You know your own business best, of course," said Walter stiffly, and with determination he put the question of blackmail out of his mind and began to think only of his beloved.

Lee, in contrast, was trying very hard not to think about Eleanor. She had come flying into the courtyard as the men were preparing to leave. The flush in her cheeks from running down the stairs made her eyes brilliant and her heavy brown hair was threatening to escape from its pins. It made his heart catch to see her. Instantly, he had led his horse away from

Walter and Diana, so that when she had stopped in front of him, they were well out of earshot.

"What made you do it?" she asked.

"What have I done now, brown hen? I rather thought I had been behaving better today—no breaking of roofs or stealing of kisses."

Eleanor ignored her own blush. "Why did you return the letters?"

"Why not? I decided I preferred your mother to Sir Robert."

"That doesn't make any sense."

Lee grinned wickedly. "Am I required to explain myself to you? I don't believe you have ever returned the compliment."

"The answer to that is easy. With me there's nothing to explain. I am as transparent as glass and as simple as a lunatic."

"Ah, yes, I had forgotten. You're just a schoolgirl, aren't you?"

"Mr. Campbell, if I and my family weren't already involved in your machinations, I wouldn't give you the time of day, believe me. But since I am, I think you owe me something other than pat phrases and evasions."

He idly took her hand and bending in a deep bow, kissed the tips of her fingers. "Alas, Lady Eleanor," he said. "That's all you're going to get. Infuriating, isn't it?"

"Oh, stuff! You don't matter enough to warrant more than indifference, sir!"

The violet eyes laughed into hers. "That's what I like about you, Lady Eleanor. You are so calmly consistent. It's a great virtue in a female."

"Virtue!" said Eleanor. "You wouldn't know it if it bit you!"

Lee swung onto his horse's back and called out to Walter, who with a last meaningful look at Diana, turned his horse to join the black.

Then Lee had leant down and given Eleanor a wink. She had gazed back at him with her eyes full of justifiable indignation. It had cost him every bit of self-control he had to make his smile light and his voice flippant. "You had better support my poor sister," he had said. "Love has her in its blind grip. Diana is about to have the vapors."

"For God's sake," said Walter. "What the hell is this?"

Lee brought his attention back to the present and skillfully edged his horse onto the verge. A carriage was ponderously rolling toward them. Pairs of outriders in elaborate livery rode before and after the vehicle. On the box sat not only the driver, but two servants armed with weapons to guard against highwaymen, and one with a loud and piercing coaching horn to warn other travelers out of the way. Lee and Walter were immediately honored with a blast, startling their horses so that Walter was almost unseated.

"Good heavens," said Lee with evident delight, though the black also shied and then bucked. "I hope my sister is feeling strong."

"What do you mean?"

"Unless I am very much mistaken, Mr. Downe, those are the colors of the Duke of May. It would follow, therefore, that the inhabitant of this splendid equipage is none other than his son, your rival for the hand of the fair Lady Diana: the infamously charming, wealthy, and eligible Roger Waters, Lord Ranking."

Ten

Eleanor firmly shepherded the drooping Diana back into the drawing room. To her relief Lady Augusta's eagle eye was distracted at that moment by an apparently casual comment from Lady Acton, and Eleanor's high color met only her brother's shrewd black gaze. What did Richard guess? Thank goodness there wouldn't be any chance for a private word! When he took his leave she was able to blandly hug and kiss him, and wish him a safe journey back to Helena as if nothing were wrong. Then while Lady Acton made her own goodbyes, Eleanor returned to her room so that her mother could enjoy the last few minutes with her eldest son. At least, that's what she told herself. For she had the strongest desire to be alone and gather her thoughts. Devil take the infuriating Leander Campbell! But the luxury of reflection was denied her. There were rapid footsteps running up the stairs and a hammering at the door. Eleanor opened it to find Diana, her eyes wet with tears.

"Oh, Eleanor, it's all quite dreadful! Now Walter has gone back to London, when shall I ever see him again?"

"Very soon, don't you think?" Eleanor was not feeling very sympathetic. "Mama and I go to town, too, and surely you and Lady Augusta follow immediately?"

Diana dropped onto Eleanor's bed. "Yes, and that's the worst of it! Your brother Richard barely trotted out of the driveway, when a carriage turned in. It has the May arms, Eleanor! Lord Ranking is here!"

"Di, pray don't be a watering-pot. It makes your skin blotchy. Not even your formidable mama can make you marry Ranking if you don't want to."

"But he'll fawn over me and pay me attentions, and I can't bear it! What if he should try to propose?"

"Refuse him. It won't cause an international incident—merely a tempest in the domestic teapot."

Lady Diana mopped at her eyes and smiled. Then she looked at her friend with her heart in her eyes. "You said you would help me, Eleanor. If you were nice to Lord Ranking, maybe he wouldn't want me, after all. You're so much braver than I am, you could cope with him. And anyway, you're not in love with somebody else, so it wouldn't be nearly as upsetting to your sensibilities. I shall die if he takes us to London. Get him to escort you and Lady Acton instead. Say you will, please?"

Eleanor laughed. "According to your brother, only heroines in romances would rather die. Anyway, it's highly unlikely that Lord Ranking would transfer his attentions from a blond angel to a brown hen."

"Why?" said Diana. "I don't think he's ever noticed what I look like. He just wants a suitable wife. And in so many ways, you're a better catch. Your father has all kinds of influence and standing. You're an Acton!"

"Do you think Ranking so mercenary? I thought he was captivated by your beauty."

"Lord Ranking was never captivated in his life. He's a toad! Oh, say you'll help me, Eleanor!"

"I don't see how I can. Really, Di! I've never had any practice at captivating before."

"Think of it as a challenge," said Diana. "Just enough to make him leave? Please?"

Eleanor looked at the genuine distress on her friend's lovely face and felt a rush of remorse. She reached out and squeezed Diana's hand. "Of course I'll try," she said. "What-

ever I can do to help you marry your Walter Feveril Downe,
from this moment I promise it shall be done."

"How can Lord Lenwood ride away without a coat?" said
a petulant voice as the girls came down. "Your son cares
nothing for his health, Lady Acton?"

A tall, drooping young man stood in the hallway beneath
them. His skin was pale and a little flaccid as if he rarely
saw fresh air, and he was unwinding several layers of woolen
scarf which had been wrapped about his neck. He seemed
unaware of the resulting crushed cravat and bent shirt collar
that thrust up crookedly beneath it.

"Richard is never ill," said Eleanor's mother, with her
most incisive smile. "We Actons enjoy the soundest constitution."

"Which is most fortunate for you!" stated Lady Augusta
as she motioned the company back into the drawing room.
"To my way of thinking, you are very wise to take no risks,
Lord Ranking. Why, Lady Acton herself had to be brought
back in the carriage after walking too far from the Park. It
is so foolish to expose oneself to a raw wind on a blustery
day."

Lord Ranking turned to the countess. "Did you indeed,
my lady? Why, I am always subject to a horrid inflammation
of the lungs after the slightest exposure. I am known for the
delicacy of my organs. No one has to be more careful. Ah,
Lady Diana!"

The girls had joined them. Diana made a stiff curtsy and
introduced her friend to her unwelcome suitor. Lord Ranking
immediately produced a quizzing glass and surveyed Eleanor
from head to toe, before taking her extended hand. "Most
delighted, I'm sure. I hope you will forgive my not bowing
too deep, Lady Eleanor? Nothing aggravates a delicate chest
more certainly than to disturb its natural elevation, I find.

And once irritation sets in, only the most determined care can cure it, and then, alas, but temporarily!"

Eleanor swallowed her smile and replied as gravely as she was able. "Red flannel is the answer to such problems, Lord Ranking. Worn as a preventative against chills and sudden upsets, nothing is more effective. I have it on the highest authority."

"Red flannel is all very well, of course." Lord Ranking gazed at her with serious interest. "But a posset of treacle and boiled milk is very comforting—unless one fears ague, in which case nothing can answer better than elderberry ague-ointment. You have consulted Culpeper's Compleat Herbal?"

"Of course," said Eleanor wickedly. "But in this case it was a Norfolk laborer called Frank Garth who recommended red flannel most highly."

Lord Ranking seemed oblivious to her teasing. "I understand. Wisdom may be found in the most unlikely places. You are a fellow sufferer, no doubt?"

"Lady Eleanor was abed with a dreadful fever at Acton Mead during Christmas!" added Diana quickly. Since it had been only a simple cold, this was a most iniquitous exaggeration.

"How extraordinary! I myself suffered just the same thing," said Roger Waters, immediately drawing Eleanor aside.

She sat beside him on the couch, and for Diana's sake began to display the deepest interest in his ailments. For the first time in her life, Eleanor discovered that it was really quite simple to be captivating after all. Nothing more was needed than to allow the victim to talk endlessly about himself. When it was someone as empty-headed as Lord Ranking, it was simplicity itself. Thus to Lady Augusta's horror and Lady Acton's amusement, by the time that tea had been served, the heir to the dukedom of May had not once paid the slightest attention to Diana.

Then when the tea dishes were cleared away, he suddenly declared himself unable to stay in the damp drafts of Norfolk one second longer than necessary. He would accompany the Acton coach up to town on the morrow and the Harts could follow as they wished. There was nothing that Lady Augusta could say to make him change his mind. Diana's profuse and ardent thanks were to be Eleanor's only reward.

And her cold comfort during the next two weeks as Lord Ranking seemed determined to become a regular visitor They had arrived safely in London, where the Earl of Acton was already ensconced in Acton House on Park Lane. Lord Ranking had indeed accompanied them up from Norfolk, yet to his chagrin had found that the Actons had no intention of sharing either carriage. He had been with them, however, for every meal and stop to change horses, and there Lady Acton had unmercifully teased him about his fastidiousness, his health, and his sensibilities. It had only added to her delight that Lord Ranking seemed impervious to her meaning. Lord Acton of course had never been a cramp on his wife's style, and whenever he saw the sprig of the Duke of May approaching the front door, Eleanor's father instantly retreated to his study—but the countess was having a wonderful time.

"Lord Ranking can't forget the tender solicitude you first showed him at Hawksley, Eleanor, when you advised him about the red flannel. It's your own fault that he hangs about your skirts," she had said with glee when Eleanor finally complained.

"Then I wish you would discourage him, Mama. I have more than done my duty by Diana. Surely I don't have to pay for it by accepting morning calls from Lord Ranking for the rest of the Season?"

"Nonsense, take it as a compliment. His attentions make the other young men take notice."

Which, perhaps fortunately considering Eleanor's fragile

heart, was not proving to be true. Although it was still early in the Season, every night was filled with balls and routs, soirées and assemblies. Eleanor found she must dress each evening in various pale shades of silk and attend an endless round of events. Somehow, she was supposed to attract a suitable swain. So far, only Lord Ranking seemed to be impressed. Leander Campbell, the one man she could not get out of her mind, was nowhere to be seen. Yet his name was often mentioned. Eleanor gathered that although he wasn't invited to the kinds of assemblies considered suitable for girls like herself, he was sought after by every hostess for her private dinner parties. Sometimes the ladies would mention him with a breathless little sigh, but it seemed that he was generally held in the highest regard, and it was with some regret that he was not accepted everywhere. *It only goes to show what a consummate actor he is,* she thought angrily.

The very first week had culminated in her presentation, along with a white-clad flock of other young ladies, to the Queen. She had indeed worn a feather in her hair and the required hooped dress, worn only at court, as had they all. "We looked like a flock of ducks," she said later to Diana. As expected, Lady Augusta had also brought her daughter to town in order to pursue the elusive Lord Ranking. Unlike Eleanor, Diana was the center of a crowd of admirers at every turn. Walter tried hard to pay her no more attention than was acceptable. Only Lord Ranking seemed to have entirely lost interest, and every day, much to Eleanor's disquiet, he called at the Acton town house.

Thus Lady Acton, Eleanor, and Roger Waters sat one afternoon in the upstairs gilt and ivory drawing room at the front of the house, above the incessant rattle of carriages on Park Lane.

"It is a great misfortune," said Lord Ranking gazing damply at Eleanor—who was trying to avoid his eyes by admiring the frescoes above her head—"that Lady Diana

Hart should have such a half-brother. I passed Mr. Campbell as I arrived at Hawksley, you know; he barely had the courtesy to move his horse from the road. Then today I was forced to acknowledge him at my club; one of the fellows invited him in as a guest. Far from being humbled by the honor, he behaved with the greatest insolence! A vagabond fellow, but then what can you expect from someone so situated? Nothing of the kind has ever happened in our family, I am grateful to say."

"Your family has always been such a model of propriety, hasn't it?" said Lady Acton instantly. "I recall your father in his youth. Wasn't there some problem with Lady Hare or was it the Marchioness of Withy? I forget now, perhaps it was both."

Eleanor had resolutely ignored Lord Ranking's comments about Mr. Campbell and was idly admiring the bulbous limbs of the painted Athene on the ceiling. Surrounded by cherubs in fluffy pink clouds, the noble Goddess of Wisdom forever threatened to burst from her draperies. In what extraordinary corner of the realm had the artist found his model? Or had he created the poor lady purely from imagination? And then Lady Acton made her comment about Lady Hare and the Marchioness of Withy. Eleanor concentrated very hard on the owl by the goddess's shoulder to avoid disgracing herself with unseemly giggles.

Roger Waters dabbed at his nose. "I cannot answer to that, Lady Acton. Yet I trust my father went about his concerns with impeccable manners. Mr. Campbell can hardly be expected to appreciate the standards of persons so far above him in life as we are. He can never be accepted as an equal by any real English gentleman."

"No, Mr. Campbell follows only his own code of honor," said Lady Acton. "Inherited from his Highland forebears, no doubt, if his father and yours were examples of the English peerage in which you take such pride. Imagine if we allowed personal integrity to count for more than birth and privilege! Society would fall apart at the seams, don't you agree?"

Her sarcasm this time could not be ignored, even by Lord Ranking. He colored a little and soon took his leave. "Thank God!" said the countess, suddenly bursting out laughing. "What a pompous fellow! How I wish I had been a fly on the wall when Leander Campbell gave him a set-down."

Eleanor turned from the window where she had gratefully gone to watch Lord Ranking's carriage finally pull away. "Don't say you admire Mr. Campbell, Mama? How can you defend him after what happened in Norfolk? What is more dishonorable or despicable than blackmail? He would have bled you of everything and Sir Robert, too! He didn't know you, though that's no excuse, but he certainly knew the major! The man taught him to ride. He rescued him from Ireland! It seems incredible to me that you can link Mr. Campbell's name with the idea of honor!"

"Dear child," said the countess seriously. "I do believe you have hold of the wrong end of the stick. It is not Mr. Campbell who wanted my money and my jewels, believe me."

Eleanor looked at her mother with wide eyes. "It wasn't? But he brought the letters back!"

"For which I shall be eternally grateful. But Mr. Campbell wasn't the blackmailer, Eleanor. Good God, the man risked a great deal to get them back for me."

Eleanor's heart had begun to dance oddly in her breast. If Lee hadn't blackmailed her mother, then she had been guilty of an appalling misjudgment. She blushed to think of the things she had said to him. "Then who was?"

Lady Acton sank gracefully into a chair. "You don't really need to know, do you?"

"No, I suppose not." Now, why, amidst the tumble of other emotions, should her initial chagrin be swamped by this overwhelming feeling of happiness? "You're sure it wasn't Leander Campbell?"

"I swear it to you, my dear. I went to see Sir Robert, as you may remember, the morning we left Norfolk, and I know the truth. I promised the major I would never reveal it and that's a promise I shall keep. But for heaven's sake, not only do I owe my rescue to Leander Campbell, I find I like him a great deal." Then Lady Acton looked closely at her daughter. "You're not indifferent either, are you? He's a charming young man, but don't succumb, Eleanor, you know it's impossible."

"Succumb!" said Eleanor indignantly. Good Lord, he might not be guilty of blackmail and for that she was genuinely glad, but he had still used her as casually as a milkmaid. "I'm pleased for Diana's sake to find that her brother isn't really a black villain, but I still think he's an out-and-out rogue."

"Well," said Lady Acton, taking up her fan and idly opening and closing it. "Thank goodness for that!"

Lee rode quietly through the park. He realized idly that it was the first day of May. Some of his acquaintance publicly acknowledged him, some did not. He was used to it. The fertile brain was involved with other matters. He had indeed received no satisfaction from his confrontation with the major. They had faced each other across the table at the Dog Inn two weeks before. Major Crabtree's features had been familiar to Lee since childhood, yet he had spent most of the years since out of England. How well did he really know the man?

"I would like you to know, sir," Lee had said, "that I am aware of the work that Frank Garth's brother did for you many years ago. I took the liberty of examining the rosebosses in the library for myself."

Major Crabtree's honest face colored above the military mustaches. "Then you know of certain papers pertaining to your birth?" he said at last.

"Indeed, sir. But you will be relieved to know that the most critical of those papers no longer exists."

Sir Robert looked away for a moment while different expressions raced across his features. Lee watched him carefully. It seemed for a moment that the predominant emotion was anger, but that made no sense, so he dismissed it.

"You destroyed them?" said the major at last. His voice was choked.

"The marriage papers are burned. Did you think I would proclaim the contents to the world? My father was a bigamist; my sister is a bastard. Is this why you kept it secret from me? Good God, I would have thought you could have trusted me better than that. And if you didn't, why not destroy the papers yourself?"

Major Crabtree had put his head in both hands so that Lee couldn't see his face. "It wasn't my place," he mumbled.

"Well, I thought it was mine," said Lee coldly. "You have kept silent about this for twenty years, sir. I trust nothing will change now?"

The major glanced up. He looked ill. "Of course not," he said.

"You should also know that I am aware of your predicament over Lady Acton's letters."

"For God's sake, you young puppy!"

"Frank Garth told me of other hiding places in the house besides the library, you see."

The major glared at the younger man. "Then you know that I have already recovered the letters myself," he said at last.

"So it would seem, sir. They are now in my pocket, along with a copy of a note demanding ransom sent to Red Lion Street. I have already been to the bookseller. He knows nothing, except that he expects a packet from Lady Acton to be picked up by a gentleman who will identify himself. It's a popular spot, of course. Every gentleman in Norfolk goes in at one time or another. But since the letters have been returned, we can hardly expect him to show. I gave instructions for the packet to be sent back to Lady Acton. You will have no objection to my delivering the letters to her forthwith?"

Lee had discovered the letters with genuine surprise. He had searched the house for evidence about Manton Barnes, and instead found Lady Acton's letters hidden in a cupboard upstairs. How had they come to be there, at Deerfield, when the major had said they were stolen? For God's sake, his childhood mentor could hardly be involved in blackmail—wasn't he a victim himself? That left only one explanation, and reassuringly the major had just given it: he'd already recovered the letters himself. Yet why had Sir Robert hesitated even a moment to send them back to Lady Acton?

The major was now very white, but he had his voice well under control. "I should be happy if you would do so, of course, since that was my own intention. Yet I am still within my rights to damn you for an interfering cad, Mr. Campbell. I happen to be in love with the lady. If I could return the letters myself as I had planned, maybe she would forgive me. Now I doubt she'll even give me the honor of a farewell."

"Oh, spare me, Major," said Lee lightly.

Sir Robert leaned across the table and took Lee by the wrist. "You've never been in love, have you? I hope it comes on you like a thunderbolt, and the lady spurns and despises you."

"All ladies spurn and despise me, Major. That's why I seek solace with females of a different kind." Lee had shaken off the major's restraining hand. "Would you feel at liberty to tell me who originally took Lady Acton's letters?"

The major sneered. "Certainly not! Let me just say that it is someone closer to you than you think."

Lee had looked at him for a moment. He would never forget the expression on Sir Robert's face. It was in that moment that he knew that the major had indeed become an enemy. He would get no more out of him.

Sir Robert had stayed in Norfolk, but he was shielding

someone. Who? Someone who had access to Deerfield, someone who could visit Red Lion Street without notice and, if his suspicions of a connection were correct, someone who had known Manton Barnes. Only one name came to mind. Walter. He dismissed the thought as fast as it came. That was the worst of this damnable business: anyone was suspect. Surely he had missed something? Something obvious. Finding the copy of his mother's marriage lines had bothered him more than he thought, and when he tried to relax and allow his mind full rein to speculate, all he thought of was Eleanor. Well, he had given up, quite deliberately, any possibility of ever winning her. Surely he had more self-control than to regret it?

Thus it was that April passed into May.

Lee looked up as a carriage passed him, then he suddenly pulled the black to a halt. Accompanied only by a groom, a supple young lady was riding toward him on a spirited dun. She had said she had ridden to hounds with her brothers. As he watched her handle the mount, he didn't doubt it. Eleanor looked beautiful on horseback. At the same moment, she glanced in his direction and her face flooded with color. Lee gave her a sardonic grin and the faintest nod of the head. He expected her to cut him dead. Instead, with a quick word to the groom who stayed well behind her, she set her horse straight toward him.

"Is this wise, Lady Eleanor?" asked Lee as she came up.

"I've never been wise, remember?" replied Eleanor. She had just observed the way so many members of the *ton* tactfully ignored Mr. Campbell. The open snobbery made her suddenly very angry, which gave, had she known it, a very becoming color to her cheeks. "I wanted to talk with you."

The black champed at the bit and tossed its head. Lee raised a brow. "Indeed? Do you think I'm in particular need of reproof? I can't think of anything I've done recently that's so very bad. Or at least, not much worse than usual."

So he was going to make this difficult. Eleanor wasn't

surprised. She turned her horse to fall in beside his. Lee could do nothing but allow her to ride on with him, the Acton groom following discreetly behind them.

"I owe you an apology," she said, her cheeks still flaming. "Please have the grace to accept it."

"Good heavens! Now you have me completely at a loss. For what small transgression could you possibly feel remorse?"

"Stop it," said Eleanor bluntly. "This isn't in the least bit easy. But when I've wronged someone, it's only right to say I'm sorry. I know now you never took my mother's letters and instead somehow recovered them from the real blackmailer. Mama told me so two days ago. I'm sorry for ever accusing you and I want to thank you for what you did. You saved Lady Acton from certain ruin."

Lee laughed. "Very well, I am found out. I tried so very hard to act the villain. Instead you have discovered that I'm really a saint."

Eleanor turned on him, her eyes blazing. "I didn't say that! I don't think you're at all saintly. There're still innumerable things I shan't forgive you, but I did wrong you over this one thing, and I had no right to accuse or even suspect you."

" 'There's ne'er a villain dwelling in all Denmark / But he's an arrant knave.' You had every right, brown hen," said Lee lightly. "I was a likely enough rogue. This apology is entirely unnecessary, since I myself allowed you to continue your suspicions. And I had already shown you my true colors at the Three Feathers, where you found me drunk, maudlin, and totally irresponsible."

Eleanor wouldn't allow herself to think about how she had felt when he first kissed her, nor the passion that had flared between them for a moment at Deerfield. If she did, she'd never get through this. "Why did you ask me about blackmail?"

"As an idle amusement, of course."

"You mean you can't tell me the truth. Very well. It's none of my business. I suppose it's to do with Manton Barnes."

Lee pulled up his horse. "Now, how the devil did you hear of him?"

"Walter told me he was a friend of yours who died in an accident and that's why you were drinking at the inn. I'm sorry. I thought perhaps his death was connected to all this, but I had no right at all to mention it, and unless you forget I did so this instant, I'll have to apologize for that, too."

"Your remark remains unsaid, my lady. Nevertheless, I am completely cast down that you won't forgive the rest of my foolish behavior."

"And that," said Eleanor, truly meeting the violet gaze for the first time, "really is arrant nonsense. Your behavior may be many reprehensible things, Mr. Campbell, but I suspect that it's never foolish."

"Very well. We'll leave foolishness to the schoolgirls. Talking of schoolgirls, how do you like the marriage mart?"

"Not at all, as it happens."

"Alas! As Dr. Johnson said: 'When a man is tired of London he is tired of life; for there is in London all that life can afford.' I could introduce you to a much more intriguing world, you know."

"No doubt you could. I don't suppose my mother would approve?"

And then Lee genuinely laughed. "I can't say," he said at last. "I doubt she would even approve of your talking to me in the park. Your youth and innocence will be all that saves you. The gossips will happily lay the blame for such an indiscretion at my door."

"You're not accepted at very many places, are you?"

"Brown hen, don't say you are dredging up wells of compassion for the poor landless orphan? I am welcome at all the interesting places, I assure you." Eleanor knew she was blushing again. He was deliberately blocking her attempt to make even limited amends. "Save your concern for poor

Lord Ranking, Lady Eleanor. He needs it a great deal more than I do."

Lee tipped his hat and put his heels to the black. In a few minutes, he was out of sight. Eleanor suddenly became aware of the curious glances she was getting.

"For heaven's sake, my dear Lady Eleanor," said a voice behind her. "It can hardly be wise to be seen talking openly to Mr. Campbell. A man of his birth? You won't take it amiss if I drop a friendly word in your ear? Not the done thing at all."

Lord Ranking sat in a pony cart, muffled to the ears in cloaks and wraps.

"Nor is it wise for you to be out, my lord, on such a brisk day. Even balsamic elixir won't save you if you should catch your death," she said, spinning the dun and riding away from him.

How dare they! Leander Campbell was an earl's son. And, as only she knew, he was also in truth the present Earl of Hawksley. Why had he really burned those papers? Until she had come to London, she'd had no idea how much he had given up. But the importance of rank and wealth was now being daily brought home. The content of a man's character meant nothing without it and less with it. It wasn't right, but it was the way of the world. If Leander Campbell had claimed his birthright, even Lord Ranking would be fawning over him. Instead Lee had willingly destroyed his own future to save Diana's. There was really no other motive that made any sense. Eleanor felt a confused wave of indignation sweep over her. It was absolutely none of her business, and anyway, the man was impossible.

Eleven

"It shall be the saddest crush of the Season," said Lady Augusta. "We'll invite everyone! The ball that I gave last year will be nothing to it. What do you say, Diana?"

"As you like, Mama." Diana was idly staring from the window of the town house which had once belonged to the late Earl of Hawksley. Eleanor watched her with guarded concern. Lady Diana Hart seemed truly unhappy of late.

"I declare, Felicity, these girls will be the death of us!"

Lady Acton smiled and softly waved her fan. It had not escaped her notice that Diana was in a positive decline. Eleanor's beautiful friend seemed to care nothing for the delights of the Season, even though she could have taken her pick of any of the most eligible beaux. The reason was obvious, of course, to everyone except Lady Augusta, and it went by the name of Walter Feveril Downe. Eleanor's lack of interest in the entertainment offered was harder to explain. Her daughter was usually the soul of good sense, and she had never looked more attractive. Yet she seemed to go through assemblies and balls in a distracted dream, and none of the desirable bachelors was anywhere close to offering for her, in spite of the Acton name and fortune.

"No doubt a grand ball will lift all our spirits," she said serenely.

* * *

Eleanor had been provided with a new gown for the occasion. The curved neckline swept low in fine folds of silver gauze, embroidered with a pattern of tiny flowers. As was the fashion, a high waistline further accentuated the curve of her breasts, and beneath them the skirts fell to the floor in a shimmer of silk. Long evening gloves covered her arms to the elbows, and delicate white silk slippers peeked beneath the hem. She thought she would be entirely indifferent to the result, but when her maid had finished dressing her hair, and she saw herself for the first time in the long mirror, she was amazed. The soft fabric made her creamy skin look as smooth as satin, and her maid's hour of brushing had brought out deep russet highlights in her hair. She would never be a beauty, but the overall effect was almost presentable.

"You are ravishing, dear child," said Lady Acton with approval from the doorway. "Now, let's hurry. It's one thing to be fashionably late, but hardly the thing to miss supper."

The earl was to escort them. Eleanor's formidable father had laced himself into his stays and poured the overflow of his bulk into white silk breeches. He would undoubtedly spend the evening in the card room. The countess, it went without saying, would be among the most beautiful ladies there.

They had barely handed their wraps to the footmen and entered the ballroom, when Diana hurried over and whisked Eleanor away.

"Walter will be here," she whispered. "And I shall dance a waltz with him. Perhaps Mama mightn't notice just one. We can hardly ever meet privately; it's been torture! Oh, Eleanor, there he is now. Did you ever see anyone who looked so distinguished?"

Eleanor followed her friend's gaze and knew the color was draining from her face. Walter looked perfectly unexceptionable, dressed quietly and correctly for the evening's dancing, his blond hair yellow in the light of the candles. He was handsome enough, but she would hardly have described him as distinguished. That word would, however, fit to perfection the gentleman standing beside him.

"Your brother is here?" she said at last.

"I made him come. I wouldn't let Mama give me a ball unless he did. Everybody is so stuffy about him, except for the young gentlemen, of course. And Lee probably won't dance, out of consideration for the dowagers' sensibilities. It's enough to give the mamas apoplexy to think that their daughters might fall in love with someone so ineligible."

Eleanor watched him for a moment. It was outrageous. It was less than a week since she had last seen him, yet Leander Campbell could still make her heart behave like a drum set. Then she was forced to acknowledge the suitors who came swarming after Diana and herself. Soon her dance card was almost filled, and she was being led into the first set. However, she hardly noticed her partners. Instead her eyes were drawn to that dark head and wicked smile, until he disappeared into the card room with some other gentlemen.

At last she found a moment to herself, and she slipped into a chair behind a potted palm. It was now very hot, and Eleanor fanned her cheeks with her pearl-and-ivory fan as she watched the dancers swirl by. The faint smell of moist dirt from the palm was cool and refreshing compared to the heavy scent of hot wax and perfume that otherwise permeated the room.

"Well, brown hen," said a familiar voice behind her. "Has the marriage mart improved?" Eleanor spun around. Lee was leaning on the back of the empty chair beside her. He seemed perfectly cool and relaxed, the starch of his high collar and cravat still crisp and white, the cut of his jacket accentuating the breadth of his shoulders. "I am being discreet, as you can see," he added lightly.

"Don't be ridiculous," replied Eleanor instantly. "Do you mean that it wouldn't be politic to be seen sitting beside me, so instead I must crane my neck like a goose to talk to you? This palm tree would screen an elephant."

He moved around the chair and sat beside her. "You *want* to talk to me?" he asked, surprised.

Eleanor looked away from the violet gaze and steadied her breathing. Let him mock her if he must! An idea had been slowly crystallizing in her mind, and now it suddenly came to her how it might work. Only Lee could help, if he would.

"Something must be done about Diana and Walter," she said firmly. "Your sister is pining away. She barely eats and I know she's not sleeping. It makes her all the more beautiful and the beaux are hounding her to death, but if it doesn't change, she'll really become ill."

"She is sick with longing," said Lee quietly. He allowed his eyes to drift slowly along the curve of Eleanor's neck. "She needs him like a desert dweller needs a well. After a few days away from him the thirst becomes overwhelming, and without another draught, the sands will bury her forever. It's known as love. They should elope."

Eleanor spun back to face him. "They never will and you know it! But can't we at least help them see more of each other? Lady Augusta watches over Diana like a hawk. She's even afraid to have more than one dance with him tonight, and Walter never comes to call because Diana can't bear the thought of her mama finding them out. Yet I can go places with her. Can't you arrange for Walter to be there and meet us?"

"I am stunned," said Lee simply. "I had no idea you were a conspirator."

"I want to help Diana and it's the only thing I can think of to do."

"You have a kind heart," he said seriously.

"Oh, fiddlesticks! I just don't want to see Diana make herself ill. Say you will help, Mr. Campbell?"

"Kind enough to override your own distaste for my person

in order to help your friend," he continued. "Of course I will. If I'd known you would feel this way, I'd have suggested it myself."

"Send me a message at Acton House," said Eleanor. Then she tried valiantly to conceal her feelings. "And now I suppose I must go and circulate again. It's not at all the done thing for we flowers of the marriage mart to hide behind palm trees, especially in order to conspire with wicked rakes. I'll never find a rooster for the brown hen like this! What is the matter?"

Lee had closed his eyes for a moment, but they flew open and met hers as he laughed openly. The deep blue was dark with self-mockery. "I am only thirsty," he said lightly. "Now, let me slip away before we cause a scandal."

He moved off, but not in the direction of the refreshment table, and Eleanor was left sitting in the chair. She felt suddenly bereft. Good heavens! So she must still be suffering this ridiculous schoolgirl crush for him. Well, it didn't matter, did it? As these last few weeks had made devastatingly clear, anything serious between them was impossible. With determination, she stood up and went to join her mother, who sat at the side of the room with the other mamas and the dowagers.

"He looks so like his father. You remember the late Earl of Hawksley, don't you, Lady Acton?" said one of the ladies as she came up.

"La! Who doesn't?" replied another high voice. "Hawksley was a devil and so is his son! I'm amazed that Augusta allowed him to attend tonight. One can't be too careful about maintaining the proprieties."

"I remember Gerald Hart well enough," said Lady Acton lazily. "Yet I believe his son is nothing like him."

"Worse, no doubt! It's a scandal that Mr. Campbell is here, in a room full of innocent young girls."

"Why?" said Lady Acton. "Do you think he might abduct

one of our daughters from under our noses? He refrains from dancing, yet I really see no reason why he should."

"You think a partner from a respectable family would give countenance to the by-blow?" said the first lady. "When his mother was some peasant girl from the Highlands? I'm afraid nothing can save him. He will sink inexorably to the gutter. Circumstances of birth always tell in the end."

Eleanor unconsciously clenched her fists. How dared these mean old biddies disparage Leander Campbell. She knew him to be a rake and accepted it, but she was also slowly coming to realize that what Richard had said must be true. Her brother was a superb judge of character, and his friendship wasn't lightly given. Over and over again she had thought about that extraordinary night when Lee had burned the evidence of his mother's marriage. *Which means that Lord Hawksley's marriage to Lady Augusta wasn't valid and that Lady Diana Hart of Hawksley isn't a Lady and doesn't belong to Hawksley at all.* He had done it to save Diana from the stigma of illegitimacy which he had borne unfairly all his life. No one knew better than he what that meant, yet he had sacrificed everything for his sister. Eleanor could think of nothing in her experience that was a finer or more selfless action. And then he had rescued her mother from someone who would have blackmailed her, perhaps at some cost to himself. Choked with anger, Eleanor spun on her heel and walked directly after Lee.

He turned with surprise when she appeared at his elbow. The gentleman to whom he'd been talking raised both eyebrows, but bowed and took his leave. Several pairs of eyes began to swivel in their direction. Eleanor didn't care.

"I would like to ask you to dance, Mr. Campbell," she said.

"What on earth has brought on this sudden desire for unsuitable exercise, Lady Eleanor?" he asked with a smile.

"The unfairness of this whole place," she said indignantly. "Why shouldn't you dance?"

"Because the band is striking up a waltz, for a start," he replied instantly.

"Does it make a difference?"

"Perhaps not. After all, I am expected to sweep ladies into my arms every day. Why not include Lady Eleanor Acton? Of course, the waltz offers a most discreet embrace, though so very public. Surely you can understand that I prefer those which are both less elegant and more private?"

"You are deliberately trying to embarrass me," said Eleanor, furious that he could so easily make her blush.

"On the contrary, I am trying to make you retract your request, brown hen. Do you always charge in with the cavalry when you think something is unfair?"

"I hate meanness."

"And I think I prefer being the recipient of your heavy guns to being the beneficiary of them. It's simpler."

"You're impossible, aren't you?"

"Of course," he said with a devastating smile. "I take pride in it, remember?"

"Then damn you for a stiff-necked . . ."

"Bastard," he finished. "Now retract your invitation to this waltz, or I shall make you very seriously regret it."

"How?"

"Good God, brown hen! Do you really think I can't make good on my word?"

Eleanor was already very bitterly regretting her impulsive action. She had no idea what he might do, but there was no question in her mind that he had no intention of dancing with her, and the more she persisted, the less dignity she would have left.

"All right, you win! I am suitably humiliated and chastened. And anyway the next dance, being a staid promenade, is promised to Lord Ranking. I suppose I should go and prepare myself to be mauled about like a piece of dough."

She turned and left him. Lee watched the silver skirts as they retreated toward the ladies' powder room. Her neck rose

like a slender column from the perfect skin of her shoulders,
shadowed only by her brown hair. She was wearing the gold
locket that he had found at the Three Feathers: the one she
had so bravely been prepared to rescue from the clutches of
a rogue.

"I say, old chap, are you all right?"

Walter stood beside him, his open face unusually clouded
with concern. Lee turned to his friend and laughed. "A devilish thirst has come on me—like a thunderbolt, you might
say. Lead me to some fine brandy and a gaming table, for I
think I'm ready to lose a great deal of money. What say you
to hazard?"

Eleanor managed to survive the rest of the evening, yet
not even Lord Ranking's absurdities were able to lift her
spirits. Why on earth should it bother her how Diana's profligate brother might behave? She had been a fool to once
again expose herself to him when she knew that it would
only cause her pain. Yet she was involved, because Diana
was her friend. If only Lee's father had waited another two
months to marry Lady Augusta. Then Lee could have been
recognized as Earl of Hawksley and probably already wed
to an heiress, and Diana could freely marry Walter. Eleanor
remembered the spiteful comments that the dowagers had
made about Lee's mother. What kind of girl had Moira
Campbell been? Surely Blairmore was more than a cottage?
Even if it was the simplest place in Scotland, Moira had still
won marriage to Gerald Hart. How could she have known
he would abandon her?

For Eleanor knew that Moira Campbell must have been
entranced by her lover. It was his son, wasn't it, who had
spoiled her for all these other suitors? Because of Leander
Campbell, she wasn't interested in any of the beaux she was
meeting on the marriage mart. It was the most humiliating
thing to have to admit to oneself. His smile, his eyes, the

way he moved—however disgracefully he acted, everything about him bewitched her. Well, besotted or not, Lady Eleanor Acton was not going to sit about and mope. The morning after Lady Augusta's ball, she pulled out a fresh sheet of paper from her writing case and sharpened a new pen. If she wanted to find out about Moira Campbell, if that would somehow help lay to rest this insistent longing for the Highland woman's arrogant son, then there was no better time to start than the present.

It took several drafts before she had penned something tactful enough and with a sufficiently plausible reason for her curiosity. Eventually she sanded and sealed the final version, and addressed it to the minister who had witnessed the wedding in Strathbrae, Scotland. She remembered quite clearly all the details she had read before Lee had burned the marriage lines, and knew the man's name. The only problem was that she had no idea if the fellow was even still alive.

The message from Lee arrived the next day. She unfolded the paper which on the outside had been clearly and correctly addressed in the finest penmanship to Lady Eleanor Acton, Acton House, Park Lane. Inside it was short and to the point, and she could almost imagine one violet eye half-closed in a wink.

"By the Curzon Gate. Wednesday morning at ten. L.C."

Wednesday morning dawned bright and warm. The girls went together arm in arm to the park. It was not the innocent walk that Lady Augusta assumed, for Diana very soon spied a closed carriage waiting at the corner by the Curzon Gate.

"Oh, look!" she said. "It's Lee's man!"

"It is?" replied Eleanor. "Then he's waiting for us, silly. Come on!"

Lee's footman helped them into the dark interior. Five minutes later, they were being shown into an elegant set of rooms where Walter eagerly awaited his beloved.

"Welcome to my humble lodgings, Lady Eleanor," said Lee with a grave bow.

Eleanor looked around with only the slightest dismay. If they were seen entering or leaving, it was almost unexceptionable that a lady should visit her half-brother, even if he did keep bachelor apartments. That Lady Augusta wouldn't see it that way, however, accounted for the discreet carriage and the careful servants. Immediately, Diana sat beside Walter and he took her hands.

"Perhaps it will be politic to leave them?" Lee asked Eleanor. "Poor Mr. Downe loses all faculty for polite conversation when in the presence of my sister, or even when thinking about her. Love makes people so tiresome." He gave her a wicked grin. "I have a very fine library here. You have an interest in libraries, do you not?"

Eleanor refused to be fazed by the reference. "I should be very happy to admire your books, Mr. Campbell, but may I trust your manners?"

"Of course. You refer to my disgraceful behavior at Deerfield? Would you believe it was only a moment of madness, or would you prefer to think I wanted to make my wicked point? Either way, I would never dare kiss a lady when Shakespeare, Milton, Bunyan, and Chaucer were in the room, not to mention any number of medieval saints and scholars. Their dry disapproval robs even me of nefarious intent. Come, you are quite safe and you should see my collection."

She followed him out of the room and into the library. Instantly, Eleanor was enchanted. From floor to ceiling, on every wall and in rank after rank of free-standing cases, there were books. It didn't take very long to realize that many of them were of remarkable antiquity and presumably extremely valuable, but Eleanor was more enthralled by the sheer beauty of the volumes that Lee began to take down and show her. He laid a large vellum tome on the table in the center of the room and unclasped the metal hasps that held it shut. Before he carefully began to turn the pages, he pulled on a pair of fine white cotton gloves to protect the ancient parchment. The action only drew Eleanor's attention to the elegance of his hands. Beneath his gentle touch, the pages revealed breathtaking illuminations in rich blue and red and gold. Something about the deft and tender way he touched them made Eleanor's heart catch in her throat. It was the caress he might give a lover, she thought blindly. Can he tell that it makes my pulse race just to stand next to him like this? But then, that was the way all girls felt during their first crush, wasn't it?

"You really do love these books," she said after awhile.

Lee glanced at her and smiled. "Of course. You find that odd, don't you? I wonder why? Because it seems strange that I haven't sold this collection to support my dissolute career? And you find that even odder, because you believe me incapable of loving anything, perhaps?"

Eleanor couldn't look up at him. She let her eyes feast instead on a tiny vine which trailed around an entire page of the manuscript. Every leaf was perfect. "I wouldn't deign to offer an opinion of your character," she said quietly.

And then she had to glance up when he laughed, even if the sight of his smile turned her limbs to water. "Then you are in a particularly reticent mood," he said. "I can't remember you being too shy to offer your judgment of me before today!"

"Well, then, I can only have become even less concerned!" she snapped.

"And I am properly put in my place. You realize of course, the indifference of a lady I have kissed is the most terrible insult imaginable to my pride?"

"Fiddlesticks, Mr. Campbell! Since I'm sure you bestow your attentions in a purely random manner, it can hardly matter, can it?"

He closed the book and carefully carried it to its case. "Ah, brown hen, it's a sorry thing to be a rake," he said. "You will choose your acquaintances more carefully in the future, won't you?"

Eleanor pretended not to hear him. Instead she was looking about with a new and dreadful suspicion. This collection was indeed immensely valuable. In which case, how had he acquired it? An officer's pay and the proceeds of his success at the tables might be enough to keep him in horses, and send a little extra down to Hawksley to Frank Garth, but it could never have purchased the most famous book collection in London. Had her mother been wrong? Was Lee the blackmailer after all? Yet Lady Acton had said that Sir Robert had told her the villain's true identity, and that it hadn't been Lee. She could hardly doubt that. When he left for Belgium and then India, as her brother had said he intended, it would no longer matter, she supposed.

"Richard told me you might live abroad some day," she said, as casually as she was able. "What will you do with all this when you leave?"

"It could go into storage, of course, for I want to think that these volumes await my eventual return. But scholars should continue to have access to it. I intend to put the books out on loan to a museum."

He was quite serious. Eleanor gazed at him as he moved through the room. His lean hands rested for a moment on the spines of a row of volumes, and the dim light softened his dark hair to a shadow. She felt the most disturbing rush of desire. How could she have thought that he could forget all honor and sink to blackmail because he so loved his books? It wasn't possible. Yet he was a rogue! She could make no sense out of it at all. All that was left was the most insistent wish that everything had turned out differently. *She is sick with longing,* he had said about Diana. *It's known as love.*

* * *

Lee watched from the window as his sister and her friend climbed back into his carriage. Walter had left immediately after the ladies and was already striding away up the street.

"I owe you my sincerest gratitude for arranging this meeting," he had said as he refused Lee's offer of brandy and took up his hat and cane. "And you have it. But I'll be damned if I want to hang about and be victim to your dashed odd mood and that sarcastic tongue!"

"Indeed, you had better go, my friend," Lee had replied. "Otherwise you'll no doubt be the recipient of unnecessarily wanton remarks about your feelings for Diana."

Lee cursed silently as Eleanor looked up one last time toward his window and the sun caught her profile. Then he stepped back and returned to the library. Very deliberately, he took down the vellum he had shown Eleanor and kissed the cover. Whether it was in benediction or farewell was impossible to say. And so Leander Campbell was left to his thoughts.

As Eleanor was left to hers. As soon as she went over everything she knew, she was convinced that her mother couldn't be mistaken. Lee was not the blackmailer, whatever else he might be. And for Diana's sake, she would see him again, whatever it did to her own composure. The next note came the following morning.

"Vauxhall Gardens. Saturday evening at nine. L. C."

Twelve

Lady Acton expressed no surprise at her daughter's sudden desire to see the famous gardens and Diana, of course, knowing what was planned, longed to go. Lady Augusta, however, didn't think it quite suitable unless the girls were properly chaperoned, yet she was afraid her own sensibilities and the dignity due her station would preclude her from attending.

"Vauxhall Gardens is becoming far too popular. All manner of City men are taking their wives and daughters there these days, I hear. Persons of real refinement will soon shun it."

"Then I shall take them," said Lady Acton. "You were not so fine in your taste last summer, Countess. You accompanied our party to Vauxhall yourself when we were escorted by Major Crabtree. Viscount Jasper and Mr. John Mallard were with us, and Miss Blanche Haricot suddenly joined our party, white as a sheet. Surely you remember?"

"Yes, I do, Felicity. And as I recall, the result was a thorough soaking for all concerned. When the weather is so unsettled, it cannot be prudent to seek amusement outdoors."

"Lord Ranking will be in our party," said Lady Acton. "You cannot object if he escorts Diana, surely?"

Eleanor had looked at her mother with dismay, but if that's what it took to get Lady Augusta's permission for Diana to come with them, she would have to accept it.

"Of course, as son of the Duke of May, he lends consequence to any situation. Diana may go if she wishes, but I hope you will understand if I do not attend."

Lady Acton ignored the insult and laughed. "How very sorry I am to hear it," she said wickedly. "We shall have a dull evening without you."

Lord Ranking, it seemed, was to be their only male escort, and to Eleanor's relief, Lady Acton insisted he take her own arm and allow the girls to follow behind them. The heir to the Duke of May, however, could not relax.

"I am very afraid it may rain, Countess," he said to Lady Acton. "I cannot abide the least exposure to rain."

"Oh, nonsense, my lord! I think the night augers very fine. Let us take a seat here under this canopy if you are worried." Then she laughed aloud. "Why, how very odd and unexpected! I do believe it's Mr. Downe and Mr. Campbell."

The countess waved to the young gentlemen and winked privately at Eleanor. At which point Eleanor realized that her mother had plans of her own, and was by no means averse to aiding Diana's courtship with Walter, if for no other reason than to annoy Lady Augusta. It wasn't surprising, therefore, that within fifteen minutes Eleanor and Diana were walking with Lee and Walter down the tree-lined pathways toward the bandstand, leaving Lord Ranking fretting about the night air and how it might affect his lungs, much to the wicked delight of Lady Acton.

"Your plan succeeds, Lady Eleanor," said Lee. "My sister is once again blissfully enjoying the private company of her beloved. Unfortunately you have overlooked one small drawback to this conspiracy."

"Which is?" said Eleanor. She walked stiffly beside him, stifling the longing to take his arm and lean into him as Diana was doing with Walter ahead of them.

"That you have to put up with me, of course, and there's no telling how disgraceful I might become."

She glanced up at him. He seemed to be deliberately baiting her.

"I'll endeavor to stand it," she replied acidly. "We are only here for Diana's sake, after all."

" 'For some must watch, while some must sleep; / So runs the world away.' "

She would not let him get away with it! "I think you do more than watch and sleep, though, don't you, Mr. Campbell? I know you fought in the Peninsula. My brother told me."

"Did he?" said Lee. He laughed and the bitter edge to his voice dropped away. "Your brother is a good man, brown hen; he only sees the best in those around him."

"Richard is more than that, he's a reformer. If you claimed your birthright and became earl, you could help him do a lot of good. I don't know that Diana would care, if she could marry Walter. If he loves her, he'll take her even if she is illegitimate."

"You are full of brave plans to see Diana wed, aren't you? Even to declaring her a bastard? What of my stepmother?"

Eleanor hesitated. Why should she want him to let the world know his real birth? Did she somehow think that if he could be shown to be an earl's rightful heir, then he couldn't have been capable of wickedness? "Yes, I know, but Lady Augusta is a horrid dragon of a woman."

Lee stopped and turned to her. "A cruel deed is a cruel deed whether done to the wicked or the good, don't you think? It's not by the character of the victim that we judge the perpetrator."

"And have you never done anything cruel, Mr. Campbell?"

"Too many times and sometimes deliberately, when the occasion warranted. And so have you, though unwittingly." Eleanor gazed up at his face. She couldn't read his expression, but her heart thudded wildly in her breast. Violet lights danced between his dark lashes as he smiled back. "It's cruel for you to have such eyes, brown hen. And to be so very tempting to touch."

"I'm not in the least tempting," she said, choking.

He laughed. "Don't you think you should let me be the judge of that?" He was slowly guiding her away from the public path into a little shaded grove of trees. The light from the lanterns was broken and scattered like drops of water across the ground. Somewhere in the distance the band was playing the tune of a pretty popular song. Eleanor knew some of the words: "Oh, don't deceive me. / Oh, never leave me. / How could you use a poor maiden so?"

She knew what was going to happen, and if she wanted to resist, she knew he wouldn't force her, but instead she allowed him to gently touch the side of her face with his hand. They were entirely shielded from anyone passing by.

"For old times' sake, Eleanor," he said softly, bending his head and taking her mouth with his.

She clung to him, drowning in sensation. More than anything, she wanted this moment to go on forever, but too soon he released her and once again gently stroked her cheek with his long fingers. "You are the memory of England I shall take with me," he said. "And all the guilt of using you so selfishly is mine. Marry for love, Eleanor."

"That's what Helena said to me," Eleanor replied shakily. "Because she's lucky enough to have been found by Richard. You know it's impossible advice." Then she gathered her courage. "Don't you think Lord Ranking would be a perfect match for me?"

"Unless you swear this instant that you'd rather die an old maid, I shan't be able to go."

Her heart stuck in her throat. "Go? Go where?"

"To Belgium where our troops assemble. Napoleon gathers an army in Paris. Wellington and the Allies can't attack France before July, but Boney may move first. If he does, I must be there. I have purchased a new commission and next week I go to Brussels. There's a great deal that I leave unfinished behind me, but I can't help that. In the meantime, it's traditional for a soldier to steal what kisses he may."

So Richard's prediction that Lee would rejoin Wellington was coming true immediately. She couldn't bear it! "From any girl who crosses his path, I suppose," she said blindly.

"No, only from those who cross swords with him, of course. Now, we had better catch up with my sister and her swain before I decide I need another keepsake."

He took her hand in his and tucked it into his elbow. Eleanor followed him back onto the public path. He was leaving to join the army. What had Richard said? *There will be another terrible battle, I'm afraid.* What if Leander Campbell was killed? And if he wasn't, he was going to India, wasn't he? So it had been a farewell kiss. The thought sunk into her heart and turned it to ice.

"You leave Diana and Walter to their own devices?"

"Now your mother seems to have become a willing conspirator, Lady Augusta's cause is doomed. There is nothing more I can do. They'll wait for each other. Diana may pine, but she'll not give in. I predict my sister will be Mrs. Feveril Downe within the year. Meanwhile, I have duties to my country."

"Don't you have other responsibilities in England?"

His face looked bleak. "I thought I did, but they have come to naught." Eleanor said nothing. It wasn't her place to pry. She was amazed when he went on. "I made a promise to myself when my friend Manton Barnes died, but I'm going to break it."

"What kind of promise?"

He smiled. "One of pride, perhaps, or revenge. I apparently underestimated my opponent: the man who blackmailed your mother. I still don't know his identity."

There was no question he was telling the truth. Eleanor stopped, forcing him to halt also. "But you got the letters back from him!"

"Not directly. In fact, Sir Robert had already retrieved them."

"My mother knows who he is. Major Crabtree told her."

"Lady Acton?" He began to laugh. "Why didn't I think to ask her? And why do I think she would never tell me? Especially now that a dangerous rake such as myself has taken the liberty to kiss her brown-eyed daughter, more than once."

"She would think that it's valuable experience for me, and since I have a sound head on my shoulders, I won't refine too much upon it," said Eleanor desperately.

"A very sensible attitude," replied Lee with a laugh. "I like your mother, brown hen."

"Everybody does." Eleanor was vainly trying to make sense of this whole evening. "But she likes you and that's more rare."

"But I am prepared to wager," he said, glancing up at the sky, "that she doesn't take kindly to rain."

"Oh, good heavens!" A large drop fell on the back of Eleanor's hand. "Poor Lord Ranking! He'll catch a chill and have to wrap his feet in mustard plaster!"

"Come on," said Lee, laughing and catching Eleanor by the hand. "We'll rescue them."

As a distant growl of thunder rolled overhead, the crowds on the walks began to scatter. Diana and Walter came hurrying up, and they all raced back to the canopy where Lady Acton and Lord Ranking had stayed to admire the illuminations.

"Does no one have an umbrella?" said Lady Acton as Eleanor and Lee reached her. "Surely you didn't come unprepared, Lord Ranking?"

"You said it wouldn't rain," moaned the duke's heir. "I cannot abide wet! I shall be abed this fortnight if I am soaked!"

"Here, take my wrap," said Eleanor, gallantly handing

over her shawl. "Come, Mr. Campbell, have you no protection to offer poor Lord Ranking?"

"Let me offer you my coat, my lord," said Lee instantly, stripping off that garment and holding it over Lord Ranking's head. His shirtsleeves shone white against the dark canopy overhead.

"You will be soaked yourself, Mr. Campbell!" cried Lady Acton gaily. "Oh, dear! Must I have to witness gentlemen giving up their own cloaks for another every time I come to Vauxhall? Last summer it was Sir Robert gallantly protecting Blanche Haricot and now it's to benefit Lord Ranking!"

"Major Crabtree knew Miss Haricot?" said Lee with sudden intensity.

"Oh, indeed! She was engaged to his nephew. Oh, good heavens, that was your friend that you mentioned to me at Hawksley, wasn't it? I never met Manton Barnes, as I told you, but I knew Blanche, and Sir Robert seemed to know her very well. She was upset over something, almost hysterical. The engagement had just been broken off, of course, yet this was some very dreadful distress. Sir Robert took her home. It was very touching to watch. He offered her such a gallant and sympathetic ear; I believe she must have poured out her heart to him. Of course, very shortly afterwards, she went to America."

And Manton Barnes received his first blackmail note, thought Lee with an absolute certainty. So as he'd suspected long ago, it was Blanche who'd told Barnes's secret to the blackmailer. This was the proof! How could he have been so very blind?

"I can't bear it anymore," said Diana sadly. Eleanor sat with her friend in the drawing room of Acton House. She was trying to busy herself with some embroidery but it wouldn't go right. Impatiently, she pulled out the last row of stitches. Ever since the meeting with Leander Campbell three days before, she hadn't been able to concentrate on anything else. And now he seemed to have disappeared. At least no further messages had arrived from him.

As if to echo her thoughts, Diana went on, "And now Lee's going away. I shall miss him so much. If only he had been the heir! If I were just a younger sister to the Earl of Hawksley, Mama couldn't stop me marrying Walter."

Eleanor looked down. Diana was indeed a younger sister to the earl, but an illegitimate one, and Lee would never do anything to change the situation. "Your brother is confident you and Walter will be married within the year, Diana dear; he told me so."

"Your mother is being very kind to us," Diana replied. "Walter is to call here while we visit, did you know?"

"Then that must be him now," said Eleanor, hearing footsteps in the hall. "Oh, fiddlesticks! I am out of blue thread. I shall have to go and get some." She gave Diana a wink. "You won't mind being left alone with him for a bit, will you? It'll only take me a moment."

Eleanor met Walter in the doorway and showed him in to Diana. As she turned to go to her own room, she saw her friend run into her lover's arms. It wasn't proper, but who would ever know? Firmly she shut the door behind her.

It may have been half an hour later when Eleanor suddenly became aware of a commotion in the hall. Running to the banister, she leaned over to see Lady Augusta handing her gloves to the maid.

"My daughter is here, is she not?" said the booming tones.

"Yes, my lady," replied the maid with a curtsy. "Lady Diana is in the blue drawing room with Lady Eleanor. Allow me to show you up."

Eleanor raced to intercept them, almost colliding with Lady Augusta at the head of the stair. "Oh, good morning, Lady Augusta!" she said, as loudly as she dared.

"Is something the matter with your voice, young lady? I

am not deaf. There is no need to shout. Most unseemly in a young girl. Where is your mama?"

"Oh, she's out, Lady Augusta." Eleanor positioned herself between the dragon and the drawing room door. "Perhaps you would like to wait for her in the morning room? I'll ring for refreshments."

"I do not require refreshment, Eleanor. I have come to find my daughter. Isn't she with you?"

"Diana isn't well. She's lying down. If you would like to sit in the morning room and wait, I'll fetch her."

"Stuff and nonsense! The morning room is at the other end of the house as I recall. I shall wait in here!"

Without more ado, Lady Augusta thrust Eleanor aside and took the doorknob. As it turned, Eleanor exclaimed as loudly as she could, "Why, isn't this the loveliest May ever, Lady Augusta?"

She had failed. Oblivious to the world, Diana and Walter were entwined together on the couch. Wrapped in her lover's arms, her blond tresses mixed with his, Diana was being passionately and very thoroughly kissed by Walter Feveril Downe. It was equally obvious that she was kissing him back. Lady Augusta screamed.

From Vauxhall, Lee had ridden his black charger through the night, as urgently as if he had despatches to deliver for Wellington. By the time he arrived at Deerfield, he had long worn out his own horse and left a string of used-up rented nags behind him. He had stormed into the study, thrusting aside the footman who answered the door, only to be met by the surprised butler, hurrying up from the pantry where he had been polishing silver.

"Where is the major?"

"Why, we didn't expect you, sir! Sir Robert left for London not these five hours since."

At which Leander Campbell had sat down in one of the

expensive chairs, thrown back his head, and laughed. After a moment, he had looked up into the astonished face of the servant. "Tell me what I need to know," he had said savagely. "Or I shall tear this place apart, every floorboard, every mattress, every fashionable and costly item in it. And if I don't find what I'm looking for, you will be next."

The smelling salts and the burnt feathers had been applied to both Lady Augusta and her distraught daughter. Walter valiantly tried to defend his beloved, but Eleanor managed to grab him by the arm and insist that he leave.

"There's nothing you can do while hysterics reign, sir. Believe me, if you try to protect Diana it'll only make things worse. Pray wait in the study. I'll report everything, I promise."

His jaw clenched, Walter strode from the room.

"How could you?" cried Lady Augusta. "My only daughter! How long has this been going on?"

Diana couldn't reply. She had her face buried in her handkerchief.

"They're in love, Lady Augusta," said Eleanor bravely. "They want to marry." If only Lady Acton were here to handle this.

The Dowager Countess of Hawksley drew herself up like a drill major. "Love!" she exclaimed. "An emotion for servant girls and milkmaids. Never did I think I would live to see the day! How could my daughter be so lost to everything that is suitable?"

Diana choked. "I shall marry him, Mama. I'll die if I don't!"

"Stuff and nonsense! You are an heiress, Diana. Pray remember whose blood you carry in your veins. What if this adventurer had gained his way with you! I shudder to think what might have transpired had I not arrived."

Diana paled. "Mama, Walter would never have . . ."

"I saw for myself what this jackanapes would do, young lady. Shocking, contemptible behavior! But the answer is simple. You will never see him again."

Diana dropped her head in her hands and sobbed. Eleanor put her arms around her friend. She longed to tell Lady Augusta exactly what she thought of her, but nothing could be better guaranteed to make an already bad situation worse, so she held her tongue. Her relief was overwhelming when the door opened again and she heard the cool tones of another countess.

"Good heavens!" said Eleanor's mother lightly. "What do we have here?"

There was silence.

Lady Acton smiled and crossed to the mantel. "I do know, as a matter of fact," she said to the two woebegone faces and the other, stiff with disdain. "I have just spoken with Mr. Downe in the study."

"Is Walter all right?" asked Diana through her tears.

"As well as might be expected, considering the news I just gave him."

"What news can have any importance, considering what I have just witnessed here!" cried Lady Augusta. "My daughter with a viscount's younger son! In jeopardy for her reputation! Under your roof, Felicity!"

"Oh, pooh!" said Lady Acton. "Some minor indiscretion, no doubt, unless you choose to publicly refine upon it. A mere trifle. You may have forgotten, Augusta, but we were all young once."

But Eleanor could read her mother better than that. Something had happened. Something which had upset Lady Acton very deeply.

"What news?" she asked bluntly. "Is someone hurt? Did someone die?"

Her mother turned to Eleanor. "Not yet, dear child. But I'm very afraid that someone is about to."

Eleanor's heart leapt into her throat. Richard? Helena? Not Lee? Surely not Lee?

Lady Augusta took Diana by the elbow. "It cannot concern us," she said brutally. "Come, Diana. We are going home."

"Oh, but it concerns you more than me," said Lady Acton immediately.

Lady Augusta stopped and raised her thin brows. "Indeed?"

"He is a member of your family, after all," said Lady Acton. "Mr. Campbell has been arrested."

"Arrested?" said Lady Augusta indignantly. "What depraved crime has he committed now?"

"I have no idea what he may have committed, Countess, but he is in Newgate. As you may imagine, the *ton* is agog with such a delicious *on-dit*. They say Mr. Campbell rode into town yesterday evening as if the devil were at his tail. He was immediately arrested. He is reported to have offered to draw his pistol on the Bow Street men, but then to have started to laugh instead. He went quietly to Newgate where he is to be held until he stands trial. His accuser is your neighbor, Major Sir Robert St. John Crabtree."

Eleanor held on to the arm of the sofa as if it were a lifeline. She thought she might faint, though she had never done so before. It was through a sick haze of blurred vision that she heard her mother continue. "The crime is murder, Lady Augusta—the killing of one Manton Barnes. Our friend Leander Campbell faces the gallows."

Thirteen

Eleanor did not faint. In fact, nobody even noticed that she had turned white. Lady Augusta swept out with Diana in tow, only pausing long enough in the doorway to deliver the parting shot.

"I have known for twenty years that it would come to something like this!" she cried viciously. "And to think that this unscrupulous Walter Downe is his friend! No doubt the entire distasteful scene I was forced to discover here was Leander Campbell's doing. Let him be hanged! We should all have been better off if Sir Robert had never brought him back to England and better yet had he never been born."

Lady Acton insisted that Walter stay and take a glass of brandy. Eleanor joined them in the study, and had no hesitation in gulping down a glass of white wine herself.

"Your concerns over Lady Diana can wait, Mr. Downe," said the countess firmly. "What is this matter of Manton Barnes?"

"I know nothing about it," said Walter, his face stiff with shock. "I shall have to go and see Lee, of course."

"To get his permission to speak of it? Nothing is more exasperating than these ridiculous codes of honor to which you gentlemen adhere. How can I help him, Mr. Downe, if I don't know the facts?"

"You can't," said Walter dully. "He's a commoner. He'll

be tried in the common court, whatever any of us do. None of the privileges of our class apply to him."

"I am aware of that," said Lady Acton, getting up and pacing the room. "But don't be concerned that he will be left for months to rot in jail. I can at least see that there's no delay so that the trial takes place immediately. He is innocent, surely?" Walter looked down into his glass and said nothing. "Oh, Good God!" exclaimed the countess as there was a noise in the hallway. "Acton is back! I must go and distract your father, Eleanor."

She left the room and Eleanor boldly took up the brandy decanter and refilled Walter's glass. "You must tell me, Mr. Downe," she said. "I know that someone has been black-mailing people and Lee tried to stop him. You told me before, when I first met him, that Lee was upset about Manton Barnes's death, and he said something to me then about blackmail. I have no idea what the connection is, but surely Mr. Campbell is innocent of murder?"

"Manton Barnes was being blackmailed and he told Lee about it," said Walter, standing and going to the fireplace so that she couldn't see his face. "He couldn't meet the demands. When the blackmailer threatened to expose him, he shot himself."

"Oh, I'm so very sorry! But surely the authorities knew it was suicide?"

"Lee wanted to protect Manton's family. He rearranged things so that it would look like an accident. Several fellows witnessed what happened, of course, but they won't speak up unless Lee asks them to and he can't."

"Why not?"

"Because then it would come out about the blackmail."

"But Mr. Campbell wouldn't go to the gallows in order to protect the reputation of someone who's already dead?" asked Eleanor indignantly.

"I don't know," replied Walter, gazing dully at the grate. "He might."

"For God's sake," said Eleanor. "My mother is right. You gentlemen are totally absurd."

Walter looked across at her. He had set his shoulders rather stiffly and his face was completely rigid. "I shouldn't have told you. I'm sorry, Lady Eleanor. There is no way you could be expected to understand."

And Eleanor saw suddenly why Walter must be allowed to leave right away. His eyes were suspiciously bright. It would be the cruelest thing she had ever done to allow him to break down in front of her.

"Of course," she said quickly. "You had better go and see him. Good day, Mr. Downe."

Eleanor went straight to her own room and found herself marching up and down in front of her bed, actually wringing her hands. In spite of everything, she laughed at the absurdity of it, and forced herself to sit sensibly at her desk and try to think things through. When she had first met Lee at the Three Feathers, Manton Barnes had just died. Lee was in both shock and grief over it, she realized now, and he must also have been determined to discover the blackmailer. *I made a promise to myself when my friend Manton Barnes died, but I'm going to break it.*

What kind of promise?

One of pride, perhaps, or revenge.

And he believed the man to be the same villain who had blackmailed her mother. He must have known there was a connection between Manton Barnes and Lady Acton. He had already recognized Richard's portrait in the locket and knew who she was when he had asked her about blackmail. He'd had no intention of blackmailing her himself, he'd just wanted to know if she knew anything about it. For some reason, she was relieved to at last understand it. Yet no wonder he had been so ruthless with her.

Her mother knew who the blackmailer was, but she had promised the major never to reveal the name. Although Lady

Acton might make fun of the gentlemen's code, she would never break her own word either. The only one who could save Leander Campbell from this absurd mess was himself. Surely he would see that he must tell the authorities that Manton Barnes's death was a suicide? The poor major must have heard something which had caused him to grasp entirely the wrong end of the stick. Doubtless he would drop the charges as soon as he knew the truth. Yes, Lee must tell the judges what had happened, then his friends could witness it and he would be released. Feeling a great deal better, Eleanor went down to join her parents. She felt confident she could discuss the latest town gossip with equanimity.

Of course, she hadn't allowed for the fact that Mr. Campbell's arrest would be the latest gossip. Her father spent the evening talking of nothing else. With every word, Eleanor's optimism shrunk. Finally, she was forced to conclude that Walter had been right. Lee would never reveal that his friend had been blackmailed, and neither would anybody else. Gentlemen were enmeshed in their promises to themselves and to others, and they would never break them.

Newgate Goal was notorious. Most of the prisoners were packed together into overcrowded cellars on the Common Side, men in one wing, women in the other. Pimps and pickpockets, prostitutes and petty thieves, all awaited the hangman without distinction. The only circumstance which could relieve this stinking misery was the possession of sufficient money to buy a private room and one's own food in the handful of cells around the Press Yard—strictly speaking not part of the prison, but attached to the Governor's house. A generous payment to the Keeper ensured clean sheets and frequent visits from one's friends. Never had Leander Campbell been so deeply grateful for his skill at hazard and his prudent use of funds. Lee had even been able to send for some of his books.

Now, however, his stock of coin was about to be rapidly depleted. The favor of the Keeper was expensive.

"There's someone to see you, sir," said that gentleman several mornings later.

Lee looked up from the ponderous tome in which he had been absorbed for the last hours. "Then show him in, by all means."

The Keeper gave a crude wink. "It's not a man, Mr. Campbell, but a female. Unless your gentlemen friends have taken to wearing skirts?" Lee raised a brow, but gave no reply to this coy statement. "And a lady, if I'm not mistaken. I'll leave you lovebirds alone, shall I?"

"Five guineas?" asked Lee calmly.

The Keeper pocketed his bribe and stepped out of the cell. A lady muffled from head to toe in a capacious cloak slipped in, and the heavy door clanged shut behind her. She was carrying a basket. There was an audible grating sound as the key turned in the lock. She dropped the hood of the cloak and smiled nervously at him.

"Good God!" said Lee, closing the book he had been reading, and standing. He gave her a stiff bow and motioned her to the one chair in the room. "Forgive my simple accommodation, brown hen. I wasn't expecting polite morning calls from earl's daughters. To what misplaced schoolgirl charity do I owe this honor?"

"If you're going to be difficult, I shall leave again and not give you any of the things I brought you."

"No, since you are here, stay by all means. If you have any decent brandy or fresh fruit, I'll tolerate you as long as you like."

Eleanor set down the basket. "That repulsive Keeper has already pawed over everything, I'm afraid, in case I was bringing you a file or something . . ."

"A pistol would be more useful," interrupted Lee.

"But here are some early strawberries from our greenhouse and apples out of the store. And this is French, I believe. At least, Father likes it very well." She held out a bottle of the very best brandy that King's Acton could furnish from its cellars.

"Your father gave this up willingly?" asked Lee. He seemed to have relaxed.

"No, I stole it."

"Brave Eleanor! Won't the butler be in danger of losing his position?"

"Oh, no, Father trusts him implicitly. He's been with us since long before I was born. Father wouldn't know if our butler was stealing him blind."

"Or his daughter?"

Eleanor colored a little. "I never have before. But isn't this a good cause?"

"Decidedly," said Lee, carefully opening the bottle. "It's very good brandy anyway. Will you join me? I believe I have two glasses."

"I never drink brandy."

"Then this," he said, leaning forward and grinning at her, "is an excellent time to start, don't you think? I don't imagine you've ever been locked in a Newgate cell with a murderous rogue before either."

Eleanor took the glass of dark liquid he offered and sipped at it. Her nerves were definitely a little shredded. It hadn't been that difficult to get here unnoticed, but it had taken a certain amount of courage and ingenuity. And Lee was making it plain that he was thoroughly aware of the impropriety of the whole thing. The brandy settled with a warm glow. "I can see why you like it," she said.

"Excellent. Now, my brave child, why are you here?"

"To stop you nobly going to the gallows, of course. I know about Manton Barnes and the blackmail, you see. I figured most of it out and then tricked poor Walter into telling me the rest. Don't blame him for he was outgunned and I caught him at a disadvantage. If you don't tell everyone that your friend committed suicide and wasn't murdered, I shall. For Diana's sake, since your sister is foolish enough to love you."

Lee gazed steadily at her face for a few moments. Eleanor looked down to escape the violet eyes. If she wasn't careful, he would discover just how much she cared herself. "I believe you would, brown hen," he said at last. "Very well. Then you must know the reason why you won't do that, and I shall tell you."

She glanced up at him. He seemed perfectly calm. "There are no threats you can make that will stop me!"

"I wasn't intending to make threats. I thought instead I would tell you the truth. There's nothing else that will content you, is there?"

Eleanor stared at him. "No," she said. "I don't suppose there is."

He sighed and ran his fingers through his hair. "This is going to be difficult," he said with a sudden laugh.

"Just begin at the beginning," said Eleanor. "I am perfectly comfortable and no one will miss me for hours. I said I was going shopping."

"Manton Barnes was engaged to a lady called Blanche Haricot," he began. "She was young and lovely and eligible. Yet there were reasons why it wasn't a suitable match. I convinced Manton to ask her to release him from the betrothal."

There was silence for a moment, as if Lee couldn't quite find the words to go on.

"He was in love with someone else?" said Eleanor helpfully.

"Yes, I suppose you could say that. Several other people, in fact."

Eleanor was puzzled. "He was in love with more than one lady at once?"

Lee looked up at her and gave her a wry smile. "Except that they weren't ladies, Lady Eleanor, they were other gentlemen."

Eleanor digested this in silence for a moment. It wasn't something that she knew anything about, but she remembered a hushed conversation Richard and Harry had been having once about something of the kind. Men could prefer other men to women. The army and the navy took extreme measures against it, and Richard didn't approve. Eleanor was extremely hazy about the details. "I'm not sure I understand," she said. "But I think I know that such a thing can happen."

"Well, it happened to Manton Barnes. He fought against it, but I think it was just his nature. He was a friend of mine— I'd known him since Eton, for God's sake—and I couldn't hold it against him. Yet I wouldn't let him marry Blanche Haricot in order to protect himself. He didn't love her and he confided in me that he knew he could never bring himself to consummate the marriage. She would have been trapped in a terrible bond, without a real husband and without children. I can think of no worse fate for an innocent young girl."

Eleanor still wasn't quite sure what he was talking about, but she was wise enough to limit her question. "Why should he want to protect himself?"

"Because such love between men is forbidden. It's a capital crime, in fact. Had Manton ever been found out, he and his lovers would have faced the hangman."

"But he was found out," breathed Eleanor, "and black-mailed over it. How very cruel!"

"As cruel as the punishment of Prometheus—that was how he put it. So finally he killed himself."

"And you tried to make it look like an accident and covered up the suicide?"

"I destroyed some letters and his diary." Lee sounded perfectly calm, though Eleanor knew that this was costing him some effort. "And whatever other evidence I could find. I had to make sure that no probe would be made into his motives. I did it not only to protect Manton Barnes's family, but also his lovers. If the truth comes out, they will hang."

"So you'll die instead?" said Eleanor angrily. "And leave Diana without a brother. They're a bunch of cowards!"

"They are men with families: innocent mothers, sisters, some even have wives. I have never met most of them, but they are men who have done nothing except follow their nature and love the wrong person. Meanwhile, some of them are philanthropists and reformers and educated, caring men. England needs them. The crime is that we cannot tolerate their private behavior. They haven't come forward because they have no idea they are in any danger. Besides, I have no intention of dying."

"What can save you? No one escapes from Newgate!"

He seemed to feel nothing but amusement. "Then there'll have to be a first time, won't there?"

Eleanor stood and began to pace up and down the narrow room. "It's outrageous! You would risk death for these strangers."

He smiled. "If I wasn't languishing here in jail, I'd soon have been facing death on the battlefield. I shall protect those innocent men and their families, but I don't intend to hang at the Old Bailey."

"For God's sake," said Eleanor. "Diana is innocent, too. She's distraught!"

"Diana enjoys drama; by all means reassure her. But if you really want to believe that I am nobly offering myself as a final sacrifice, you at least ought to behave accordingly."

Eleanor stopped and faced him. "What do you mean? I have already made a secret journey in a dark cloak clutching a basket. Isn't that what all the heroines do in the romances to save their best friend's brother?"

"Of course. But they usually bring some elaborate escape plot to free the prisoner: a bundle of clothes, so he may escape as a washerwoman; a rope made of hair; a magic potion that will make him invisible. If not, they at least grant him his final wish."

"What's yours?" said Eleanor tartly. "Since I so foolishly forgot the pistol, what else can I arrange? For you to be accompanied to the gallows with choirs of maidens throwing rose petals?"

He reached out and caught her wrist, then spun her onto

the cot beside him. "One maiden will suffice," he said. "And I can think of much better ways to say goodbye than dismantling flowers or shrill singing."

He bent her body back against the pillow and trapped her beneath him, supporting himself on one elbow. She could feel the warmth of him and his strength enveloped her. Gently, he smoothed her hair back from her forehead.

"You already said goodbye at Vauxhall," said Eleanor desperately. The clean masculine scent of him filled her nostrils. It made her blood burn under her skin.

"Yes, but that was just when I went to face Boney's guns. Now, it's the certainty of the gallows-tree, don't you think we should do it again?"

"Mr. Campbell . . ."

"Leander. He swam the Hellespont nightly to reach his beloved Hero at Sestos. She was a priestess of Venus. Think of the vows she was breaking! It was a most unsuitable match."

"And on his death, she drowned herself."

"Well, that's taking things a bit far," said Lee, laughing quietly. "But I am already drowning in your brown eyes, fair lady. And you must have known perfectly well that if you allowed yourself to be locked up with a rake who had nothing left to lose, he would take advantage of the situation."

"I did know," said Eleanor, as he bent his head to hers and kissed her with complete abandon.

Another day had passed before Eleanor ventured a visit to the Hawksley mansion. Unfortunately there was company, and the talk was of nothing but the imminent trial. Eleanor folded her hands and tried to blot it out. Diana was still pale, but she looked better for Eleanor's news that Lee was in such good spirits and so confident of a safe outcome. If only she could share that confidence herself.

"The case comes rapidly to trial," said Lord Ranking with a damp sniff. "I hear that Mr. Campbell intends to represent himself. He runs low on funds, no doubt. I don't imagine such a profligate can maintain his style very long in Newgate Prison."

"Mama! It is all so frightful!" cried Diana. "He must have a barrister! Can we not sell something at Hawksley? Or take out a mortgage?"

Lady Augusta looked shocked. "Certainly not! Hawksley owes nothing to Leander Campbell."

Eleanor kept silent. She had already talked with her mother and discovered that Lady Acton was quietly ensuring Lee's private room. The countess knew perfectly well, of course, that the proud Mr. Campbell would never take money directly, but her influence and her purse went a long way toward preventing a thousand petty indignities. Thus the Keeper had become assiduous about decent food and hot water for a prisoner with such exalted connections. He had even personally made sure that Mr. Campbell had access to whatever he wanted in the way of books and writing materials. Eleanor also knew that Lady Acton had confronted Lady Augusta about it, but it seemed that Hawksley was impoverished. It was odd that such a grand and naturally rich estate didn't provide more ready cash for either repairs or its owners.

"You are bearing up very nobly, Lady Augusta," Lord Ranking went on. "Such an affliction for you and your family. Anyone with a delicate sensibility cannot help but be affected. What can illustrate more clearly that character is formed by nobility of birth?"

Eleanor could take no more and she stood up to go. She had only come to comfort Diana and reassure her that Lee was well and cheerful. Walter was forbidden the house, but Eleanor brought secret messages from him. Mr. Feveril Downe was acting as a go-between with Major Crabtree, attempting to get that gentleman to drop the charges against Lee without revealing any details of Manton Barnes's circumstances. So far he had not met with success. And meanwhile, safely hidden in her writing desk at Acton House was the letter from Strathbrae which had arrived that morning. The minister who had married Lee's father and mother was not only alive, he had responded immediately.

"Blairmore lies some distance from here and the family is not known to me," the minister had written in a tight, orderly hand. "Yet well do I remember Moira Campbell. She was very lovely and certainly a lady. If anyone could be said to be sick with love, it was she. The young couple arrived here at Strathbrae without warning and threw themselves on my mercy. I had heard of Ian Campbell, for her father was a dour and hard man with a certain reputation. Gerald Hart possessed a charm and a gift with words that we Scots don't readily associate with the Sassenach. He was able to persuade me to marry them then and there by declaration. They came with her maid, and I called upon the local gamekeeper who happened to visit at the time to witness their marriage. It was a binding contract before man and God, yet she returned to her father's house and he to England. They swore me to secrecy, for Moira thought she could yet win over her father, but as was my duty, I wrote the details of the wedding into the records of this parish. Alas, Gerald's promises were as the dew and melted away as quickly. He never came back. Some years later, Moira died near Loch Linnhe and was buried there. I heard that all the village laid flowers on her grave—wildflowers from the hills—while the local piper played the pibroch and the music carried away over the calm blue water. I had never known there was a child. If you know of him, he would now be a man grown and should have this:"

And from the packet had fallen a document, duly signed and witnessed. A copy of marriage lines, identical to the one that Lee had burned. Of course, there might be several copies. *It was a binding contract before man and God.* Eleanor had proof that Lee was Earl of Hawksley.

Fourteen

It was extremely hot in the Court of King's Bench. The judges were in their heavy robes and most of the solemn long-jawed faces shone damply in the dim light. In front of the judges several benches were packed with bewigged lawyers who had come to hear the case. It was a dusty black assembly and the atmosphere was solemn. A handful of flies buzzed disrespectfully in a sunbeam that illuminated the courtroom. Leander Campbell stood quietly in the dock. With thanks perhaps to Lady Acton, he looked impeccable. His shirt collar and cravat were crisp and white, his close-fitting jacket the height of fashion. He seemed perfectly composed, even a little amused by the proceedings.

In the visitors' seating set aside for members of the Quality, Eleanor watched him. He had inherited every bit of his father's fatal charm; no wonder she had proved so vulnerable to it. On one side, her mother fanned herself gently, and on the other, Diana wrung her hands together in her lap. There was a black cloth lying on the desk in front of the Lord Chief Justice. Should he pronounce sentence of death, he would set it on top of his powdered wig. There was, however, a great deal to get through first.

"You are here to answer a charge of murder, sir," said a dry voice. "What say you? Are you guilty or not guilty?"

"I will not answer the plea, my lord," replied Lee with a respectful bow of the head.

"Does he stand mute?" asked someone in a whisper.

Eleanor looked helplessly at her mother. She had no idea what all this legal jargon meant, but this question was enough to send a shiver around the courtroom and several of the lawyers leaned their heads together to whisper to each other. How could Lee be so foolish as to go through with this without legal counsel?

"I warn you, Mr. Campbell," said the Lord Chief Justice, leaning forward from the Bench, "these are proceedings of the utmost gravity."

Lee smiled at the judge. "Indeed, my lord. No one could take them more seriously than I. It is after all my neck which is being wagered, is it not? Instead I claim the right to prove my innocence directly against the man who brings this appeal of death: Major Sir Robert St. John Crabtree. Major Crabtree brings these charges without evidence, my lord. His only grounds for involvement are his relationship to the deceased. He was Manton Barnes's near relative, his uncle."

There was a sudden silence.

"Is he here?" said the judge at last.

Major Crabtree stood up and bowed.

"I really can't understand," said Lady Acton idly, "what anybody can see in that man."

Eleanor gave her mother a surprised look and received a slow wink in exchange. She bit her lip. Her mother was unrepentant and incorrigible—even her disastrous affair with the major only gave the countess another chance to laugh at herself. Then she looked back at Lee. The violet eyes met hers and he smiled. Instantly Eleanor felt color flood her cheeks and glanced down. Surely he would find it natural that Diana was here and that Lady Eleanor Acton should accompany her friend?

"Your honor," said Lee, giving his full attention back to the Bench. "I demand instead that this matter be settled by wager of battle."

Sir Robert turned to the judges. "I think the man is mad, your honor! What kind of answer to the charges is this?"

"One which has been legal in England since the Middle Ages," said Lee merrily. "And still stands on the law books of this kingdom. We shall fight, Sir Robert."

There was an uproar among the spectators. The Lord Chief Justice was finally forced to hammer his gavel to restore order. "If there is further outburst, I shall clear this court," he thundered. "What are you about, Mr. Campbell? This is a court of law. Dueling is not an option!"

"I do not suggest a duel, my lord. I demand legal trial by combat. If the court will honor me with its patience, I shall be happy to demonstrate that this remedy is still a valid choice in this realm. Allow me to prove my innocence in wager of battle with Sir Robert. If he prevails, thereby—according to the ancient law—proving my guilt, by all means take me away and hang me. On the other hand, should I prevail or hold out until starlight, you must in duty proclaim my innocence."

There was instant pandemonium. Within five minutes, Lee had been taken back to Newgate and the visitors' gallery cleared. Once glance at Eleanor's white face was enough for Lady Acton to declare that her daughter should not be allowed to attend the court again.

Yet every day brought further talk of the trial. All the ancient books of law were being ransacked. It was decided that Lee was correct: the right to demand trial by combat had never been repealed. The Earl of Acton shook out his napkin at breakfast with the news that the law required the presence of the judges at the fight, and that the battle must begin at sunrise. By dinner, he announced that both contestants must take an oath to employ no witchcraft.

"It's barbaric!" cried Lady Acton. "A remedy for the Dark Ages. Surely this battle won't truly go on!"

"Trial by combat has been legal in this country for ten centuries, madam. An absurd law may sleep unnoticed, but until it's changed by Act of Parliament all free men must support it."

Two days later, it was discovered that the judges must also lay down the required dress to be worn by the accuser and accused. Eleanor had to suppress a wild vision of Leander Campbell in full armor and chain mail. Would he and the major be required to joust in the lists, or fight with mace and battle-ax? Her surmise was wrong. Trial by combat would be neither so dashing nor so romantic. Three days after that, Lord Acton proclaimed that the required weapons were cudgels.

"No doubt the exact size and weight are specified by law?" asked Lady Acton idly.

"I cannot say, madam. The contestants must provide their own weapons. Mr. Campbell may be happy that a broadsword is not required, for it would seem that he must finally have run out of funds. I have it on the best authority that he is at last selling his collection of books."

Eleanor looked up at her father in dismay. She couldn't let her parents know, of course, that she had been privileged to see the famed library. It must be terrible for him to sell his books. Was Lee in fact so desperate? She could still see those strong hands gently turning the illuminated pages. Yet if her mother was sending money to pay for his room and board, why should he sell his wonderful books, the books he loved like children? What could have happened to change his mind?

Lady Acton raised a perfect brow. "And you cannot conceal your delight. You have coveted such rare volumes for years. Will you make an offer?"

"If they come onto the open market, indeed I shall. Though it's going to cost me a pretty penny, I'll warrant."

"Is Mr. Campbell's collection so very valuable?" asked Lady Acton. She folded her fan and tapped it against her cheek.

"Worth a small fortune, madam. Of course, he did not purchase the entire collection himself."

"He didn't?" asked Eleanor faintly.

The earl was in an indulgent mood. He smiled kindly at his oldest daughter. "No, indeed! The greatest part of it was a gift from Lady Went after her husband's death. Lord Went took a fancy to the lad when he met him at Oxford—thought he had a brilliant mind, or some such nonsense—and when he died, Lady Went fulfilled his wishes about the books. Extraordinary that Campbell was never tempted to sell off before. The fellow likes to live like a lord, for all he's a commoner."

Eleanor bit her lip. Her father's statement laid to rest the last of her doubts about Leander Campbell. There seemed to be no end to the surprising things she continued to learn about him. Lady Acton leaned forward and smiled at her husband.

"If he weren't a commoner, he wouldn't be facing this trial, dear Acton. Instead he'd be sitting before men like yourself and the late Lord Went in the House of Peers and be acquitted. No doubt you'd dismiss such trumpery charges against one of our own class."

"Humph! He's an odd chap, by God. Had nothing but his soldier's pay and lives at the gaming tables, when all the time he was sitting on a dashed great fortune. And now he insists on facing a fit and active man like Major Crabtree with nothing but a cudgel!"

"Yet he hires no barrister," said Lady Acton thoughtfully. "I wonder what he intends to do with all that money?"

It was enough. Whatever the consequences, the whole thing must be stopped, and only Eleanor could stop it. With her face set and her bonnet only slightly awry, at the earliest opportunity she marched into the beautiful town house belonging to the earls of Hawksley. The butler showed her into the bright parlor where Diana sat alone, blindly staring out of the window.

"Eleanor!" cried Diana, leaping to her feet and flinging herself into her friend's arms. "What shall we do? How can we stop this barbaric fight? The major will beat Lee to death! I know he will! With a sword or a pistol, he could never prevail—but with cudgels!"

"Sit down, Di, and calm yourself. There is a way to stop it, if you really want to."

"Oh, Eleanor, you clever thing. You have a plan?"

"Yes, I do. But it's up to you, really. Listen, you said once you wished that Lee were legitimate, rather than you. Did you mean it?"

"Of course I meant it! Hawksley ought to be his, and if only I weren't an heiress, Walter and I could marry right away."

Eleanor looked down. She was about to do something that would break every tenet that men like Lee and her brothers lived by. She would demonstrate that her word meant nothing, that when circumstances demanded, she would break it. Yet she couldn't stand by and do nothing, and if she sacrificed her own honor, that was her choice, wasn't it? Diana had only echoed her own fears. Major Crabtree outweighed Lee by two or three stone, and she had learned from her father that he was practicing daily, boxing with Gentleman Jackson. Meanwhile, Lee was confined to a prison cell with no chance for exercise, where his lithe strength must be ebbing away from disuse. All that athletic grace and skill would count for nothing against an enraged opponent, more heavily built and in peak condition, armed with a cudgel. She forced herself to meet Diana's eyes.

"Then you should look at this," she said simply. She slipped the marriage papers from her reticule and laid them in Diana's hands.

"I don't understand," said Diana at last. She laid the papers in her lap and gazed up at Eleanor with her heart in her eyes. "My father married Moira Campbell? But how wonderful! Where did you get this?"

"It's a long story and the details don't matter, but you do see what it means, don't you? There's also proof that Moira died after your father married Lady Augusta; so, you see, your mother's marriage wasn't valid. If you wish, I'll destroy the document right now and we can pretend it never existed."

"No, you shan't." Diana's face flushed with color. "It means I am really the bastard, doesn't it? I'm glad! Walter won't care and Lee always deserved Hawksley. I wish I'd known it sooner!"

"Then you think we should let the world know? What about your mother?"

"I don't know!" Diana wrung her hands. "If Lee is acknowledged Earl of Hawksley, everyone would know she was really only our father's mistress. It will be dreadful, but Lee will take care of her."

Eleanor found herself clutching Diana's fingers. "It also means this horrid trial will stop. As earl, Lee would have to be tried in the House of Lords and my mother will make sure that it's all thrown out."

Diana stared at Eleanor's strong hands which were preventing her from wringing her own. "It's not really such a hard choice," she said after a moment, and she gave Eleanor a tremulous smile. "There's hardly a cost to me that I would care about; it's just my mother's pride against my brother's life. Let's take the papers to the judges."

"Alas, such a solemn bunch," said someone behind them. There was just the faintest edge of sarcasm to the smooth tones. "I shouldn't take anything of any interest to judges, if I were you."

Eleanor spun around and, snatching the marriage lines back from Diana, she thrust them into her reticule. She knew that her face had gone scarlet, and she fervently wished to be anywhere but in Diana's sitting room at this moment. Yet at the same time, it was as if a whole orchestra had struck up a victory march of happiness—for Leander Campbell stood nonchalantly in the doorway. His blue morning coat was impeccably tailored and the folds of his cravat demonstrated the skill of those clever fingers.

"Lee!" squealed Diana, leaping up and propelling herself toward her brother.

"Good God!" he said after a moment, as he extricated

himself from her enthusiastic hug. "Am I so changed? So wasted? Do you think two weeks in prison has altered me forever? Alas, I shall bear the scars of the chains to my grave!"

"Don't tease, Lee, please! It has all been so dreadful!"

Lee laughed at his sister's woebegone expression. "Dreadful?" he said gaily. "When I never had so much fun in my life?"

"You escaped?" asked Eleanor bluntly. She could think of no other explanation for his sudden appearance.

"Escaped the gallows, dear Lady Eleanor, but not the jail. No one escapes from Newgate, remember? My dear friend the Keeper unlocked the cell door and bowed me into the street. I was even allowed to take my effects. It was all perfectly legal. His Majesty's justices were pleased to dismiss the case."

"You mean they let you go, just like that?" asked Diana. "There won't be any fight?"

Lee drew her over to the sofa and let his sister sink back down beside Eleanor. He then took an elegant side chair and straddled it. "The trial is over. This is 1815, dear Di, not the time of the Lionheart. There was more than one technicality to tie them all into knots, and enough pure absurdity to entrance the best legal minds of the realm. Trial by combat! It may have accidentally been legal, but the Court of King's Bench wasn't about to let it happen. Although you have to admit it was amusing to try."

"It wasn't amusing at all," interrupted Eleanor furiously. "Everyone has been worried sick!"

"Everyone?"

"Diana and Walter, even my mother!"

"Lady Acton was never worried sick, dear Lady Eleanor. I imagine she enjoyed following every minute of the process."

"She and half of London," said Diana. "How could you do such a thing, Lee?"

He raised a brow. "I didn't accuse myself and lock myself in Newgate, you know. Yet once there, I decided I'd rather not hang, after all."

"Why was the case thrown out?" Eleanor wanted not to care, not to be involved, but she couldn't help herself. The rich lashes narrowed slightly over the violet eyes as he looked at her. It completely masked his real feelings.

"Because Major Sir Robert St. John Crabtree withdrew the charges. I suggested trial by combat in order to buy enough time to persuade him to do so, and to create such a diversion that everybody would forget about the victim, poor Manton Barnes. Fortunately, it succeeded. I had no real desire to try to batter Crabtree to death with a cudgel, you know. After all, he rescued me from the nuns in my mewling infancy."

Eleanor refused to give up. "He withdrew the charges? Why?"

"Lady Eleanor, you really should curb your curiosity. A most unseemly attribute for a young lady. I made a bargain with him, that's all."

At the cool disinterest in his tone Eleanor looked down at the hands in her lap. She had no right to pry into his affairs and even less to interfere as she had done. He must think her a gauche schoolgirl, indeed. And soon he would leave for Belgium. In which case she might never see Lee again. Her thoughts were shattered by the shrill cry of a newcomer.

"Leander Campbell! Good heavens, sir! You dare to bring the taint of the prison and the shadow of scandal into my drawing room?"

Lady Augusta swept into the room. Her gown rustled stiffly about her as she walked. Since Lee was impeccably dressed in the cleanest possible linen and smelt faintly of soap, her comment seemed absurd to Eleanor. The dowager countess ignored the indignant looks of the two girls and raised her voice once more to her stepson. "You have brought disgrace and opprobrium to this house, sir. It is enough! I will thank you to say farewell to my daughter and pledge never to see her again!"

"Mama!" Diana leapt to her feet. "You shan't forbid Lee the house!"

"I shall forbid what and where I like, young lady! Mr. Campbell has trespassed too long on the generosity of Hawksley. It is his influence that brought you to lose your senses over that Feveril Downe boy. I will not have him in this house again!"

Diana was pale, but she seemed seized by a newfound courage. Eleanor and Lee both watched in astonishment as she stood up to her formidable mama for the very first time.

"You can't forbid him the house, Mama," she cried. "It's his house! Everything here is his! That chair and this sofa and the curtains and the fire irons—everything!"

Lady Augusta paled. "Whatever do you mean, Diana? You forget yourself!"

"No, I don't. Father married Lee's mother before he married you, and she was still alive at your wedding! I'm not an heiress at all, and Eleanor's just shown me papers to prove it! They're there in her reticule. Lee is the real Earl of Hawksley!"

It was as if Lady Augusta had been felled by an ax. She crumpled and would have fallen, had Lee not caught her and helped her to a chair. The countess began to moan softly.

"For God's sake, Di!" Lee said sharply. "Get some salts!"

But it was Eleanor who held the smelling salts under the fire-breathing nose. After gathering her courage for the outburst, Diana seemed appalled at what she had done and sat white-faced as Lee and Eleanor tended her mother. Yet she was changed. Diana wouldn't be afraid of her mother again.

Meanwhile, Eleanor wanted to disappear, but nothing could change the inevitable now. Lee calmly knelt next to her, supporting his stepmother. She could smell the faint scent of his clean linen and her eyes seemed transfixed by the shape of his hands. Yet it was as if the marriage papers hidden in her reticule were some terrible treasonous documents. She knew perfectly well what Lee must think of her now he knew what she had done. She had promised at Deerfield never to reveal his mother's marriage to anyone; yet at the first sign of trouble, she had gone running to Diana and put the papers straight into her hands. That she thought she was doing it to save Lee's life was made totally irrelevant by the fact that he had already been released. Yet if the situation were the same, she knew she would do it again.

After a few minutes, Lady Augusta sat up and straightened her cap. She seemed to have totally regained her composure, but the fire was gone. "It was bound to come out," she said dully. "When Gerald took me to the altar, he already had a wife. How can one ever forgive such perfidy?"

"You already knew?" breathed Diana.

Lady Augusta stared grimly at her daughter. "I have known for more than twenty years. Ever since Sir Robert brought that little boy back from Ireland. He looked so like Gerald! It was enough to break my heart. The major showed me the birth certificate and the marriage lines, and he knew when Moira Campbell had died. It proved without doubt that Leander was the true heir. How could I face it?"

"You were with child yourself," said Lee gently. "It was none of it your fault."

Lady Augusta looked at him, her small eyes damp with tears. "It might have been a boy. And then when Diana was born, she was such a lovely baby. So innocent. How could I live with bringing a child into the world who was shamed, disgraced, disinherited."

"You mean Major Crabtree knew this all along too?" asked Diana. "Why didn't he tell anybody?"

Lee had moved back to his chair. He dropped his head in his hands as his stepmother turned blankly to stare at her daughter.

"Because I paid him not to, of course!" said Lady Augusta. "How do you think that he could afford Deerfield?"

And suddenly it all made sense to Eleanor. This was why Deerfield was so lavishly kept and why there was no extra money at Hawksley. Why Lady Augusta's steward pinched the purse and why repairs were delayed until Lee paid for them. All the wealth of Hawksley for twenty years had been drained off to support the major's lavish lifestyle, and all because he knew the secret of Moira Campbell's marriage.

"You were being blackmailed by the major?" Diana was still struggling to comprehend what had happened.

"But it has stopped now," said the dowager countess. "Sir Robert told me yesterday that I would receive no more demands from him. It has been such a relief. I thought I was free at last."

"How could you do it, Mama? You have cheated Lee all these years."

"Hush, Di," said Lee firmly. "Lady Augusta did it for you, and at a huge price."

Diana was flushed, but with her newfound confidence, she stuck out her chin. "Then it's over now. Eleanor has the marriage lines. The truth shall come out, and you must claim your rightful inheritance."

Lady Augusta was now staring at Eleanor. "Why should you have anything to do with this?" she said. "Why must the Actons always win?"

"Lady Eleanor has not won anything, my lady." Lee's face was impossible to decipher, but his voice was gentle. He stood up and moved to the window. "Nothing has changed."

"What do you mean, Lee?" asked Diana. "Everything has changed! You shan't hide the truth because of me."

Eleanor had never seen Lee truly angry before, but he spun on his heel and faced his sister. Diana lost her courage instantly and dropped her eyes.

"Then you would reveal to the world that our father was a bigamist? You would happily ignore your mother's sacrifice and suffering for the last twenty years? You would hold her up to the ridicule and persecution of society, and strip her of her portion, leaving her in penury, dependent on my charity? If there is one person beside yourself who is an innocent victim in this mess, it is your mother! And do you care nothing for my precarious honor? Lady Augusta took me in and raised me when I was five years old, knowing that I embodied the possibility of ruin. You would have me return that by showing her to be a harlot, and my sister nameless and penniless, her position ruined? And what of Walter's career? Link his name with yours, and you would involve him in a sordid scandal that will rock London. A bastard isn't the most suitable wife for a bishop! If you try to publish this bizarre story, I shall maintain that it is all a farrago of nonsense. Whatever papers the Actons may have in their possession I shall demonstrate to be forgeries. If necessary I shall go to Scotland and destroy the records at their source, then I shall leave the country, but this time forever. You will neither hear from me nor see me again. I repeat: you will forget this. Lady Augusta may sleep easy in her bed and you, Diana, shall remain heiress of Hawksley."

"I won't!" cried Diana, her face as white as her muslin dress.

"You will," said Lee, "and you will never breathe a word of this to anyone. Neither will your headstrong, interfering friend, Lady Eleanor Acton."

"If you are to order me, sir," said Eleanor, desperately gathering her courage. "You might do it to my face."

He had been avoiding her. Lee could face his stepmother and Diana, but how was he to control his emotions when he confronted his brave brown hen? He had already guessed how she had obtained the papers, and he assumed she had done it in a naive attempt to help Diana marry Walter. It had also occurred to him that the minister at Strathbrae would have a record of the marriage. At any time, it could have been discovered, yet it was unlikely, and he had not had time yet to do anything about it. A small church, buried in the Highlands; a minister who had no idea why the marriage was so important; and an unclaimed earl who was about to leave for Belgium and India—it hadn't been worth worrying about. Yet, as he had threatened, he could still go to Strathbrae and destroy the church records. Only Lady Augusta had ever understood the impossibility of his claiming his birthright under the circumstances. Maybe in twenty years once Diana was safely settled and Lady Augusta gone to her grave, maybe then. But now? It would be a tainted legacy. He would rather die a pauper. Yet, God help him, it would cost him Eleanor. She sat stiffly on the sofa, her brown eyes bravely waiting for his wrath. He reached deep inside himself to find it.

"Your busy fingers are in every pie, aren't they, Lady Eleanor?" he said. "How noble of you to try to disinherit your friend. Your promise didn't last long, did it? Yet you have overlooked the type of creature you would elevate to the peerage: one who prefers the gutter to the drawing room, a gaming hell to a seat in Parliament, and the charms of a whore to those of a lady. Better let him remain a bastard. That way he can die un-remembered as he wishes, drunk under a table."

Ignoring the shine of tears that Eleanor couldn't keep from her eyes, he spun on his heel and stalked to the door. He stopped for a moment and looked back at his stepmother. "You had better give your consent to Diana's marriage to Walter Feveril Downe, Lady Augusta. He's an honorable and good man, and though he isn't a duke, his family credentials are impeccable. If you try to force her into wedlock with someone like Lord Ranking, that is the one thing that might make me change my mind."

Eleanor barely registered that this one goal at least was achieved. She had known that he would never forgive her if she interfered in his mother's marriage. Yet she couldn't help herself then and she couldn't help herself now. Since in spite of it all, she knew now that her feelings for him were no schoolgirl crush. She was deeply, everlastingly, and impossibly, in love with him.

Fifteen

Diana would not be moved. With a set face she agreed to remain silent about what she had learned. Yet when her mama capitulated and agreed to her marriage with Walter, then suggested that Viscount Clare be invited to come and discuss the marriage settlements, she wouldn't hear of it.

"It would all be a falsehood," she declared. "I shan't marry Walter under false pretenses. I'm not really Lady Diana Hart, am I? What name should we put on the register?"

And thus Eleanor discovered that it still wasn't over. For herself, she would never interfere again with Lee's affairs, but she had promised to help Diana wed Walter. If the present state of affairs didn't change, Lee was taking his sister to the sacrificial altar with him, rather than ensuring her happiness. She was too deeply involved to back out now. Once again, it was up to her. What did she have left to lose?

Sir Robert had taken rooms in Piccadilly. Eleanor grimaced to herself as her carriage stopped in front of his door. Only a couple of short months before, she had been looking forward to an ordinary coming-out. Instead, since she had discovered that her best friend had a half-brother, she had been embroiling herself in ever more disreputable adventures. Well, making a morning call on a gentleman who was old enough to be your father and had once been your mother's lover, was nothing compared to visiting a notorious rake in

Newgate. How could she have thought she respected Major Crabtree? The man had been blackmailing Lady Augusta for years. Whatever her opinion of Diana's mama, the cruelty of the act sickened her. It had not taken long to realize that he must also have been the villain in Manton Barnes's case, and, incredible as it may seem, her mother's. The clues had been there, all along. Since Lee was not the blackmailer, who else was there?

The butler seemed less surprised than she expected. Perhaps the major had all kinds of victims of his nasty hobby coming to call? Eleanor was shown into a small study and she composed herself to wait. If Sir Robert thought he had a monopoly on Lee's secret, he was wrong. She wasn't sure how that could help, but it might be worth something. In the meantime, he might still hold evidence about Manton Barnes, and that was another weapon he could hold over Lee. Perhaps if she could convince him that Lee intended to go away, he would give it up. It really didn't make sense. She could feel her palms becoming clammy. Lady Eleanor Acton had barged in once again with no clear plan of action.

There were voices in the hallway.

"By all means go ahead, sir," said the major's voice. "But I think there is nothing else to discuss. I have agreed to your terms. Indeed, I am gratified at your generosity. Pray wait in the study while I secure the papers. I shan't be a moment."

The door opened and Eleanor stood up to face him. But it was not the major who entered, it was Lee.

"Well, well," he said with a lift of the brow. Then he grinned. "It's the stalwart, chivalrous scion of the house of Acton, girded, accoutered, and armed in steel. Prepared once again to do battle on the side of the angels, no doubt. Do you bring cannon this time, brown hen?"

She collapsed back into the chair. Lee sat carelessly on the corner of the major's desk, his long legs stretched in front of him. It seemed impossible! Was Lee guilty after all? "You are in league with him?" she said faintly. "All along you were accomplices?"

He gave her a genuine smile and her heart turned over. There was no anger there at all, even at such an outrageous accusation. "So you know that Major Crabtree is our original blackmailer. It wasn't too hard to figure out, was it, brown hen, although it took me an unconscionable length of time. And to think I pride myself on my powers of reasoning! I was more blind than the proverbial bat. But no, we are not accomplices."

"Sir Robert found out Manton Barnes's secret from Blanche Haricot, didn't he?" Eleanor asked. "After that night at Vauxhall when they were caught in the rain. Miss Haricot confided in Manton's uncle, thinking he'd be sympathetic, but he only used the information to destroy his own nephew. He began to blackmail him then."

"He did. And when your mother and the major became friends, Manton found out about it from his uncle and guessed she'd be the next victim. Yet how could he warn her? They had never met. Instead he tried to warn me, though it was too late by then."

"But now you help him? When for twenty years he's been draining Lady Augusta. It's horrid! Why has he now decided to stop?"

The answer did not come from Lee.

"Because Leander Campbell has the oddest ideas of family loyalty, Lady Eleanor. He is being kind enough to pay me instead." Major Sir Robert St. John Crabtree had quietly opened the door and joined them.

Eleanor spun to face him. He was smiling under the splendid mustaches. "You don't deny it?"

"Dear lady, why should I? But pray don't share the glory of my enterprise with Mr. Campbell. He has never been anything but a victim, I assure you."

"Then why is he here?" asked Eleanor.

"Mr. Campbell brings papers for our final arrangement.

He signs all right and title to his book collection over to me. I have already been the beneficiary of some most welcome funds from the advance sale of some choicer volumes. Now, I shall have the whole."

"I don't understand!" She turned to Lee. He seemed completely relaxed. "Your books! I thought you said you loved them? Is that all that love means to you? Something to enjoy while it's there and dispose of when it's convenient? Why are you paying this monster?"

"Surely it's obvious enough? I told you we made a bargain."

"You pay him to keep silent about your own birth? Is that why the demands on Lady Augusta have stopped? Your funds replace hers? And this bargain is why the charges against you were dropped?"

Lee inclined his head.

"Don't you think he owes me something?" asked the major. "Thanks to his interference, my lovely little scheme with Lady Acton came to naught before it began."

"It's the most despicable thing I can think of, to so use my mother!" said Eleanor indignantly.

"On the contrary, it amused her. As for Lady Augusta, Hawksley is drained anyway," added the major complacently. "The proceeds from the sale of the bulk of Mr. Campbell's collection will keep me in sufficient comfort for a long time, and there are a couple of volumes I have coveted for myself for years. My needs are really quite modest. Such old-fashioned sensibility is so rare anymore, but Mr. Campbell wishes to protect his stepmother and his sister from my avaricious grip. I believe that's how you put it, isn't it, sir? The source of the blunt matters not to me. Mr. Campbell's gold is as good as Lady Augusta's. But what an odd fellow, to be sure! I had been so confident he would seize his inheritance, if the truth ever came out. But there you are. It's deeply moving, too, how he cared for poor Manton Barnes, when he shared nothing of the fellow's sadly illegal predilections. I am most distressed myself, of course, that my nephew met such a sad end; nothing could have been further from my intentions, but he was a weak reed."

"How can you give up your books to a Judas like him?" Eleanor asked Lee.

"Does it surprise you to learn that I love Diana a great deal more than the books?" Then he smiled with a warmth of reassurance. "It wasn't hard. What use would such volumes be to me in India?"

Eleanor turned once again to the major. "So you must have known that Manton Barnes committed suicide and why! It was your fault! What sense did it make to bring charges of murder against Mr. Campbell?"

"Simple, Lady Eleanor. I am surprised you have not guessed it. As soon as Mr. Campbell knew that it was I who had blackmailed Barnes, he realized what a delightful weapon the possession of the marriage lines must have been to hold over Lady Augusta. Mr. Campbell was then impetuous enough to tear Deerfield apart. He eventually found all the evidence he required, of course: papers pertaining to my nephew's lovers, which he informs me he has anonymously returned to the gentlemen in question; records of my receipts from Lady Augusta. Your mother's letters, of course, he discovered some time ago. Yet while he was so busy, my butler sent me a warning message. I thought Mr. Campbell would slay me on his return to London, which is why I had him thrown in jail. But of course, I have never understood the intricacies of his fertile brain. He only wanted to pay me instead. Touching, isn't it? If hadn't been so suspicious, we could have made our little agreement much sooner and saved all that business of the trial."

"And deprived the town of so much entertainment?" asked Lee with deliberate irony. "I couldn't wait to see you with a cudgel, Major."

Sir Robert ignored him. "Now I can hardly believe we

have anything more to say to one another, Lady Eleanor. No doubt Mr. Campbell will see you home. Good day."

The major bowed himself out.

Eleanor turned to face Lee. "Did you suspect him at Deerfield?"

He answered her with simple honesty. "I don't know what I suspected. I wondered if he knew about Manton Barnes's lovers, of course. That's why I came to Norfolk in the first place. They hadn't been close, yet Manton had no nearer male relative left alive, and it was possible he had confided in his uncle. His father died years ago. I'm not sure why, but I felt that Sir Robert was holding something back from me. I tried to get him to give himself away more than once."

"The attack on the practice grounds," breathed Eleanor. She closed her eyes for a moment. She could still picture that careless and magnificent horsemanship. If she and Diana had not arrived when they had, would Lee have achieved his goal then?

"Yet I could never find a shred of evidence. And I was reluctant to believe it, I suppose."

"He rescued you from the nuns with the white sails; yes, I know. But only because when he saw the papers that came with you he must have known they represented a fortune."

Lee's smile was more sad than bitter. "I even believed his explanation about why your mother's letters were hidden at Deerfield."

"You found them there?"

"I came back that night to look for anything that would cast light on poor Barnes. I found you and learned about Lady Acton's letters. They were hidden in another of those little cupboards. When I confronted him, Sir Robert told me he had himself recovered them from the blackmailer. Then he tried to cast suspicion on Walter, of all people."

"But when my mother said that he had known Blanche Haricot, you knew for sure, didn't you?"

"As if the proverbial scales had fallen, brown hen."

"Why don't you fight a duel with him?"

"Because I would kill him, and nothing would be achieved by his death. Do you think I should take it upon myself to be judge, jury, and executioner of the man who taught me to shoot? He gave in to this nasty temptation and innocent people have suffered for it, but he has also given years of his life in service to his country. For God's sake, I loved him dearly as a boy; I thought him Hector and Sir Bevis all rolled into one. Nothing can bring Manton Barnes back to life, and he had many causes for despair besides the blackmail, you know. Sir Robert certainly never wished him dead. He appears callous about it, but in fact I believe the suicide shocked him very deeply—he never pursued any of Manton's lovers, after all. Your mother is safe. Only Lady Augusta can still be harmed, and I have made sure that her secret will never be told."

"By drawing up papers and signing over your books?"

He smiled. "Indeed."

"I thought you swore revenge? A lead ball would solve that for you, wouldn't it?"

"Which is why I can't use it, brown hen. And now you will give me your solemn oath that you will forget all about me and my sordid affairs."

"I can't," said Eleanor. She could feel tears pricking behind her lids.

"Nevertheless, you will."

"Because if I don't you will make me?"

"Because you know it's the right thing to do, Lady Eleanor."

"But it's not! You think you are trapped and you're nobly going to make this sacrifice for Diana and Lady Augusta. But who knows what the future might bring? The major might have an attack of the apoplexy! Lady Augusta could die of a fit of the pique! And Diana refuses to marry Walter under the circumstances. She says it would all be a sham. She'd rather you were earl. And so would my brother."

"Richard would rather I died fighting with Wellington, than so betray my sister and stepmother."

"Then do whatever you must! You've left your sister in an impossible quandary. You care so much for your own precious honor, yet you give no thought to hers. She says it would be a falsehood to marry Walter without telling him, and you have made her swear never to do so. I am such a sorry creature that I break my word as often as I break a dinner roll, but Diana never will. You're the most stubborn, opinionated, arrogant man I ever met!"

"Had you not taken it upon yourself to meddle," he said quietly, "Diana would know nothing of it. But I am confident that she'll change her mind once she sees that I'm a hopeless case. She longs for Walter and he for her; she'll give in and marry him soon enough, and I guarantee they'll be very happy. But now that you have made up your mind as to my character, perhaps you will do me the favor of staying out of my affairs?"

"I regret bitterly that I ever became involved in them, sir!"

The violet eyes were unfathomable. "Save your regret. I now remove myself from the scene. I am leaving for Brussels tomorrow. Now, let me escort you back to your remarkable mother, before it is surmised that you have been abducted like Persephone."

And lost in the Underworld, thought Eleanor.

Eleanor walked into Acton House in a rare discomposure, only to be greeted by her father. The Earl of Acton was beaming.

"Come with me into the study for a moment, Eleanor. I have remarkable news."

"Yes, Papa?"

"A most eligible match, my dear! Well done! A triumph in your very first Season! I gave my consent at once, of course."

Eleanor was genuinely puzzled. "A match, sir? With whom?"

"Why, Lord Ranking, of course. He asked for my permission to pay you his addresses only an hour since."

And then the earl was thrown into complete confusion as his eldest daughter broke into sudden peals of laughter. He even suspected that there was a very slight hysterical edge to her merriment, but Eleanor was always the sensible one, so that couldn't be.

"What, miss? What's this? Laughter is hardly a prudent or considered response!"

Eleanor recovered herself with an effort. "Oh, Papa! Surely you're not serious? Lord Ranking?"

"What's afoot now?" asked the countess in cool tones from the doorway.

"Your daughter, madam! Ranking has asked for her hand and she has the effrontery to laugh about it! There'll not be a better offer. When old May pops off, the lad will be a duke. May Castle, think about it!"

"I am thinking about it, and the very idea gives me the vapors!"

"Don't tell me you'll take Eleanor's part in some silly schoolgirl fancy, Lady Acton!" glowered the earl.

"I think our daughter is neither silly nor a schoolgirl any longer, Acton. She will marry Ranking over my dead body."

"Thank you, Mama," said Eleanor firmly, and before any more could be said, she slipped from the room. The sound of her father's raised voice followed her up the stairs.

Once in her room, she sat down and took a deep breath. Instantly, she dismissed the news about Lord Ranking. All her thoughts were for Lee. How did you face yourself when you had just made the only man you would ever love feel nothing for you but contempt? Of course Lee couldn't lay claim to his inheritance under the circumstances, and of course Diana would quickly give in and marry Walter. Meanwhile, Leander Campbell would take ship for Belgium and join Wellington to fight the final battle with Napoleon. She knew with certainty that it would be a terrible slaughter. In spite of all the years of war, the two great generals had never met face-to-face on a battlefield. How many deaths would result when they did?

Idly, Eleanor played with the quills on her desk and scratched little doodles with black ink on her writing paper. How had she fallen in love with him? It seemed now that she had felt this way ever since that night at the Three Feathers on the Norwich road when he had kissed her the first time. But perhaps it had been when he rescued her parasol from the barn roof, or when he rode the farm horse bareback to fetch the carriage for her mother. She closed her eyes and pictured the dark hair blowing about his forehead and the long lines cut deep beside his mouth when he laughed. The shapes made by her pen had turned into a sketch of the cut of his nostrils and the shape of his chin. Furiously, she tore it up. Women are only too vulnerable to such rogues, aren't they? she asked herself. As Moira Campbell had fallen prey to his father. What had the minister said? *If anyone could be said to be sick with love, it was she.*

Eleanor reached into her desk and pulled out the letter from Strathbrae. Slowly, she began to read it again. Poor Moira, who never saw her own baby, dying alone by Loch Linnhe and being laid in her grave by the Highland villagers. At least they had brought flowers. She read the words again: *wildflowers from the hills—while the local piper played the pibroch and the music carried away over the calm blue water.* She could picture it as clearly as if she had been there.

And then it struck her. Shaking with excitement, Eleanor reread the entire letter again. Could the minister be right? Was it possible that all their distress and all the sacrifice had been unnecessary? She would be forced to interfere again and Lee might truly never forgive her this time, but he had to know this! And if she didn't act, she'd never see him again anyway, so what could it matter? It would mean going to his lodgings this instant, by tomorrow he would be gone.

"Eleanor?" said her mother's voice at the door. "Are you getting dressed for an afternoon engagement?" Eleanor thrust the letter back into her desk as Lady Acton came in. The lovely face reflected nothing but amusement. "I see not," added the countess. "Just as well. Your father is determined, my dear. Unless you agree to accept Lord Ranking's suit, you are to keep to your room. Lord Acton is afraid you might meet Roger Waters in public and give him the snub. I'm sure it will be only a day or two before I can bring him around. Apart from listening to his suit, your father has never exchanged two words before with Lord Ranking. I shall just throw them together. That should do the trick! Meanwhile, I suppose you must languish here. Do you mind?"

Eleanor stared at her mother. "I'm not to go out?"

"Well, you have hardly seemed interested in the dances and parties we have carried you to of late. I begin to despair of your success this Season myself."

In spite of herself, Eleanor grinned. "Then you don't call Lord Ranking's offer a success, Mama?"

"Eleanor! Pray, be serious!" Lady Acton leaned forward and tapped her daughter on the wrist with her fan. "If you should have accepted him, I'd have thought you had windmills in your head. Now, be patient. I shall bring Acton around. He's sulking like a bear robbed of honey, but it won't last. In the meantime, be a good girl and act contrite, won't you?"

With a wink, the countess rose and left the room. Eleanor gazed at the door. If she wasn't to go out, how could she take the minister's letter to Lee? And if not now, when? Could she send him a message? Would he come? Perhaps not, and she couldn't take that risk, could she? Nor could she put something so important into anyone else's hands. Could she somehow sneak secretly out of the house and make it by herself to his lodgings? For the entire afternoon, while her parents were in the house, she could never escape unnoticed. If she waited until they had gone out for the evening, it would be getting dark. It had been one thing to hire a cabriolet to take her to Newgate or to the major's. Then it had been bright morning and it had been assumed she would be shopping. A maid had waited protectively in the cab for her. But she couldn't take one of the maids when her father would undoubtedly tell the staff she wasn't to leave the house. Which left no alternative except to venture alone into London at night. It simply wasn't done, and for more and better reasons than those of etiquette. *Come, Eleanor,* she said fiercely to herself. *What on earth is the use of being descended from crusaders and cavaliers, if you can't act with decision when necessary?*

Sixteen

There was nothing left to delay him. After all, Lee had been ready to go and join Wellington before he had been arrested. His horses, his servant, and most of his luggage had already gone on ahead, except for the solid charger he had just bought, who would carry him eventually into the mouths of Boney's guns. The business with Sir Robert was completed. He had made sure that the major would not indulge in blackmail again. So Lee was free at last to fulfill his professional obligations—and about time! There would be one succinct comment from the Iron Duke when he arrived, then no more would be said, but Lee had no doubts about Wellington's justifiable reaction to all this delay. He was not really just another officer and, although the long truce of the last several months had rendered unnecessary his special skills, the Duke was expecting him now.

Lee stretched out his legs and smiled a little grimly. He had no illusions about what kind of engagement was likely to result when the Iron Duke met Napoleon on a battlefield for the first time. When it finally began, it would be sudden and absolute. Either Wellington would sweep into France, or Boney would sweep into Belgium. Either way, it would be without warning, and the armies would clash together like battering rams. Leander Campbell would be wherever he was most needed: carrying orders unprotected across the field, taking up slack wherever he found it, rallying men to stand and face gunfire that mowed them down like wheat, until he was either mowed down himself or it was over. He wouldn't be surprised if Wellington put him in the front of the action, as a little reminder not to loll around England warming jail cells when his country required him overseas. Lee stood up and shrugged into his evening coat. Either way, he wouldn't see his brave brown hen again; for if he survived, he would go straight to India. The thought brought a pain that made him think for a moment that it might be better to die on the battlefield. Then he laughed at his own absurdity. He was damned if he was going to sit here and indulge himself in memories of her! He would go out and mend his depleted purse at the gaming tables one last time.

It was late when Lee came back, but not as late as it would have been if he had not been going to take ship the next morning. He had wanted diversion, but he would need a clear head for traveling, so although faintly inebriated, he was not entirely foxed. He had just turned in to the street by his lodgings, when he heard a shrill scream. Some dark figures were struggling together in front of his own door, their shadows leaping black against the buildings in the glare from the new gaslights. Since one of the combatants seemed to be wearing skirts, he took off running toward them. He was almost there when the woman screamed again. Her assailant cursed roundly and he violently thrust her away. The woman went sprawling onto the street.

"Damn you for a most particular doxy!" said the man who had grappled with her. "Isn't my money as good as the next man's?" Then he looked up just in time to meet Lee's fist. He went flying back onto the pavement.

"Are you all right?" Lee sharply asked the woman.

"Oh, there's nothing I love better than to sit in the dirt, sir!" She seemed to be strangling, for her voice was extremely odd, but she managed to get to her feet. She was wrapped from head to foot in a rather shabby cloak.

The man on the pavement sat up and shook his head. "Damn me," he said. "Devil take you and your damnably efficient fives, sir! Only wanted a little professional company."

"But the lady doesn't like your looks or your blunt, sir. I suggest you try another for your evening's entertainment."

The gentleman rose unsteadily and gave Lee a wobbly bow. "Take the hussy. You're welcome to her. I like my harlots willing. I only tried a little kiss, and she reacted like a bloody vestal virgin!" He rubbed his hand over his bruised jaw and staggered away up the street.

Lee turned to the girl, who was now vainly trying to sink back into the shadows. For under the hood of the cloak, her face was lit clearly by the street lamp and her brown eyes had turned into pools of black.

"For God's sake," said Lee, and then he laughed. "The vestal virgin, indeed! Welcome once again to my indecorous bachelor quarters, Hero!"

"The priestess of Venus at Sestos?" asked Eleanor. "I can hardly lay claim to a resemblance, can I? I thought she waited romantically by the Hellespont, draped in Grecian robes and thinking of prophecies?"

"Well, I doubt seriously if she wandered the streets of London inviting gentlemen to brawl over her! May I ask what you are doing here?"

Even in the flat light, Lee could tell that she had colored. "I wasn't inviting anything," she said.

"My dear Lady Eleanor, the presence of a female alone here at this hour offers only one interpretation. Thank God your admirer was on foot and not in a carriage, or you might have been carried away and met the fate you deserve. I begin to think you really are full of windmills, brown hen!"

"Do you?" replied Eleanor. She hadn't been afraid to walk through the dark to Deerfield, but this had been entirely different. For most of the way, she had attracted unwelcome attention and vile comments. At last it had culminated in that man who was drunk enough to physically attack her and force her to kiss him. She was fighting back tears, though she would happily have been dragged though fire before letting Leander Campbell see it.

"Oh, devil take it! For God's sake, come in. We had better clean you up before I return you to your long-suffering parents."

He put his arm firmly around her shoulders and helped her up the steps. He had seen instantly that she was close to breaking down, but for both their sakes, he must keep her from so doing, or from guessing that he knew it. Two minutes later she was sitting stiffly in an upright chair in the room where Walter and Diana had pursued their courtship, sipping at a welcome glass of brandy. Lee watched her from his post by the fireplace, his shoulders thrust firmly back against the mantel.

"Very well," he said at last. "Explain this latest cavalry charge, Lady Eleanor. I am to surmise that your gallant tilt at Sir Robert this morning wasn't enough? What were you doing in what must be your maid's cast-off cloak, fighting with strangers in front of my door?"

Eleanor assumed wrongly that the tension in his voice must come from anger. Here she was, interfering again! "Unwelcome as it may be, I had to come to see you before you could leave, for Diana's sake," she said bravely. "Something else has come up."

Lee wrung his hand through his hair. His voice was filled with irony. "I feared as much. Is Diana threatening dire acts of self-sacrifice? That's supposed to be my role, not hers."

"Diana doesn't know anything about it. She would think it most shocking that I am here. This is remarkably good brandy, isn't it?"

"I should hope so. It's what's left of the robbery from your father's cellar that you brought me at Newgate. I save it for special occasions."

"Oh," said Eleanor. How had she thought she could bear to face him?

"Now why, my dear, are you creeping about in such ramshackle clothing in the middle of the night, instead of politely making an afternoon call like a civilized person?"

"Because, like the Pearl of Brittany, I was languishing in my room, a prisoner. Lord Acton has been imposing his parental authority. So I waited until he and my mother had gone out for the evening and bribed my maid. That part wasn't hard. She's known me for years. The hard part was that I didn't dare try to hire a conveyance in the dark, and it wasn't fair to make her come with me; the earl would have turned her off with no character. So I walked here alone and now I've got blisters."

"They are well deserved," said Lee with a grin. "How did you escape? Surely the Earl of Acton's butler didn't allow you out unescorted at night? I believe you told me he was trusted?"

"I climbed out of a window."

"The library, no doubt?"

"No, the morning room. It gives onto the garden. And then I had to climb over the wall, but it's quite low by the stables."

"You know it's not at all the done thing for young ladies to visit gentlemen in their rooms so late in the evening, especially when those gentlemen are three sheets to the wind."

Eleanor wrinkled her brow. "You've been drinking?"

"Like a lord. A regrettable state of affairs, but one you might have predicted."

"Should I? Why?"

"You are less perceptive than I thought, brown hen."

The light from the candles played over his face and outlined the clean strong curve of one hand where it hung relaxed from the mantel. Eleanor looked down. She longed for him to take her in his arms and kiss her. "I don't claim to be perceptive at all," she said. "But I had to see you before you left. I assure you it's important."

"And so you—less than discreetly—come to my rooms at

night? There is only one outcome that both parties normally expect."

Eleanor looked up again. His smile was teasing, yet his words offered no mercy. "What do you mean?"

"That the lady surrender her virtue, of course."

Her heart beat heavily in her breast and she knew she was scarlet. "I thought you liked your ladies with a little more polish and a lot more experience?"

"Yes, but I've been known to take what's available. Inexperience can be a refreshing change, after all. And when I think of all those routs and soirées you've been attending— not to mention Vauxhall Gardens—and the intrepid adventures you have plunged into headlong! You have, in spite of yourself, acquired a certain amount of polish and experience in the last several weeks."

"Nowhere near enough for someone of your educated taste, surely? Why, only moments ago I was biting the hand that offered to feed me and sprawling in the gutter."

"But you displayed some very charming petticoats and a delectable ankle."

"Which you should have refrained from noticing!"

"Then you don't think I should take you to my bed?"

Eleanor took a deep breath. "I think you are deliberately punishing me for coming here like this!"

He leaned back and grinned. "No doubt you are right."

She would never know what it cost him to tease her about it, for there was nothing he longed for more than to take her in his arms and kiss her until she surrendered. And there lay his bedchamber, one door away, with the fresh herb-scented sheets on the great feather bed. Lee closed his eyes for a moment. He could imagine the feel of her silky flesh beneath his hands, and knew quite clearly how honest and passionate would be her response. It would be an exquisite rapture to take this one last night and teach her the enchantment of wanton abandonment. His desire was urgent and compelling enough to almost unnerve him. With genuine surprise, he realized that he had not enjoyed a lover since before that night at the Three Feathers. Had his bold Eleanor spoiled him for any other woman? He had fallen in love, as completely and helplessly as Romeo. He loved her bravery and her quick mind; he loved her humor and her brown eyes. She might not be society's idea of a great beauty, but the sweet curves of her body entranced him. He knew without question that if he moved one step toward her, there would be no turning back.

Lee crossed his arms and focused on the hard edge of the mantel cutting into his back, until he felt the pressure of his desire abate a little. She could have no idea, of course, of the torture she put him through to come here like this. For God's sake, it could not be long after he landed in Belgium that he would face Napoleon's guns. Once again, he would have to greet Death and discover whether that gentleman intended only a passing salute or a permanent embrace. And he must face Azrael celibate this time. What a splendid irony! It was only fair, wasn't it, that he should have just the smallest revenge?

Eleanor was gazing at him. His expression seemed closed and remote. "I know I am right. It seems to be a favorite pastime of yours to threaten to ravish whatever female is foolish enough to cross swords with you. What you don't know is that I have a knife."

And then he burst into genuine laughter. "Do you indeed? Then the gentleman who accosted you in the street was fortunate to escape with no more than tooth marks! Do you think you could prevail against me, should it come to a fight?"

Eleanor found herself grinning. She knew without question that the little blade her maid had made her carry was useless as a weapon against someone of his agility and training. "I never thought that for a moment, but I could plunge it into my heart in order to save my virtue, couldn't I? Death before dishonor?"

"Pray, do nothing so dastardly, dear lady. I should have to face your brother Richard over it! You win. You may keep your virtue. Now why did you really come here?"

"To show you this," said Eleanor. She pulled the minister's letter out of her reticule.

Lee took it and read it over carefully. "For God's sake!" he said after a moment.

"It is important, isn't it?" asked Eleanor.

"Damnably so! You realize, of course, that I have passage booked to Belgium on a troop ship in the morning, and that I have already delayed joining my regiment innumerable times this last month?"

"Then you will have to delay it again. You can't go without knowing the truth about this. You owe it to Diana, whether you care or not for yourself!"

"And that I have already sent my horses and gear on ahead?"

"Surely a servant is with them?"

"And that if I miss this ship, the next one mightn't take me there until after it's all over?"

"The Duke of Wellington will have to win without you."

"Without question he will do so. But I will have shirked my duty and earned his just displeasure."

"Earls have other duties besides being slaughtered by Napoleon, and brothers have duties even more important than that. Wellington will get over it."

"You don't give up, do you, brown hen?"

"Diana is my friend," said Eleanor, looking down. Then gathering her courage she stood up and faced him. "And in the meantime, you are stuck with an earl's unblemished and importunate daughter in your rooms. Think of the scandal if it were found out! If you take advantage of the situation, my reputation is ruined. If you don't, then yours is. But if you don't promise to look into this first thing in the morning, I shan't go home and you will have to ravish me after all."

His eyes narrowed, but he was smiling. She had no idea

what she was saying, of course. Nor of how very tempted he was at that moment to forget all honor and restraint and pull her into his arms. The memory of the taste of her lips flooded his tongue and sent tension throbbing through his body. He did not move. Instead he forced heavy sarcasm into his voice. "You *want* me to steal fire?"

"Like Prometheus? Why not? If you will only make things right by your sister, you can go to Timbuktu for all I care. I want you to find out the truth about your mother, and free Diana to marry Walter Feveril Downe. If that means letting go of your damnable willingness to sacrifice yourself, then so be it."

He hesitated for a moment. The words which ran through his mind were Romeo's: *Why such is love's transgression. / Griefs of mine own lie heavy in my breast.* Sweet Lady Eleanor Acton, who would risk all to help a friend. If only she would do it for him, for once. He did not speak the words aloud. Instead he smiled with a sarcasm honed by years of practice. "I surrender, brown hen. There are some members of a Highland regiment waiting now for passage to Belgium who can give me a new translation of the Gaelic. I never had cause to doubt it before, but you are right. The minister's letter raises damnable questions. If the Highlanders confirm what we have always believed, I shall join them on the ship. For though Wellington can do fine without me, he rather likes his officers to keep their word. But if something new is to be discovered, I will at least send a message to Diana before I traverse the Sahara to such a dust-ridden hellhole as Timbuktu. Now, are you satisfied? For it's all you will get. And if you will kindly gird up your maid's charming cloak, I shall take you back to Acton House forthwith."

"Unravished?" questioned Eleanor. She was shaking. "You are noble, aren't you, to sacrifice your reputation for mine?"

If he did not stop her this instant, he would not be able to control himself. "Don't offer me your virtue, Lady Eleanor," he said coldly. "I am not sure that I could handle such a plain brown virago in my bed, after all."

With exquisite pain, he watched his words wound her to the soul. They did not speak again as they hurried through the silent, dark streets. Lee helped Eleanor up onto the garden wall beside the stable, then turned on his heel and walked rapidly back to his lodgings. There on his desk lay the letter from Scotland. What if the minister was right? The prospect made him dizzy to contemplate. Yet what could it matter, when with Eleanor it was too late?

Diana came to call the next morning. The butler showed her into the sunny morning room where Eleanor sat at an embroidery frame. No stitches seemed to have been added for quite some time. Instead, what should have been gay little bunches of pink flowers around the bonnet of the shepherdess lay still innocent of their silk garnish, and Eleanor's hands lay idle in her lap.

"I missed you at the rout last night," Diana began. "Do say you were not ill?"

Eleanor looked up and laughed at her friend. "Oh, no! I was confined to my room. Haven't you heard the news? Lord Ranking has offered for me."

"Eleanor! You told your papa you would refuse him, I trust?"

"Well, of course! If I'd had any idea it would come to this when I agreed to your scheme at Hawksley, I'd have told you to take care of him yourself."

"Oh, it is all my fault! I'm so sorry! And now your papa is angry?"

"Oh, pooh! He thinks I should be honored. Yet one earl's daughter is much like another to Ranking, I'm sure. Luckily my mother seems to concur in our sentiments. It is Mama's scheme that I avoid him, so I don't have to refuse his offer to his face. She plans to thrust him into Papa's company until the Earl of Acton decides he really doesn't want Roger Waters for a son-in-law. In the meantime, I recline at home on a couch and refuse social engagements. Now, enough about me. When will you marry Mr. Downe?"

Diana flushed and clenched her hands together. "How can I? I am sworn to silence about Lee's real birth, so I can't tell Walter. Yet how could I marry him when he doesn't know that I'm illegitimate?"

"Easily, you ninny. He wouldn't care. And if it ever came out, he would understand that you had given your word to Lee."

"And now Lee's gone away. Oh, Eleanor, what if he should be killed? I can't bear it!"

"Oh, fiddlesticks!" said Eleanor with more conviction than she felt. Surely now that she had been brave for so long, she could hold herself together for a few more days? "He's been through years of campaigns. Why should one more prove fatal?"

There was a slight disturbance behind them. Lady Acton stood in the doorway. She turned and laid her hand on the scarlet sleeve of a man in uniform and said something to him. He had to bend down to hear her. Behind them, the dim light of the hallway shone on the blond hair of Walter Feveril Downe.

"They're in here, Major," the countess said gaily.

The embroidery frame crashed into the hearth as Eleanor leapt to her feet. "What are you doing here?" she cried, her heart in her mouth. "What have you discovered?"

Seventeen

"I have come, Lady Eleanor, to see that my sister marries this poor honest churchman." Lee turned to Diana who sat blushing in her chair. In his crisp uniform, he looked splendid. Eleanor had never expected to see him in his regimentals. It gave him an authority and a distance she had never imagined. Major Leander Campbell! A man that other men obeyed without question, not only because he had a natural power, but because it was backed by genuine compassion. Yet the smile he gave them was still that of Lee, Diana's impossible half-brother. "Walter will take you, willy-nilly, Di, whether you are heiress or pauper, bastard or duchess. Since as it happens you are none of those things, he will happily take you as you are: the entirely legitimate half-sister to the present Earl of Hawksley, who will provide you with his blessing, his brotherly advice, and a suitable dowry."

"What are you saying?" asked Diana faintly.

"I was right?" Eleanor could feel the pulse pounding through her body. "About the minister's letter?"

"You had better sit down, dear child. You are the color of table linen. I can't allow a daughter of mine to succumb to the vapors." Lady Acton took a chair and waved the gentlemen to do likewise. "It would seem that there's no end to life's wonderful surprises. You had better explain, Hawksley. My little brown hen is about to expire from suspense."

Lee's violet eyes met Eleanor's. His expression was guarded, as if he still could not really accept what he was about to say. "You were entirely correct, Lady Eleanor. The Highlanders had been carousing most of the night and were lost to the world. It was a splendid waste of time to wake most of them. Luckily the piper was sober enough to give me his expertise in his native tongue, then I had the good fortune to have it confirmed by one Captain MacDonald. It would seem that Lady Augusta's marriage to my father was perfectly in order."

"You mean I am legitimate, after all?" Diana seemed stunned.

"Indeed, dear sister."

"I don't understand," said Diana. "How can I be, if you are earl?"

"Ask your busy friend from Miss Able's Seminary, sister. It was her doing."

Diana turned to Eleanor, whose face was still as white as the linen in her embroidery frame.

"I know it was none of my business," began Eleanor slowly, "but I wrote to the minister who performed your father's marriage to Moira Campbell. He sent me the marriage lines that I showed you, but he also told me about Moira's death. He said there were wildflowers laid on her grave, and that the sea was blue and calm. Because of the translation on the back of the original Gaelic letter about her death, we had all believed that Moira Campbell died in November, a month after Lady Augusta's wedding to the Earl of Hawksley. But how could there have been wildflowers blooming so late? And surely the sea was never calm and blue in Scotland in November? The translation had been confirmed by Sir Robert, but obviously he couldn't be trusted about this. So your brother has taken the original to the Highlanders and had them give him a correct English version."

Lee walked over to his sister and gently kissed her forehead. "Moira did die when the flowers were blooming and the sea was blue. She died in June. Thus, although I am indeed the legal heir to our rascally father, you are also his entirely legitimate daughter. Whatever his faults, he wasn't a bigamist. His first wife had gone to her grave four months before he married the second. I wonder if he knew?"

"Oh, good heavens! It will save Mama!" exclaimed Diana. "She's still the rightful dowager countess, isn't she? She'll always be able to hold up her head in society."

"I have already informed her of that fact. She is rather put out that you have lost the complete inheritance, though I assured her that I would do right by you. Yet I think on the whole, relief that her marriage was honest overrides all other factors. She has confirmed her consent to Walter paying you his addresses, and though reluctantly, sends her blessing."

"Yet it is your consent I need," Diana teased. "You are now head of the family. And there's no money left for a dowry, so Walter will have to take me without one."

Eleanor felt a sudden rush of envy at her friend's clear-eyed confidence in Mr. Downe's love. Walter had taken the seat next to Lady Diana Hart and had taken her hand in his.

"No, he won't," grinned Lee. "It has been an excessively busy morning and it began before dawn. Several players in our little drama lost some sleep, I'm afraid, besides the piper and his comrades. I have also been to see Sir Robert. His side of our bargain—the one that made him drop his murder charge against me—was a signed confession of his persecution of Lady Augusta. I made him do it in case he broke faith in spite of taking my money. He gave it willingly, of course. His confidence that I could never use it was boundless. Now, however, the dowager countess is out of danger, and Major St. John Crabtree is in trouble up to his neck. He has agreed to quietly leave the country. I allowed him some funds, but first I obtained his gift of the deed of the bulk of his property and the return of mine. I have passed some of it on to you, Di. Deerfield is yours now, whether you want it or not."

"Deerfield?" asked Walter, looking up in surprise. It was obvious that he hadn't known of it until this moment.

"Now don't get squeamish, Downe. It's the cost of marrying an earl's daughter. You must take her property without quibble. It's a charming house, you must agree, though at present in need of some minor repair. I rather tore things apart three weeks ago. Did you know it was full of the most cunning little hidden cupboards?"

Diana stood up and threw her arms around Lee. "You dear thing!" she exclaimed. "We shall be neighbors! What could be more amiable?"

"It's more than generous of you, old chap!" said Walter. "I'll have to become a bishop to justify living in such a place! And now, I suppose I had better formally request your permission to marry your sister. For I realize that in spite of everything, I've never yet done so."

Lee leaned back lazily in his chair. Sun streamed through the window and flung his dark hair into brilliant relief, though it shadowed his features. "I don't know if I can," he said idly. "Unless Lady Eleanor would agree to give me her hand. Doesn't that seem like only justice?"

Eleanor leapt out of her chair and walked swiftly across the room. How could he! To offer the importunate schoolgirl her heart's desire as a jest! He couldn't mean it. For he could have no idea of the depth of her emotion and the changes she had gone through in these last two months. What if she called his bluff and accepted? How would Lee get out of it? And if he did not, how would she manage when Lee became bored with her and regretted this idle gesture? He would seek a mistress, wouldn't he? Someone sophisticated and worldly. And she could never accept it! He had made his feelings clear: *I'm not sure that I could handle such a plain brown virago in my bed, after all.* She spun about and faced the ring of expectant faces. "I'm damned," she said softly, "if the new Lord Hawksley isn't more enamored of self-sacrifice than Icarus! What noble gallantry! Good heavens, I'm sure you can find a more suitable mistress for Hawksley Park than me! I'm barely out of plaits and short skirts."

And then he leaned forward and she caught the set pain of his expression as the sun lit his features. "Well, thank God for that!" he said lightly. "Now if you will all excuse me, I have a ship to catch."

"You're still going to Belgium?" breathed Diana. "What about Hawksley? You've an estate to run! And now you have your books back from Sir Robert, they will have to be inventoried and everything. Shouldn't you oversee all that?"

"Dear Di, it's the most annoying thing, I know. Duty is so tiresome. But I'm a soldier as well as an earl, my dear, and I have a commitment I must fulfill. Your mother has all the papers you need, signed by me at some ungodly hour this morning, for you to wed and live happily ever after in bliss. I trust I may come back and celebrate with you. But before I can take up the reins at Hawksley, I'm promised to the Duke of Wellington for a spell. And though I've let this absurd business detain me for too long, I'm going now. Good day, Lady Acton." He stood and went to the door. Each of them came forward and shook him by the hand. Eleanor was compelled to do likewise. He caught her hand and raised it to his lips. She could feel their sensuous touch as he gently kissed her fingers. Then he leaned forward and whispered in her ear. "Marry for love, brown hen."

"Well, I'm damned," said Lady Acton after he had left. "If your father hears you have turned down yet another eligible offer, Eleanor, you'll be on bread and water for the rest of the summer. First Lord Ranking and now the Earl of Hawksley!"

Eleanor turned to her mother and laughed, a little unsteadily. "Oh, fiddlesticks, Mama! Don't you think I should wait for a suitor of the blood royal? And if that won't do, perhaps I can hold out for a man who loves me?"

* * *

Eleanor refused to go into a decline. Her father relented and allowed her to attend all the social functions of the Season once again, although she would just as soon have sat at home. Instead, she dressed in her finest and waltzed and laughed as if nothing at all were wrong. Lady Acton had tactfully explained to Lord Ranking that perhaps her daughter was a little young yet, and he should allow her a little more time to make her decision.

"I do comprehend, my lady," he said with a noble sniff. "Lady Eleanor is of such a delicate constitution, she must be wooed with discretion and patience. I pride myself that I am a man of the most amiable temper and tender sensibility. She shall not be distressed by my honorable attentions, I assure you."

Thus Eleanor had to suffer Lord Ranking's idea of a discreet courtship, which mostly consisted of him creeping up to her at odd moments and giving her a damp but meaningful look.

If the gossips of May had been thrilled with the scandal of the trial, the news in June that the notorious Leander Campbell had been discovered to be the rightful Earl of Hawksley caused a sensation. Augusta, Dowager Countess of Hawksley, had all the necessary papers to prove it, and Lady Acton leant her considerable weight to the cause. A deputation was sent to Scotland to confirm the records of Mr. Campbell's mother's marriage to the late earl and the circumstances of her death. One of the witnesses, the maid Fiona Mackay, was found still alive. As the summer heat took London in its dusty grip, the word passed from mouth to mouth that it was all true, and Leander Campbell was indeed a peer of the realm. It was then generally agreed that no one had ever heard a more touching tale, and the dowagers vied with one another in declaring that they had always suspected it. Each one had secretly felt all along that Leander Campbell had all the qualities of a true aristocrat.

"Everyone else may have looked at him askance!" said Lady Vain one day in Eleanor's hearing. "But I always knew that he was one of us. Such a noble and distinguishing bearing. And his mother was the descendant of an ancient Scottish royal lineage, so I hear."

"Indeed. And when he returns from his duties fighting the Corsican Monster, we may be sure he'll be looking about himself for a wife."

At which, Eleanor started to walk away as the dowagers began to toss the names of various society beauties into the ring, only to hear one lady add: "And what about Lady Acton's girl? Very plain, of course, but very eligible to become Countess of Hawksley. Her dowry would do much to put Hawksley to rights. I understand the estate is much in need of repair."

That Major Sir Robert St. John Crabtree had decided to sell up and move to the Colonies caused a tiny flurry of comment, but it was not so strange as to raise further question. No one in London except the Actons and the Harts knew that the major had prospered for twenty years by blackmail. And then every other interest was supplanted. The news arrived from Europe that the French Channel ports were closed. Bonaparte was on the move. Almost every family had a brother or son in Brussels with Wellington. Napoleon was known to be the greatest general of the day. Would France overrun Belgium again? How many British soldiers could survive against the Emperor's invincible Imperial Guard?

Eleanor was in agony. Major Lord Hawksley would be in the thick of it. He could be killed or maimed. She prayed fervently for his survival. Yet if he came home to England, she didn't expect to see him privately ever again. He would marry one of those ladies that the dowagers were busy gossiping over, and if she was ever to visit Diana and Walter at

Deerfield, she would be bound to see him with his wife. The safest thing was to get married herself before he returned. Yet who was there, except Lord Ranking? No one else had shown any interest and the Season was almost over. If he did not return, of course, it would be simple. She would never marry.

It seemed that it must be the hottest June in years. Thunderstorms built and broke in torrents most afternoons. All of London society seemed caught up in the wild intensity of the weather. Mrs. Boehm's ball at No. 16 St. James's Square was to be one of the finest affairs of the Season. Eleanor was there in her best ivory silk. She was determined to smile with just the right amount of kindness on Lord Ranking. Thanks to the presence of the Prince Regent, the room was packed with the most decorative members of the *beau monde* and no expense had been spared. Mrs. Boehm smiled with gratified triumph, certain she could declare her event a sad crush. The first quadrille was just forming when a ripple ran through the dancers and they began to break apart and run for the windows. A crowd seemed to have poured into the square outside, and the noise of shouting rose to the ballroom.

A lady turned from the window. "A carriage comes! Oh, dear God! They have some of those horrid French eagles! It is news from Belgium!"

Eleanor fought back waves of panic as a stranger in a dusty uniform burst into the room carrying two flags. He thrust his way through the crowd and knelt, laying the flags at Prinny's feet.

"Victory, Sir! Victory!"

The Prince Regent was instantly overcome, and began to weep hysterically until one of the guests heroically dashed a glass of water into his face. With dripping chin, he was escorted into another room where he could read the despatches away from the crowd. Eleanor saw her father follow him in. She glanced around. More than one guest was in tears and everyone seemed to be leaving, while Mrs. Boehm wrung her hands in despair at the ruin of her party.

"Come, dear child," said Lady Acton calmly at her elbow. "Our illustrious Prince Regent will now drown his feelings in claret, but Lord Acton has just sent me a message from the inner sanctum. Wellington achieved a great victory south of Brussels on Sunday. Napoleon is crushed and flees back to Paris, our troops in hot pursuit. No doubt our facile friend is with them. But let us face it and find out. Casualty lists have been posted at the Horse Guards."

Eleanor followed her mother as they joined the flock of lightly clad ladies and gentlemen who jostled down the stairs and ran out into the street. No one had thought to put on a wrap, or worry that the cobbles might shred their delicate evening slippers. The carriage still stood in the center of a mob of frenzied people, the horses nervously tossing their heads at the noise. "Boney's beat! Victory!" cried several voices, and then the name of the village where the battle had been fought began to be shouted in triumph. "Waterloo! Waterloo!"

Lady Acton and Eleanor were swept along in the crowd. Within minutes they reached the throng around the List of Killed and Wounded. Here and there, a sob of anguish surfaced through the voices as someone discovered the name they dreaded to find on the list, and a wife or mother or daughter had to be helped away to hide her grief. Eleanor found tears running openly down her cheeks. It was Thursday, the twenty-second day of June. Lee might already have been dead for four days. Her mother had taken her hand, and was firmly holding her as they were jostled and pushed. At last Lady Acton was able to reach the list. Eleanor clung to her mother's fingers; she was blind with distress.

"It's all right," said Lady Acton at last. "His name is not there. Our difficult new earl has survived Waterloo."

* * *

The next day the news was more complete, and for several days afterward extra details arrived in London. "I have never fought such a battle," Wellington was reputed to have said, "And I trust I shall never fight such another." And then at last, there was news of Lee. He was mentioned in despatches. He was now, with the rest of the army, on his way to Paris. Eleanor felt the wildest turmoil of emotion. Lee had survived! What happened to her was irrelevant compared to that. But she could not bear it if he came home and married someone else. Lady Acton looked up from her writing desk as her daughter came white-faced into the room several mornings later.

"I have made a decision, Mama," Eleanor said quietly. "I shall accept Lord Ranking."

"Shall you?" said Lady Acton with an idle wave of her pen. "Well, your father will be pleased."

"I think I shan't do better," Eleanor stammered, as her mother's shrewd black eyes smiled into hers.

"No doubt. A duke's son. Well, well. There seems to have been such a fashion for honorable self-immolation around town this summer, but I wouldn't stand in the way of such a splendid match. But don't tell Ranking or Acton quite yet, will you?"

"Why not?" asked Eleanor dully.

"Because I have a letter from Richard. Helena's confinement is expected within four or five weeks, and she is finding the wait very tiresome. They would like you to visit at Acton Mead." Lady Acton did not say that it was she herself who had suggested this remedy to Richard and Helena. She was very afraid of what Eleanor might do if she stayed on in London. "Go down to the country for a fortnight. If you are still enamored of Lord Ranking when you come back to town, why then, we'll have a splendid wedding! What do you say?"

"That I would love to go, of course," said Eleanor. She adored Acton Mead, Richard's home by the Thames. It had been their grandmother's, and she had spent many happy hours there as a child. She also dearly loved Richard and Helena. Of course any delay to her nuptials with Lord Ranking would be welcome. And finally, it would remove her from London when Leander Campbell came back.

Eighteen

Helena, Lady Lenwood, was enormous. She came out to greet Eleanor with a huge smile. "I am all belly!" she said gaily. "I did see an elephant last year, but that was before I found myself in such an interesting condition. Do you think that the impression could have lingered so long that I am about to give birth to one?"

Her happiness was so contagious that Eleanor found herself able to bury at least part of her own misery. Acton Mead was beautiful. A riot of white roses grew over a little bower outside of Helena's own blue drawing room, and the ladies determined to spend the July days sitting in the sweet shade of the flowers sewing dainty little clothes for the expected heir. A cool breeze funneled around the house from the river and brought the scents of all the flower borders. Richard was with them often, but he had an estate to run and constant business with his tenants. He was also overseeing innumerable improvement schemes, some involving his land and some in various political organizations dedicated to saving children from intolerable working conditions.

"I should think my brother would drop all this work to be with you," said Eleanor idly one day. "Every time he goes out, it's as if he tears out part of himself and leaves it behind."

"Then I hope whatever he leaves in my care is returned complete and whole when he returns," said Helena seriously. "Being apart doesn't threaten us, you know, and marriage doesn't diminish the fact that you're still two separate people.

Yet I suppose we carry each other's souls in the palms of our hands, so love must allow absolute trust."

"Which you have always shared."

Helena gave her sister-in-law a look of genuine surprise. Then she laughed. "Not at all, I assure you! Richard trusted me so little when we were first wed that he thought I conspired his death! No, falling in love is all very well, but real love and trust must be earned every day. I have never thought that anyone could maintain love long in the face of unkindness or neglect, whatever passion may be shared."

Eleanor looked down. Helena wasn't so much older than herself, yet she seemed so calm and sure of herself. Then she gathered her own brand of courage. "Oh, well," she replied lightly. "With Lord Ranking, all it will take will be a mustard plaster and elderberry elixir, and he'll be faithful for life."

"Helena!" It was Richard's voice. He appeared at the door to the blue room and smiled at them. "I have need of your ear for a private word. You will excuse us, sister mine?"

Eleanor offered her help as Lady Lenwood rose heavily to her feet. Then as she entered the house, Richard put his arm around his wife's waist and they disappeared. Eleanor lay back and watched the bees buzzing in the roses. It was very ignoble to be jealous of your own brother's wife, wasn't it?

"Good God!" said an amused voice. "My flowers would seem to be redundant! I had no idea that you would be sitting in a veritable bower of blossom."

Eleanor jerked upright. Lee was standing under the arbor, his arms full of roses of every conceivable shade of red. He was unscathed, whole, and smiling, the dark hair mottled with broken sunlight. The new Earl of Hawksley seemed unchanged by Waterloo, that worst of battles. How long had he been back in England? It was less than a month since

Napoleon's defeat. The Allies had only reached Paris the previous Friday; Richard had received the news that very morning, five days later. Had Lee come straight to Acton Mead from France? The thought gave Eleanor a sudden rush of hope. She could not allow herself to feel it. He came up to her and dropped the flowers over her lap and around her feet until she was surrounded by their fragrant beauty.

"What are you doing?" she asked immediately, calling on sarcasm for protection. "Is this the equivalent of Jove visiting Danaë in a shower of gold?" Then she blushed scarlet as she realized the implication of what she had said.

Lee grinned. "An odd choice of comparison, brown hen. Perseus was the happy result of Jove's visit, of course. And Danaë was willing only because it broke the monotony of her imprisonment in the brazen tower. Surely you aren't an imprisoned princess here at Acton Mead?"

"No, a veritable gooseberry: merely an unnecessary witness to my brother and his wife's enchantment with each other. I thought you were in Paris, welcoming the return of King Louis. Do you visit Richard? What are the flowers for?"

He took up a dark red rose and held it to his face, inhaling the heady perfume. "I thought I was visiting you."

"Me? Why?"

"To begin a proper courtship, of course."

Her heart was racing. Could he hear it? "With roses?"

"Why not? The Sultan of Persia slept on a mattress stuffed with their petals. In Kashmir, roses were scattered on the water to welcome the return of the Moghul emperor. Heliogabalus rained them onto his guests from the ceiling. Fashioned out of the body of a nymph by Chloris with the aid of Aphrodite and the three Graces, aren't they the traditional messengers of contrition, apology, and depth of emotion? I bring red roses for true love, while you sit here beneath white ones for purity."

"I might do better with columbines," said Eleanor shakily.

"For folly? Whose, I wonder, yours or mine? No, red roses will do just fine, perhaps with a sprinkling of bluebells."

"Bluebells for constancy? Rather a red carnation."

"Sweet gillyflowers? 'Alas for my poor heart.' That is their meaning, isn't it? 'The fairest flowers o' the season / Are our Carnation and streak'd Gillyvors / Which some call nature's bastards.' Don't make it difficult for me, brown hen. I am humbly trying to start afresh."

"Lee, don't, I pray!"

"Don't what?" he brushed petals from the seat next to her and sat down. Then he leaned back and closed his eyes. Eleanor could feel her limbs tremble with the force of her awareness of him. "I spent only two hours in London, but I have your father's permission to pay you my addresses, and your mother was so bold as to wish me Godspeed. Everything is in order for a gentle and respectful courtship. However, I shan't blame you if you spurn me without a backward thought. I have behaved with total recklessness, haven't I?"

"Yes," said Eleanor. "I have felt positively trampled, and I'm not sure that either wine or perfume has resulted. If this is a wooing, it might take more than armloads of roses."

He sighed. "I feared as much. Very well then, what will it take?"

Eleanor looked at him. The dappled light played over the fine bridge of his nose and cast broken shadows on his cheek from his lashes. There was the faintest hint of darkness over his jaw where his beard had been less closely shaved than usual. It was evidence, she assumed, of the speed of his journey. Her eyes moved to the clean line of his lips. She had the most immodest desire to press her mouth to his.

"Well, it could start with an apology for your ungracious behavior at the Three Feathers."

"No, you shan't get it. I don't regret kissing you. I didn't then and I don't now. I can't change, brown hen. I'm a shameless fellow, even if I do have the misfortune to be an earl."

"I don't mean for the kiss, sir. I mean for not telling me

you had fought in the Peninsula with Richard and for thinking I was involved in blackmail. You were not at all honest with me."

Lee sat up and turned to her. "We were strangers, and I was unforgivably foxed! But my kiss at least was honest."

"As was mine," said Eleanor desperately. "You must know that I've been in love with you ever since. For God's sake, Lee! If you have been careless enough to arouse unsuitable passions in the innocent breast of a schoolgirl, pray enjoy your amusement in secret. Don't come and compound it with more idle flirtation."

He reached out long fingers and stroked her cheek. "No, I didn't know. If you mean it, it causes me only a happiness I surely don't deserve. But who said anything about idle flirtation? This is a very serious flirtation, I assure you."

She dropped her head as his knuckles caressed gently at the base of her ear. "It can't be."

"Why not?"

"Because you have barely hidden your condescension and intolerance from the beginning."

"Oh, Lord!" said Lee. "What I have barely hidden, my dear, is that I conceived an equally unsuitable passion for you. For these past months, I have been fighting the strongest desire to carry you off and imprison you myself. It was only the tattered shreds of my honor that made me desist. In fact, I would very much like to ravish you here on the spot, but I am prepared to marry you first. Now, for God's sake, brown hen, can't you believe that I love you? I was a bastard, making my own way in the world. Until I met you, it never had bothered me. But without prospects or family, how could I in honor declare myself? If there's one thing that I'm glad of about being Lord Hawksley, it's that I'm suddenly a perfectly respectable and eligible match for Lady Eleanor Acton. Now, my lady, pray do me the honor of allowing me to begin a simple courtship?"

"I don't seem to be too much of a virago?"

He looked puzzled for a moment, then he laughed. "I would like to teach you why I had to say that. I was protecting myself at your cost and humbly beg your forgiveness. No, you don't. I love your spirit and your determination. Nor do I find you plain, brown hen. I find you irresistible."

"I think this courtship is still very odd, my lord."

"Indeed, it is backward, isn't it? It should begin with a dance."

"I won't dance with you out here on the patio. There's no music."

"Very well. Then it must proceed with a walk in the Park, or perhaps a drive in my gig."

"Do you have a gig?"

"No, as a matter of fact, I don't. And we have done enough private walking together, don't you think?"

Eleanor laughed. "As I recall, very often without exchanging two words."

"I was struck dumb by your beauty."

"So the next stage is compliments?"

"Of course, to be followed by flowers."

"I have enough of those," said Eleanor, catching up some of the roses that lay scattered over her skirt.

"And then I must kiss you."

"Must you?" Eleanor looked up at him. She couldn't disguise her longing. "But we've already passed that stage too."

"No, we haven't. For it lasts forever. Say you will marry me, brown hen. I believe I have loved you since you first tried to light the candles at the Three Feathers, and then so bravely faced me down over your locket. I beg your forgiveness for every word I have ever said that was intended to drive you away. You do see why I had to, don't you? But for every careless word, I offer you a lifetime of caring ones, though I admit that it won't do either of us harm to clash upon occasion. There is no one in the world, however, that I would rather argue with than you."

"You're not going to India?"

"Nor Timbuktu, unfortunately. I shall be very much in evidence at Hawksley Park. You cannot avoid me, Eleanor, and I shall continue to seek your hand until you give in."

"Have you resigned your commission?" asked Eleanor faintly.

A subtle shudder passed over his body. Eleanor knew with a sudden insight that it would be the only acknowledgment she would ever get of what he had just been through. "Forever," he said firmly. "Now, do you think we have covered all the necessary stages of courtship, for I can't wait much longer. I love you with a depth of feeling that scares me. Sweet brown hen, will you do me the honor to become Lady Hawksley?"

"I'd have married plain Mr. Campbell," said Eleanor simply. "If he'd thought to ask me."

Richard and Helena came together through the blue room, then stopped by the French windows. Richard had his arm around his wife's generous waist and she laid her head on his shoulder.

"It would seem that your friend is having his way with your sister," said Helena with a smile.

Richard turned and pulled Helena back into the room. He caught her to him and kissed her with passionate hunger on the lips.

"I don't suppose she'd be kissing him like this, if they hadn't just agreed to marry," he said at last.

"Oh, I wouldn't be too sure of that." Helena leaned back into the circle of his arm. "I thought the man was a notorious rake?"

"He is," said Richard. "So I thank God I'm so sure they will wed. Otherwise I'd have to call him out for so abusing my sister, and the man's not only a rogue, he's a devilishly good shot."

Author's Note

Eleanor's family first appeared in *Virtue's Reward,* the story of Richard and Helena. Her brother Harry Acton, although he doesn't appear in this book, is certainly destined to be a hero in the future. Incidentally, the quotes from the Regency geography text about the *Malays, Patagonia,* and *the inhabitants of the United States* are genuine.

There was a real trial during the Regency period which provided me with the details for Lee's demand for trial by wager of battle. It occurred in April 1818, three years after my story takes place. A Mr. Ashford accused a Mr. Thornton of murder, and the latter demanded trial by combat. After extensive research in the law books, the judges decided that trial by battle had never been repealed. Only a technical flaw prevented the fight from being conducted. As Richard Rush, the American Minister at the Court of St James, reported in his diary, the case caused a sensation in society, and a statute was soon passed which finally repealed this ancient right.

The news of Waterloo did indeed disrupt Mrs. Boehm's ball as I have described. She was most put out at the ruin of her plans and the waste of her "splendid supper," which went uneaten. A guest afterward reported that the Prince Regent, in a "womanish hysteric," had to be revived first by water and then by wine.

Rogue's Reward is the third book in my series involving Wellington's intelligence officers, a group of men the Iron

Duke claimed were invaluable in his fight against Napoleon. Charles de Dagonet, hero of *Scandal's Reward,* and Richard Acton, hero of *Virtue's Reward,* both returned from the Peninsula with a particular problem to solve—Devil Dagonet had to clear his name of scandal; Richard carried a dangerous secret. Lee's dilemma, of course, has its roots in his childhood, but the men are all friends and will no doubt reappear upon occasion in future books. I hope my readers enjoy sharing their adventures. If you would like to write and tell me your favorites, I may be reached at P.O. Box 197, Ridgway, CO 81432. I would love to hear from you. Please enclose a stamped self-addressed envelope if you would like a reply.